I take out my notebook and pencil and write a quick list:

MAGIC

I know Sister Janice and everyone at school say magic is bad, but if it's that bad then maybe it's real. Maybe it's powerful. Maybe it's what I need. Maybe our new house could be magic. Maybe these things I found in the house and took home in my pockets could also be magic.

1. The brass 4 from the front door.

2. A tiny doll the size of my thumb with gold hair and a purple dress.

3. A toilet-paper roll.

Maybe if I keep one of them in my pocket from now on, the boys . . . everyone . . . will stop bothering me.

CAELA CARTER

HOW TO BE A GIRL IN THE WORLD

Quill Tree Books
An Imprint of HarperCollinsPublishers

Library of Congress Cataloging-in-Publication Data

Names: Carter, Caela, author.
Title: How to be a girl in the world / Caela Carter.
Description: First edition. | New York, NY : Harper, an imprint of
    HarperCollinsPublishers, [2020] | Audience: Ages 8-12. | Audience: Grades
    4-6. | Summary: Twelve-year-old Lydia, feeling threatened by the attention her
    changing body is getting from boys and men, finds a way to take control of her
    own skin.
Identifiers: LCCN 2019040568 | ISBN 978-0-06-267271-1 (pbk.)
Subjects: CYAC: Sexual harassment--Fiction. | Body image--Fiction. | Single-parent
    families--Fiction. | Family life--New York (State)--Brooklyn--Fiction. | Catholic
    schools--Fiction. | Schools--Fiction. | Magic--Fiction. | Brooklyn (New York,
    N.Y.)--Fiction.
Classification: LCC PZ7.C24273 How 2020 | DDC [Fic]--dc23
LC record available at https://lccn.loc.gov/2019040568

Typography by Molly Fehr
21 22 23 24 25   PC/BRR   10 9 8 7 6 5 4 3 2 1
❖
First paperback edition, 2021

For Maebh.

And for Nora, Juliette, Fia, Evelyn, Marketa,

Emilia, Veronica, Nora, and Josephine.

And for all the other girls who were born into

the world during the writing of this book.

May we use the next twelve years

to make it better for you.

CHAPTER 1

OUR HEADS TILT ONE AT A time. Mine. Mom's. Emma's. Like raindrops falling in a row. *Tilt. Tilt. Tilt.*

We're standing on the sidewalk, holding hands and staring at a ramshackle house in front of us. The entire thing looks like it's leaning onto its right side. Like it had a really tough day of work and is standing in the station, waiting for the subway, resting against one of those poles that Mom always tells me is disgusting and I should never touch.

"It's not tilted," Mom says, reading our minds. Or our heads. She's talking too fast, the way she does when it's really important that I agree with her. It's hard to agree with whatever this is. "It only looks like it's leaning because there's an extra window on the left side. Asymmetrical windows. That's why this didn't sell. Can you believe it? Well, it sold!"

Mom has bought this house. The tilting-but-not-tilting house.

I don't think asymmetrical windows were ever this house's only problem. It's set back a few feet from the street, as if there's room for a yard or a driveway or something, but all that's in front of it is dirty, cracked sidewalk concrete. It has a front stoop made of bricks, like most of the houses in our Brooklyn neighborhood. But the rest of the house is a faded green color, as close as green could get to white. Instead of brick or stone, it's covered in aluminum siding, and there are places where the siding is sliding off. There are poles for an awning over the front porch, but the awning is gone, if it was ever there. And there is exactly one shutter on each window, except the asymmetrical one, which has two. Which maybe makes it look even more asymmetrical.

Mom says we are going to live here. I scrunch up my eyebrows and tell my brain to imagine it. I can't.

"Can you believe I scooped this up before someone decided to flip it?" She keeps talking, but she's answering the wrong questions. "I mean, it's incredible. And I know the neighborhood's a little rough, but we're less than a ten-minute walk from our apartment now, so it can't be that different, right? Just a slightly longer ride to school for you girls. You probably won't have to worry about that until springtime anyway."

"I won't still be living with you in spring," Emma says, like always.

Mom shrugs, like always. "We'll see."

Then she's talking about rent versus mortgage and Catholic school tuition and the value of ownership and all sorts of things I don't care about. I hate when she talks about money.

I only have one question right now: Does this tilted house have air-conditioning?

I should have a trillion questions, I know that. Until five minutes ago I didn't know we were moving at all. There's no reason to move, really, except Mom says renting is a waste and she's always wanted to be able to buy a house. I should be wondering why this house. Why now.

But the sweat trickling down between my shoulder blades keeps me from thinking about anything else. It's ninety degrees outside and steam is rising from the sidewalks in sheets. This is August in Brooklyn.

I'm dressed in black sweatpants that used to be baggy but are now clinging to the sweat on my legs. I have my purple turtleneck tucked into them, the sleeves pulled all the way down, so that the only bits of my skin that are showing are on my face and hands.

Mom and Emma are both in shorts and T-shirts. When Mom saw what I was wearing this morning she sighed, but she didn't say anything. It's the end of the summer. She's as sick of telling me my outfits are crazy as I am of defending them.

But she's wrong. At least I'm covered. I'd rather be sweaty than exposed.

"Now, girls," Mom says. "We're going to have a lot to do once we get inside, OK? The previous owners left piles of possessions here, and we have to either throw it all away or donate it to charity. I'm going to need your help to get the house into shape."

Then she turns to me. She wraps her hands around mine and I have to look down slightly to focus on her. Mom is small and I've always known that but I'm still getting used to her being smaller than *me*. I look in her green eyes and forget about the sweat for just a second. These moments have been so rare in the year since Emma started living with us. The ones where Mom remembers that I'm her daughter and Emma is her niece. The ones where Mom remembers that it was me first, that it was just the two of us for a long, long time.

She puts her hand on my face, which is totally fine because she's my mom and all the extra fabric I've been wearing this summer has nothing to do with her.

"We did it, baby girl," she says. "We're homeowners."

A little bit of the excitement she's been filled up with spills into me. I smile at her. Despite the sweat, I shiver a little bit.

This is a big moment.

My mom and I own a house.

She hands me the keys. "Lydia," she says, "you do it. You open the door."

I nod and smile, then walk up the stairs to the front door. There's a huge crack in the top step. The railing is leaning so far to the left I can't even reach it.

I try to see this house the way Mom does. The way she says it will look when we're finished working on it. It's hard to see it as anything but a beat-up shack, especially considering the rows of pristine brownstones and brand-new, shiny high-rises in the neighborhood where we live. But I take a deep breath and I try.

I reach out to touch the heavy metal door in front of me. The two brass numbers fastened to it tell me our new address: 44 Washington Court. When I reach the door, one of the 4s falls off and I catch it in my palm. As I do, a *zing* goes up my arm. The 4 in my hand almost seems to talk to me.

Maybe this new house could be a good thing.

Maybe, once we move, Andrew and his friends will never know where I live.

I put my key in the front door and turn. It swings open too quickly, like it's made of Styrofoam.

Inside is a dark and dusty living room, crowded with boxes and furniture, as if someone tried to pack up but vanished halfway through the job. There's a staircase along the left wall of the living room and a doorway in the back of the living room leading to a kitchen with all the cabinets open, or maybe all the cabinet doors torn off.

A shiver goes up my spine. A good one.

I love this place. Not for the beautiful home Mom says it will become. But for its spookiness right now.

I've walked into one of the horror novels hidden under my bed. I've stepped into one of the movies my best friend, Miriam, and I love to scream at during sleepovers.

5

In books and movies, the answer to the problem is always in the scariest possible place. My answer is here. Somewhere hidden in this mess. I know it.

After a few hours of picking through our new creepy living room, we're walking back to our current apartment. My legs are covered. My arms are covered. My collarbone is covered. There's almost nothing left of me to look at.

As we approach our block, the chain-link fence around the park at the corner comes into view. I hear the basketballs bouncing off the backboards. I hear boys shouting. My breath catches in my throat.

Please don't look up. Please don't see me.

The boys have been at this park every day this week. I've been going to school with most of them since kindergarten, so I know they know where I live. But so far this summer they haven't bugged me when I've walked past. Maybe that's because Andrew—the worst one—has been away for the summer. Or maybe it's because I'm wearing all these clothes now.

My breath gets heavy as we walk past. *Don't look up. Don't look up.*

I rub the brass 4 from our new front door where I stashed it in my pocket. I keep pace with Mom and Emma. Then we are past them and safely inside for another day.

Our apartment looks bright and shiny with its white walls and hardwood floor and portraits of Emma and me hanging over the couch in the main room. If it weren't for the sweat and stranger-dust all over me, the whole new maybe-haunted house might feel like a dream.

"I call first shower!" Emma says, then darts into our one and only bathroom like she does every time we get home from the park or the beach or anywhere we all get sweaty. She always calls the first shower even though I'm always sweatier.

Mom raises her eyebrows at me. "It's not her fault you're dressing like it's February when it's ninety degrees outside."

"It wouldn't be fair for her to get the first shower every time even if we were dressed the same way," I say.

"She takes faster showers, Lydia," Mom says. "I need you to let this one go."

She's said that a lot since Emma moved in. It's like her mantra.

My room used to be my own—*I need you to let this one go.*

We order pizza every Friday night—*I need you to let this one go.*

You said I could get a dog when I turned twelve—*I need you to let this one go. We have Emma now.*

But Emma is not at all like the cuddly puppy I've been imagining.

I march to our room like I'm angry. But actually it's good to have a minute alone.

Emma and I have twin beds pushed up against opposite walls. I say Emma has the better side because she has the closet on hers. But the door to the room is on my side, so she's always saying I have the best one. Once, Mom told us to switch but we looked at each other and started laughing.

I check to be sure I'm absolutely alone, then pull the box out from under my bed. It's just an old shoebox, so no one would ever think anything of it. But it's where I keep my notebook, and I don't ever want anyone to look at my lists and the random thoughts I use to make things make sense because ever since last spring nothing makes sense.

I take out my notebook and pencil and write a quick list:

MAGIC

I know Sister Janice and everyone at school say magic is bad, but if it's that bad then maybe it's real. Maybe it's powerful. Maybe it's what I need. Maybe our new house could be magic. Maybe these things I found in the house and took home in my pockets could also be magic.

1. The brass 4 from the front door.

2. A tiny doll the size of my thumb with gold hair and a purple dress.

3. A toilet-paper roll.

Maybe if I keep one of them in my pocket from now on, the boys . . . everyone . . . will stop bothering me.

I shove all three new objects plus my notebook into the old shoebox and slide it under the bed before Emma could possibly be done with her shower.

I know it's weird to collect strangers' things. And it's extra weird to bring home a toilet-paper roll. But the house was covered in them. There were little piles of toilet-paper rolls in every corner. I found them on the windowsills and under the couch and in the doorway to the kitchen. I found them in the kitchen cabinets and between couch cushions and behind the empty TV stand. They have to mean something.

I hear Emma turn the shower off. It's almost my turn. I know Mom will let me go next. She always goes last.

"Hey, Mom," I call. "Is it just us three for dinner?"

"Us three," Mom says, "and Jeremy is on his way too." Her voice goes up and down in a singsong way when she says *Jeremy* because he's her boyfriend and now she's in love and that's something I'm still trying to get used to for so many reasons.

I take a deep, shaky breath and shove all the words I want to say into my stomach. "OK."

When Jeremy comes for dinner he almost always sleeps over. My mom's attention has been divided ever since Emma moved in last summer. When Jeremy's here I'm down to a tiny fraction.

Plus there are other things about Jeremy. . . .

I try not to remember the way Jeremy put his hand on my shoulder and kept it there the last time I saw him when Mom wasn't home. I try not to think about how he stood two inches too close to me.

It was probably nothing.

It was probably normal.

That's what I'm telling myself as I slip the 4 into the pocket of the jeans I will put on after I shower. Just in case there's magic in anything that comes from the house. Just in case I need protecting. Just in case the scariness isn't all inside my head.

But I know it's not real. It can't be.

Mom would never choose a not-safe boyfriend.

HOW TO BECOME A WEIRDO

YOU'LL BE RUNNING AROUND THINKING YOU'RE a totally normal good girl. Your life will be filled with homework and texting and playing tag with the boys and girls at recess. The same boys and girls you've been playing tag with since kindergarten.

Then the boys will change and the girls will change and you'll be the same old you except now that same old you is a weirdo.

Andrew will give you a nickname.

Swing.

At first you won't think that much about it. Then your friend Miriam will tell you what it means. "He's calling you Swing because he likes the way your uniform skirt swings between your butt and your knees."

"What?" you'll whisper-shout. You'll feel dirty and disgusting, like bugs are crawling around your veins trying to get through your skin.

But Miriam will be telling you this in the most excited voice in the world, almost like she's forcing herself to be happy for you. Almost like she's trying with all her friendship spirit not to be jealous. So instead of crying, like you want to, you'll smile.

Soon all the boys will call you Swing.

They'll whisper things about your legs that fill you with heavy, dark, oily shame.

They'll talk about your curvy hips and how the shadow of your bra strap shows through your white uniform shirt. They'll talk about your legs and arms and shoulders and lips and chest and knees and eyes like you are just a series of different shapes.

They'll create an "invention"—a compact mirror taped on a bendy straw.

When the teacher's looking they'll pretend it's to reflect the sunlight into each other's faces, but when she's not they'll use it to try to see up the girls' skirts.

When it's their turn, the other girls will giggle.

Maybe you should giggle too. You all wear shorts under your skirts. The boys know that. But still, this feels so disgusting.

When it's your turn, the giggles won't come. You'll press your legs so far together you'll get bruises inside your knees and ankles and you'll wonder why you're suddenly so different.

CHAPTER 2

MOM HAS MADE CHICKEN BREAST WITH bruschetta topping, homemade pita chips, and a big green salad. She always cooks like we're at a four-star restaurant when Jeremy is here. Even on Fridays when we're supposed to be ordering pizza.

When I come out of my room, Mom is pulling out our four tray tables and arranging them in the living room, trying to make them look like a real dining room table. She still hasn't showered but I can smell that dinner is almost ready. She walks to the drawer where she keeps our linens and then looks up. She stares at me for a beat. I'm dressed in my baggy blue jeans and a long-sleeved white T-shirt with black dogs printed all over it.

"Lydia," she says, "aren't you hot?"

She says the same thing every day. I hate it.

I walk to the fake table and help her put on a lilac table-cloth so that it starts to look a little more real.

"Dinner smells good," I say. I want Mom to feel good about the good things. About letting me shower before her every day and about providing everything we need by being a lawyer and about being a really good cook.

"I hope it is." She glances at the clock above the stove. "Oh my goodness, he'll be here any minute," she says. "I have to rinse off."

As soon as she's gone, the buzzer buzzes. I look at the door to our room, where Emma is lounging on her bed listening to her iPod.

Come out. Come out, I think.

I don't want to open the door. Even though I shouldn't have a problem with Jeremy. I should love how Jeremy laughs all the time, so much that his belly shakes. How he makes jokes. How he fixes things in our apartment. How he makes Mom laugh.

I should know better than to look for signs of creepiness in my mom's boyfriend.

If there's one person I should trust more than anyone, it's my mom.

Still . . . if Emma answers the door it'll be better.

The buzzer buzzes again.

I go into our room, pull out the Stephen King novel I've been reading when Mom isn't looking, and flop onto my bed.

The buzzer buzzes.

"Aren't you going to get that?" Emma says.

"Aren't you?" I ask.

It buzzes again.

"What's wrong with you?" Emma says.

"Nothing," I say. "I just want to read."

I open my book.

The buzzer buzzes again.

"You know she'll be mad at you," Emma says. "She never gets mad at me."

That's true.

I put my book down and get up, walk to the buzzer beside our front door, and press the green button. "Hello?" I say.

Jeremy's big laugh comes crackling through the speaker. "Oh, sweetheart," he says. "I was worried no one was there. Let me up, will ya?"

I press the button that looks like a door. I unlock the front door to our apartment. Then I sit on the couch.

We live on the tenth floor, which means I have about five minutes.

"Lydia, my Lydia," he says as he opens the door. I am definitely not his Lydia. He's been dating my mom for only six months. I'm Dad's Lydia. I'm Mom's Lydia. I'm not his Lydia. "It's so good to see ya!"

He's been away for a week. That's not very long for me to go without seeing anyone who isn't my mom.

Jeremy is tall and big in all directions. Big head, big arms, big legs. Mom says he's jolly, like Santa. He is usually smiling and laughing all the time, but he sometimes looks at me in a way that feels very un-Santa.

He sits on the couch next to me and slides an arm behind my neck. He's wearing short sleeves, so our skin rubs together for the length of his arm. I think about the sweaty purple turtleneck in the laundry hamper. I wish I were still wearing it.

I stiffen.

Is this weird? Or is it just weird to me?

I wish Mom could see it. She'd react if it was weird. She'd let me know if it's just my brain working too hard.

"Tell me what you did today," he says.

"Just cleaned the house," I say.

Jeremy looks around. His arm wiggles on the back of my neck. I can feel his arm hair brushing against my jaw.

I should grow my hair long. Long enough that it can cover my neck and part of my face like a brown, shiny curtain. It'll be another layer of protection. My short, spiky haircut is doing nothing for me right now.

"This place?" he says. "Your mom always keeps it clean."

I freeze. Jeremy doesn't know about the house? Mom did not tell Jeremy, her boyfriend, about the house.

I stumble for a second. I don't like lying.

Emma bursts out of our room all sunshiny. "Jeremy!" she says. He gets up and gives her a bear hug. Her feet lift off the ground. I'm so relieved to have his arm away from my neck but still queasy watching him hug her like that.

But she hugs him back, giggling.

"You got anything for me?"

"You know I do!" he says.

He slides a pack of Starburst out of the pocket of his shorts pocket.

"A sweet treat for a sweet girl," he says.

"Awesome!" she says, and does a little dance.

"Let's keep this one between you and me, OK?" Jeremy says, like always. Then he turns to me. "I have a pack for you, too," he says.

He hands it to me. I look at it in my palm.

The bottom drawer of my dresser is full of candy wrappers. Milky Ways and Life Savers and Jolly Ranchers and Airheads. Jeremy always brings us candy because he knows Mom doesn't ever let us have any. We have to hide the wrappers because Mom doesn't know about it.

Something about these Starburst in my palm makes my stomach turn, though.

"I don't like this kind," I say, even though I do. At least I usually do.

He sits back down next to me. He doesn't put his hands on me but he sits close like he's expecting me to lean on him or something.

"Are you sure?" he asks at the same time that Emma says, "Does that mean I can have two?"

I don't say anything.

Mom loves Jeremy. She always says Jeremy is the best thing to ever happen to us. And Jeremy does make her happy. And he does make life easier. But now I see so many things. Like Mom has to pretend a bunch of tray tables are a dining room table. And Jeremy has to sneak candy around her back. And Mom doesn't tell Jeremy everything either. Mom didn't tell Jeremy she bought a house.

We all hear the bathroom door open.

Jeremy grabs the Starburst out of my hand and gives it to Emma fast, and she runs into our room. In that motion he has leaned away from me so our knees aren't touching anymore.

Then Mom comes in the room.

At this moment he's not touching me even though he has been for the whole ten minutes since he arrived. I was going to look at her. I was going to use her face to tell me if the creepiness is all in my head. But now he's not touching me anymore.

Jeremy leaps off the couch and runs over to her. "Darling!" he says.

He spins her around and dips her like she's Cinderella at the ball or something. My mom laughs big and round and open and the laugh is like music and I want it to go on forever.

Jeremy cannot be like the boys at school.

Mom loves him.

I have to get control of my brain.

I wake up early the next morning. The sun is foggy through our window, lighting up my cousin's splayed limbs and the purple satin scarf that protects her hair. Emma is still able to sleep, cool in pink silk pajamas, just shorts and a tank. Mom gave us matching pairs for our birthdays in June, mine green and Emma's pink. Mine are still in my drawer with the tags on.

I squat and feel for my box under my bed. I don't pull it out because Emma is in the room. There's no way she's awake with the way she's snoring, but I don't want to risk it. I touch each item and count. *One. Two. Three. Four.*

I sneak the little doll out of the box in my palm. I stick it into the pocket of my pajama pants. They are blue with snowmen printed all over them. On top I have a white long-sleeved tee.

Before I go into the living room, I pull a sports bra out of the top drawer of my nightstand and step into it. I wiggle it over my legs and hips and then under my shirt. I wriggle my arms out of my sleeves and then down into the straps of it. I've become very good at getting dressed and undressed without exposing any skin, even in my own bedroom.

I take a deep breath and leave the room.

"Morning!" Mom whispers as soon as I close the bedroom door.

I breathe a sigh of relief. Just that whisper tells me Jeremy isn't here anymore.

Mom is already dressed. She's sitting at one of the tray tables. She's pulled it up close to the TV, where one of her cooking shows plays on almost silent. She's eating leftover chicken and bruschetta for breakfast, which Miriam would call the weirdest thing she'd ever seen if Miriam were back from visiting her mom in New Mexico for the summer. But I'm used to it. Leftover dinner is always my mom's breakfast. I didn't even realize people ate things like toast and eggs and waffles until Miriam and I started having sleepovers when I was like eight.

But sleepovers with normal breakfasts might be over now. Miriam has tried to text and email me so many times this summer but I haven't replied once. It's like I've forgotten how to talk to her now that she's normal and I'm not and she doesn't know.

"Did this wake you?" Mom asks, pointing at the TV.

I smile. I'm in the same room now and I still can't hear what the chef on TV is saying.

"No," I say.

If Jeremy were here, he'd be up with my mom. She'd be making him scrambled eggs or French toast or something else completely un-us. He'd be doing some project for her: fixing the shower so it has better water pressure or cleaning out the filter in the clothes dryer. He'd be making her laugh so loudly that even Emma would wake up. He'd tell her not to worry, that teenagers can sleep through anything.

She wouldn't be bothering to remind him that Emma's eleven and I'm twelve—we aren't even teenagers yet.

Those aren't bad things: his loudness and the way he fixes things and makes mom laugh. Those are the things I love about Jeremy. But sometimes I'm happy to have a break from him. Sometimes I'm happy to have a break from everyone except my mom.

"There's a plate for you in the microwave," Mom says. "Come join me."

I grab my own plate of bruschetta chicken. I add a side of the mac and cheese Mom made a few days ago and pull up a tray table next to my mom's.

I'm feeling warm and fuzzy. Jeremy isn't here. Emma is asleep. Mom is watching Food Network. Except for how low the volume is and how close we're sitting to it, it's almost like a normal Sunday morning.

Then Mom looks at me and says, "Christmas pajamas? Really, Lydia?"

I want to talk about something else. Anything else. It's only Mom and Emma and me here. Maybe I should go change into those green silk pj's and make her happy.

I can't.

"They aren't Christmas pajamas," I say. "Snowmen are just sculptures made of snow. They could be any religion. They don't have anything to do with Christmas."

"Lydia," Mom says.

It's her serious voice.

I look at the TV. Sunny Anderson is rubbing a brush over a grill. "What's she making?" I ask. "Steak?"

"Shrimp!" Mom says. "Grilled shrimp tacos with a cabbage slaw and pico de gallo."

21

"Yum."

We eat.

After a few minutes Mom tries again. "Tell me why you're wearing winter pajamas," she says. "It's just us right now. Tell me. Please."

I look at her. The way her short hair curls in all directions in the mornings before she combs it and puts in tons of gel. The way her pale green eyes look right at mine and it doesn't make me squirm. She's still my mom.

But I can't tell her.

There's a wall now. I don't think she realizes she's the one who built it by inviting all these new people into our lives and our home.

"What are we doing today?" I ask.

Mom wavers for a second. I can tell she's considering pushing me. But she doesn't. "I don't think you're going to like it but it's not an option," she says.

My heart races. Sometimes Jeremy pressures Mom into going to church with him. Sometimes Mom makes us go too. Worst—we always have to go to his church on the other side of Brooklyn where the priest talks about the "role of women" and Emma is always the only black person. Emma's my cousin but we don't look anything alike because my mom, dad, and I are all white and Emma looks like her mom did and her mom was black. It's got to be weird to be the one black person in a white family but my mom's usually pretty good at making sure Emma's not the only black person anytime we go out anywhere. Anywhere except Jeremy's church.

"Back to the house," she says.

I let out a breath. "All right," I say. I'm smiling.

"All right?" Mom says.

"Yeah," I say. "I like it there."

We only saw half the living room yesterday. There's a kitchen and there are bathrooms, and upstairs there are bedrooms and one of them will be mine. Mom didn't just buy a house. She bought a pile of delicious secrets. Someone else's secrets. Secrets that can't hurt me.

"I'm so glad!" Mom says. "We have to spend as much time there as we can over the weekends. It's going to take forever to clean it out."

"Weekends?" I ask.

"Well, we can't go during the week. I have work," Mom says. She's a lawyer at a small firm in downtown Brooklyn. "That's how I bought the house, after all."

And like that an idea forms in the back of my brain. One that makes my heart swell. One that gives me more hope and happiness than I've felt all summer.

Somewhere in that house I can find the protection I need before I have to go back to school and face the boys again.

I just need time to search.

HOW TO TREAT YOUR MOM'S BOYFRIEND

WHEN YOUR PARENTS FIGHT ALL THE time, it feels like it's happening to you and you alone. You pull a pillow over your head in the middle of the night so you don't hear them shouting about responsibilities and fun and how things used to be. It feels like every word is being hurled at your body and landing with painful thuds right in your rib cage.

When your parents finally divorce, it feels like that's happening to you too. Like your dad is breaking your heart by moving out. Like your mom is helping him open the wound.

It won't be until a man shows up and makes your mom's shoulders relax that you'll realize she's been holding them too close to her ears for years. It won't be until he fixes the dishwasher the first time she asks that you see how deep her frown lines have grown from all the fighting. It won't be until you hear laughing in the middle of the night that you realize all that fighting and heart-breaking wasn't happening just to you. It was happening to them, too.

And you love your parents. You love your mom. So you try try try to love the super from the building on the next block when he becomes your mom's boyfriend. You watch him closely as he surprises her with Restaurant Week reservations and tickets to art exhibits. You listen to him when he shows up right when he says he will and tries to teach you how to fix the dishwasher just to impress her. You watch as your mom turns into something even more than a mom you remember from a long time ago.

She turns into the mom you forgot to forget.

So when the man starts to hug you for just a few moments too long, you ignore it. You say it's all in your head.

When he grabs your knee under the table during dinner, you scoot away but don't say anything.

When he looks right at your legs when you wear shorts on the first warm day of spring, you just stop wearing shorts.

After all, he doesn't do anything really wrong. He doesn't do anything you could describe to someone. He doesn't cross any lines anyone else would notice. It's nothing real—just a dark feeling you can't describe, and you can't quite tell if that feeling is coming from him or if it's coming from yourself.

CHAPTER 3

I DON'T SPEND THAT DAY GOING carefully through boxes and digging for hidden treasures in our new house like I want to. Instead I get down on my hands and knees and scrub the floor. I polish the baseboards. I brush away cobwebs and save spiders by letting them out the front door. I scrub the one toilet that we know is working and work the black bits out of the tile floor of the bathroom with a toothbrush. I make sure Mom sees how hard I'm working. She has to trust me to do this job right so that I can ask her what I plan to ask her later.

Emma unearths the couch from under a pile of boxes and bags and old sweatshirts and then sits on it, slowly picking through strangers' clothes and sorting them into donation piles and trash piles.

"I shouldn't have to do this, Aunt Molly," she whines. "I won't be living here."

"We'll see," Mom says.

I scrub.

"My dad will get me as soon as he comes home and I'll go back to living with him," Emma says.

"We'll see," Mom says.

"I don't get why I should have to clean a house I'm not even going to live in," Emma says.

"Well, I'm here today and you need to be with me, so you're here too," Mom says. "But you don't have to help. If you want to sit there and do nothing, that's fine with me. But there's no internet and no television and no books here and so I thought perhaps helping me would save you from complete boredom."

I pretend not to be listening. I keep my eyes under the couch, where I'm sweeping up candy wrappers and old Coke cans and lots of sticky stuff that I don't want to know what it used to be.

"Ugh. Fine!" Emma says. She reaches into the bag next to her and pulls out a book.

"I found a book, Aunt Molly!" Emma says in a *nah-nah-nah-boo-boo* voice. "Hey!" she says. "This book is on my summer reading list."

I stop cleaning long enough to look at my mom. Sometimes I think she might be a genius.

"Guess I'm just going to sit here and read," Emma says. She leans back on the dusty couch, not worrying about someone else's couch dust settling all over her bare shoulders.

Mom half smiles to herself. I shake my head.

* * *

Hours later, when the sun finally starts to set, I'm covered in a thick layer of sweat and grime and Emma has read half of her summer-reading book.

It's mid-August. She's been refusing to do her summer reading for more than seven weeks. Now she read half a book in one day.

"I think we deserve some Chinese food!" Mom announces.

"Can we sit in the booth?" Emma and I say at the same time.

We have Chinese food a lot, but Mom usually brings it home if she doesn't make it herself. Emma and I both love to sit in the booth at the Chinese restaurant because it has a fish tank in the wall next to it with big fish lazing by. It has those cheesy menus they give you when you're kids, and Emma and I like to race to do the word finds. It has big fountain sodas with straws, and Emma and I like to blow the wrappers at each other.

Something about the Chinese restaurant turns us back into cousins instead of this cousin-sister mash-up that hasn't been working since she moved in a year ago.

Before Emma moved in we used to beg to see each other. Every once in a while Emma would spend the weekend with us and we wouldn't be able to stop giggling. My mom always took Emma's side then, too. Or treated Emma like she was extra special or something. But it was different when she was only here one night or for a weekend. And it was different because Emma always treated *me* like I was extra special.

We're only a year apart but I'm the big cousin. She always wanted to read what I was reading and watch what I was watching and do what I was doing. I used to count down the nights until she'd come to sleep over.

Everything is different now that there are no nights to count.

"I think we deserve to sit in the booth too," Mom says.

Emma jumps and wraps her clean arms around Mom. "You're the best, Aunt Molly!" she squeals.

I stand up. My muscles seem to snap at the movement. It's been so long since I straightened them out. I didn't realize how much work cleaning could be.

"Let's go," I say. I run my hand through the top part of my hair and sweat drips down the back of my neck.

"Ew," Emma says. "You're all sweaty."

"Well, maybe that's because I was actually working and not just lounging on the couch all day."

"Well, maybe that's because this is actually going to be your house," Emma says.

"It's probably going to be your house too," I say.

"We'll see," Mom says before Emma can say anything else. "I'm proud of you, Lyddie." Mom puts her arm around me, sweat and all. I can feel her bare arm on the back of my neck. It doesn't bother me. "And grateful. You did some good work."

I was going to wait until dinner, but I decide this is my moment.

"I could do some more," I say.

Mom laughs. "You will, believe me."

I turn my head to look at her. She's a little sweaty, too, despite her shorts and tank top. Her cheeks are extra pink. "No, I mean, I could come back tomorrow. While you're at work. And, you know, keep going."

"No!" Emma says. "No way!"

I look at her, trying to shoot daggers with my eyes. "By myself, I meant," I say.

"You're at your dad's the next two days," Mom says.

"Oh yeah," I say. It's hard to keep track in summer. I'm always forgetting. "Well, Wednesday, then."

Mom hesitates. "It's not your responsibility, Lydia," she says.

"I know," I say. "I just . . . I really like it here, Mom. I can't believe you bought a house. I can't wait to live here."

"Honey," Mom says.

"I want to help!" I say.

Mom takes a deep breath.

"Please?"

Mom thinks for a moment. Then nods. "You girls can come here Wednesday."

"No!" Emma says.

"I meant just me!" I say.

Mom shakes her head. "There's no way I'm letting you each hang out all day by yourself."

Mom's rule is usually that if she's at work, Emma and I need to be together. But on the days I'm at Dad's, Emma stays with our neighbor Ms. Kemp. I don't see why she couldn't do that every day so that I can clean the house. During the school year when I'm out with my dad after school, Emma just sits in our living room and watches TV alone. I don't see why she couldn't do that either.

"There's no way I'm coming inside this creepy house when I don't have to," Emma says in her extra-snooty voice.

"Well, I guess you'll have to sit on the front stoop and read, then," Mom says.

Emma rolls her eyes. "You always take her side," she says.

That's not true. It's not even true now. It only looks like Mom is taking my side. Really, she's using me to get Emma to do some of her summer reading before summer is over in two weeks.

It stings.

But it shouldn't. It shouldn't matter.

All I wanted was a chance to explore this place alone. This place that's full of magic that can help me.

Two more days and then I'll get that chance.

CHAPTER 4

AS SOON AS DAD AND I get to his little apartment in way way way upper Manhattan the next day, I walk into the tiny bedroom and change into shorts and a T-shirt. I'm sweaty from the ninety-minute subway ride in pathetic air-conditioning.

I don't tell Mom that I dress like a normal person when I'm with Dad.

And Dad never asks.

But the truth is Dad is a man and he's safe. Once when Dad picked me up from school last April, the boys immediately stopped talking about me. They walked away and started talking to Miriam and Diamond instead.

I hate that it's true, but being with Dad keeps me even safer than all the extra clothes. It's not that much help because Dad lives far away now. He's a bartender at one of the fanciest bars in Manhattan. He works every weekend so I'm supposed to see him every Monday and Tuesday. Those are his days off.

It works a lot better in the summer when I don't have school. During the school year he has to come to Brooklyn after school on Mondays and Tuesdays, which means double the subway rides for only a little bit of the time, and sometimes he's just too tired or something, but I try not to think about all those times in the summer when we're running around Manhattan having adventures. That's just one of the reasons I don't want to think about school starting again so soon.

"Guess today's adventure, kiddo!" Dad says as soon as I'm ready.

"Umm . . . ," I say. What could today's adventure be?

So far this summer we've gone to the Bronx Zoo, had a fancy picnic in the middle of Central Park, ridden a boat up the Hudson River, and taken trapeze lessons. It really could be anything.

He has something behind his back so I reach for it. Dad hops away each time my hand grabs at his wrist.

"Guess! Guess!" he insists.

I try to run around him to see but he moves to block my way.

"Daaaaad!" I say.

"OK," he says. He holds out his hands. "Mets tickets."

I beam at him.

I don't love baseball but I do love Mets games with my dad. This will be our first one all summer.

After another subway ride, we're there. It feels good to be out like a normal person. I'm in shorts that are sort of long and my Mets T-shirt is sort of baggy and fully covers my shoulders and half my arms. So I'm still wearing more than most people filing into this stadium. But not so much that people are staring at me, wondering what sort of strict religion I belong to or if I'm covering up a skin condition or something.

We walk along the inside of the stadium, dodging the crowds of people, and emerge into the sunshine at the bleachers section. I pause a second to enjoy the sun on my skin. I turn my face up to the sky. I feel the burn of it on my nose and arms and legs and I know I should have worn sunblock. Mom will be mad at me and at Dad for forgetting. But for now I enjoy the way there's absolutely nothing between me and the sun for the first time in weeks.

Dad and I get in line at one of the food carts and order the usual to bring back to our bleacher seats. A beer for him, a huge Coke full of ice for me, and a large buttery popcorn for the two of us to share.

The bleachers are crowded and my legs and hips feel too close to all the strangers as we negotiate our way to our seats in the upper deck. Way down below us, the Mets are throwing balls back and forth on the infield and outfield. The heat of the metal bleachers is almost burning me through my shorts. Dad throws an arm around my shoulders, keeping his hand free to start pointing.

"This guy, Hank Littlefield," he says, pointing to the center fielder, "he's hit a home run in every game he's played this season. It's a record. No professional baseball player has ever hit so many home runs in a row."

I nod. It's not really that I pretend to care. It's more like I don't care about baseball unless it's my dad and me at a Mets game. Then suddenly baseball is not a sport and instead it's this special thing my dad loves that he wants to share with me and I care about every word.

I take a huge sip of sticky-sweet Coke and balance it out with a handful of buttery popcorn.

Mom won't let me drink Coke. She says it stunts my growth. But Dad doesn't ask me to lie about it, so I can enjoy every sip.

Dad is still talking baseball when a person squeezes onto the bench next to me, shoving me over so that I'm closer to Dad than I ever want to be to anyone.

"Hey, man, sorry," the guy says, leaning over me like I'm not even here. "They have us shoved in here like sardines today, huh?"

He's younger than my dad, maybe college-age. He's tall and white with hairy legs and broad shoulders. He wears a plain gray T-shirt and a baseball hat and cargo shorts. I wouldn't think anything of all this if his hip weren't jammed against mine and he weren't leaning across me, almost in my lap.

Dad shrugs. "It's part of the fun, right?"

"Something like that," Too Close Guy says. "You think Littlefield is going to keep it up today?"

"Hope so," Dad says. But I'm not as interested when he's talking to this guy. I want Dad to talk to me again.

I take another sip of Coke but it tastes all wrong now, thick and syrupy like some sort of gross medicine.

"Here we go," Too Close Guy says. He reaches an arm around my waist and for an awful second I think he's going to rest his arm on me. But instead he pats Dad's shoulder hard and says, "Let's go, Mets!"

Everyone stands to watch the first batter.

I try to whisper to Dad. "Do you know that guy?"

"Huh?" Dad asks, smiling. "No. That's part of the fun. Every Mets fan is a friend today!"

When the Mets come up to bat, the first player steps up to the plate and Dad starts talking Mets facts in my ear. I try to enjoy it again. I try to care about them. I try to let the Mets magic come back to us. But it's empty now, ruined.

We all fall back into our seats and the guy next to me starts arguing with my dad about something he said to me.

I look down. I look at my knee.

His knee is touching my knee.

They are having an argument but I can't listen to it. To me it sounds like this.

The guy: "Baseball!"

My dad: "Baseball!"

The guy: "Baseball, baseball. Baseball?"

My dad: "Baseball."

My dad will say they aren't yelling. That's what he says every time I sleep over in his little bedroom and he stays on the couch in the living room with ESPN blaring on the TV.

I tell him I can't sleep with people yelling in the living room and he says, "It's not yelling; it's ESPN."

ESPN is nothing but a bunch of men yelling at each other.

And I hate the yelling. But I hate the knee more.

I wish wish wish for my jeans.

I rub the tiny doll in my pocket. The one item from the new house I brought to Dad's today.

Get his knee off my knee, I beg her.

It doesn't work.

Even she has stopped working.

Hairy Kneecaps's legs are spread wide. I'm twisted up into myself, my legs wrapped sweaty around each other, my hip jammed into my dad, trying to take up as little space as possible while this stranger's legs are spread like two feet apart and his knee is pushed into me like he thinks he deserves more space, even though he has all the space his ticket is supposed to give him plus half of mine.

Maybe he actually doesn't see me here.

Maybe I should say something.

I stare at the knee one more time. Then I look up at him and say, "So you're a Mets fan?"

He gives me a weird look. The sort of look people have been giving me when I go out dressed the way I wish I were dressed right now. Then he looks back at my dad, laughs, and says, "You'd better believe it!"

He answers my dad even though I asked the question.

My dad laughs too. Like this is funny.

I feel invisible.

The inning ends and Hairy Kneecaps's knee is still pressed into mine.

The worst thing is that I'm with my dad. And he can see it. He can totally see our knees. This is in broad daylight, daylight I was enjoying just a minute ago.

So Dad doesn't even care that this stranger's kneecap is touching mine.

That means this is OK. My dad would say if it weren't. He'd protect me if this were wrong.

This is the usual way to be in the world.

Hairy Kneecaps leans across me again to talk more baseball with my dad while the teams switch and the Mets run onto the field.

I only get a few days with my dad all summer. I only get a few hours with him the rest of today. My doll needs a little help protecting me today, I decide. I'll give it a boost. It'll do the rest.

I stand.

"Lyddie?" Dad says.

"I have to go to the bathroom," I say.

"Oh, OK," Dad says, getting up to follow me.

I step over Hairy Kneecaps's feet, holding my breath as my butt swings in front of his face. It doesn't matter. He moves his head around me to see the first pitch of the bottom of the first inning. I am nothing but in his way.

"I want to switch seats with you," I say as soon as we

reach the line for the ladies' room.

I expect him to ask why, like Mom would.

He says, "OK, sure."

When we get back to the bleachers, I sit between Dad and a five-year-old boy. The boy spills his sticky fruit punch all over me and it feels like relief.

Dad's shoulders angle away from Hairy Kneecaps. He goes back to talking baseball just to me and a little bit of the magic comes back. There is a full inch of empty space next to every bit of me: my knees, my hips, my shoulders, my arms.

But I can't help glancing over.

Hairy Kneecaps's knees are pulled closer into his own seat. They are close to my dad's but not touching.

I guess I'm the only one who doesn't deserve space.

HOW TO EXPLAIN YOUR DIVORCE
TO YOUR DAUGHTER

TELL HER THAT HER DAD PLAYS too much.

Tell her that her mom takes life too seriously.

Be careful not to say anything else.

Be careful not to say anything that could actually make sense.

CHAPTER 5

THE REST OF THE TIME WITH my dad goes by too quickly. By the time we get home after the Mets game it's late already. We go to bed and then have a long, lazy morning. Then we go out for pancakes at noon because my mom eats dinner for breakfast but on his days off my dad eats breakfast for lunch. Then it's already time for Dad and I to take the long subway ride back home.

The next day Emma and I go back to the house, alone. We stand on the sidewalk and stare at it, the way we did the first day, except not holding hands. It's hard to remember how I used to see it: broken and tilting.

Today I have goose bumps despite my sweatpants and hoodie.

I reach into my pocket and tangle my fingers in the corners of the brass 4 I brought with me. I've decided to bring a little bit of the house with me everywhere, even to the house itself.

I've decided that a little bit of house is a little bit of magic. And hopefully today I can find even more magic.

Emma flops down on the front stoop. "Good luck in there," she says. She opens her summer-reading book back up.

I don't say anything as I pull the key Mom gave me out of my pocket and slip it into the lock, loving the *click-click-click* sound.

At the last second, I scoop up the lunch Mom packed Emma to put it in the fridge with mine.

"Thanks," she says.

Emma is usually easier to take when my mom isn't around. When we can pretend nothing changed a year ago and we're cousins who would spend every second together if we could.

If it were a year ago, Emma would be following me into this spooky house.

I'd be telling her exactly why I wear all these clothes. She'd be wearing the same things as me and going to the same places.

She'd be almost a best friend, almost a Miriam. I've sort of lost them both this summer.

Emma stopped following me around once she started living with us. It's hard because I miss her all the time but I'm also so sick of her all the time.

I walk through the front door and freeze, waiting for the magic to come over me. It doesn't.

The living room looks a lot different than it did a few days ago. Mom must have gotten most of the stuff out of the back of it while I was scrubbing the front of it the other day. There's a row of garbage bags piled up on the linoleum near the front door. There's a row of boxes for charity piled up on the carpet near the door to the kitchen. The dusty couch is empty in the center of the room, but other than that we've decided to throw away or donate the furniture. Mom says we'll donate the couch, too, but that we can leave it where it is because someone will come and pick it up.

It's weird that when you buy a house, you accidentally buy everything that's in it too.

It's extra weird to sell your house without taking all your stuff with you.

Who were these people?

Did they die?

I shiver. Finally.

I have to figure it out before school starts. I have to find something that will make school . . . possible.

I cross the living room, which feels too easy with all the stuff out of the way. I go into the kitchen and put our lunches in the refrigerator, which is working and thankfully empty, like Mom said on Sunday. I'm here for secrets, not decades-old moldy bananas or deli meat or whatever. I find the dial on the wall to turn on the air-conditioning. It's dark and damp and cavelike in here but of course still hot.

The kitchen isn't quite as dark and there's not quite as much stuff in it. But then I remember: I'm alone. I can go upstairs.

The stairs are covered with burgundy carpet. There are things on them. Lots and lots of toilet-paper rolls, of course.

The head of a Barbie doll. The body of the same doll a few steps later. An unopened can of dog food. As I continue upstairs, this magic house doesn't feel like it's full of delicious secrets anymore. It's starting to feel just sad.

Maybe I won't find a solution here. Maybe this isn't where I figure out how to keep the boys away. Maybe there's isn't any magic.

At the top of the stairs the burgundy carpet turns to a rusty, pukey orange color. I'm not sure if that's damage or if it's actually a different carpet. I find four doors, all dark brown wood, all closed.

I start with the door at the end of the hallway. It's just an off-white bathroom. Boring.

I try the door next to it.

It's a bedroom with a big bed in the middle. There's faded blue-gray carpet, and the furniture—a dresser with a mirror and a desk—is modern and sleek. There's a black-and-white bedspread on the bed, and the walls are painted a trendy shade of gray. Bags and boxes are strewn across the bed, half-packed. Someone's bra hangs out of a dresser drawer. Toilet-paper rolls pepper every surface. The room doesn't fit with the house at all, except for the stuff everywhere.

I wander to the bed and run my hand over the gray bedpost.

Who were these people? Where did they go?

I walk back into the hall and open another door. This room is so full of stuff I can't even get the door open. I try the last door.

I'm blinded by pink. The walls are pink. The bed is pink with a pink canopy across the top. It has a white bedspread, and on top it's covered, completely covered, in pink teddy bears. The goose bumps come back.

This is a girl's room.

A little girl's room.

I guess I didn't think there would be kids who once lived here. It seems even crazier for kids to disappear.

My stomach flips and I suddenly wish Emma were in here with me.

I walk over to the closet and slide it open. Frilly dresses—white and pink and purple—hang neatly. I run my fingers over one of them. It looks like it would fit a four-year-old. Maybe five. Some of the dresses are bigger, some smaller, as if someone tried to freeze a piece of all the versions of the girl who once lived in this room.

I know something about this girl, whoever this room used to belong to. I know something suddenly, in my gut, like there are ghosts all around me whispering in my ears.

This girl has the magic. The magic I need to survive school again in a few weeks.

It comes from her. From whoever used to live in this room.

Where is she?

I spend a long time wandering between the bed and the closet. I spend a long time staring at pink teddy bears and frilly dresses in wonder.

"Lunchtime?"

The word makes me jump so high my head hits the top of the closet.

I turn. Emma stands in the doorway.

"No fair!" she shouts. "Are you trying to call dibs before I even see the rooms?"

There are a thousand things to say if I'm her cousin. There's one thing to say if I'm the weird thing between cousin and sister.

I should choose to be her cousin right now.

I should say, *Look at these dresses. Isn't this creepy? Who do you think lived here? Why did they leave all their stuff?*

I should say, *Forget cleaning. Do you hear the ghosts too? Can you help me listen to them?*

I should say, *Can I tell you what's been happening to me at school? Can you help me find the magic in this mess that will protect me from Andrew and his friends?*

Instead I say, "I thought you said you weren't going to live here anyway."

Emma deflates. She stares at the toes of her sneakers. "I'm not," she says.

She looks up and I see her take in the room, with its pink and frills. I see her make the same connections I just made. I see her brain asking the same questions. I wait for her to say something. Something she should say. I wait for her to choose cousins. But she doesn't either.

She says, "Let's eat on the front steps."

We go downstairs and I grab the lunches from the fridge

and sit beside her outside. We take out our turkey sandwiches. Of course they aren't regular turkey sandwiches. Mom makes her own bread and puts butter on them with just a dash of vinegar, which she says is unusual but everyone finds it delicious.

Emma keeps her nose in her book as we eat in silence. Tonight she'll tell Mom that this required reading was so boring but right now I see her eyes moving fast. I won't tell Mom she's enjoying it, though. I'll do that one thing for her.

The sun beats down on my head. I can feel sweat tickling the back of my knees.

"Man, it's hot," I say.

Emma looks up at me. "Well," she says, and she stares at my clothes.

A breeze blows by and Emma turns her face to it. I can tell she's enjoying the way it brushes against her bare arms and legs and shoulders.

She goes back to her book. I go back to my sandwich.

But after a few minutes she says, "You know, you don't need to wear the extra clothes. She's always going to love you best."

"Huh?" I say.

"You're her daughter . . . you don't need to try to make her notice you."

"You think the clothes are about you?" I ask. It maybe comes out a little mean.

"They are, aren't they?" Emma says.

"Why would you think that?" I ask.

"Because I get all the attention," she says. "But it's not that great, OK? It's not that great being stared at all the time because you don't look like your family and people wonder if your aunt is your babysitter."

She's right: she doesn't look like us and sometimes people do stare. I never really thought about what that was like for her . . . but I've also never wished for staring.

"I don't want people to stare at me," I say.

"And it's not that great being the messed-up one. You can go back to being normal."

"It's not about you," I say. "And . . . I hate attention."

"What's it about, then?"

I actually, really want to tell her. I should. I should choose cousins.

Instead I say something else I should say.

"Are you sure you don't want to explore the pink bedroom with me? It's creepy in there. It's sort of cool."

Emma looks up from her book.

Finally she says, "I'm not cleaning the house for you and your mom to live in."

I smile at her. "I didn't say anything about cleaning."

She smiles back. "Fine," she says.

Half an hour later, the pink frills and teddy bears have turned us back into cousins. We lie in the middle of the stuffed animals whispering to each other.

"Who do you think lived here?" Emma says. "Do you think this was a little girl's room?"

"It looks like it. What happened to her?" I start turning the teddy bears over to read the tags.

"What are you looking at teddy bears' butts for?" Emma asks.

We both start giggling. The sound of it is extra echoey, like we *are* in a horror movie and we really shouldn't be giggling.

"I'm not," I say. "I'm looking at the tags. Maybe she wrote her name on one of them."

"Oh," Emma says. She lies back down so she's looking up at the canopy. "You really like this house, Lydia?" she asks me.

And because in this room we're purely cousins, I answer honestly. "Yeah," I say. "I like the mystery. Like, what do you think all these toilet-paper rolls are here for?"

"That's the part I don't like." Emma pauses.

"The toilet-paper rolls?" I ask.

"No!" she says. "I don't like . . . This is going to sound stupid, but the house . . . it sort of feels like it's haunted."

I put down the teddy bear and sit all the way up, cross-legged. "Really?" I ask, too fast and too eager. "You think so?"

"I don't know if I believe in ghosts," Emma says. "But I guess . . . I guess I sort of feel them here."

"Feel them how?" I ask.

Emma sits up, mimicking my body position like she used to all the time.

"Do you want there to be ghosts?" Emma asks.

I can't answer her. Not with the whole truth. I'll sound crazy if I tell her I think there's magic in this house that can protect me. If I tell her I'm hoping there are ghosts who live here all the time. Ghosts who see everything. Ghosts who will see Jeremy's hand on my back or Jeremy hugging me too tightly or Jeremy sneaking us candy.

"No," I say. I fake a shudder. "But it would be . . . I don't know . . . exciting?"

"Exciting?" Emma asks. "I think exciting and scary are mixed up in your brain. Vacations are exciting. Sneaking candy is exciting. Ghosts are scary."

"What if they're good ghosts?" I say.

"Good ghosts?" Emma says. "Like Casper?"

She turns over a teddy bear.

I laugh. "Sure," I say. "Like Casper."

She tosses the teddy bear to me. "No wonder you're excited," Emma says. "You want to fall in love with a ghost."

"No!" I say, throwing the teddy bear back.

And soon we are having a teddy-bear fight in the pink, frilly room of a girl whose name we don't know but who may be watching us.

By the end of the day I'm more convinced than ever that the house is magic.

I don't go in the pink room at all on Thursday. I wipe the counters in the kitchen. I clean off the staircase. I lug the vacuum from our now apartment to our future house so that I can vacuum all the carpets. I stay far away from the frilly dresses and the pink canopy bed, knowing that the minute I walk into that room, I'll get lost in there again.

On Friday, I scrub the kitchen. I scrub each shelf of the fridge and polish the inside of all the cabinets. Then I start in the junk bedroom, separating things to go to the trash and things to be donated. Thursday and Friday are an investment in next week. When Mom comes this weekend, she needs to see that I've made progress or there's no way she'll let me come back.

But by cleaning up the house, I'm the one erasing the magic. By the end of the week it feels like only the pink room holds any spookiness anymore. Maybe all the ghosts have gathered in there. Or maybe there's magic in the toilet-paper rolls. They are everywhere. On the stairs and in the junk room and in the kitchen cabinets. They are in the drawers of the clean master bedroom. Under the couch and in the freezer.

I don't know why, but I start to collect them in one of the drawers in the upstairs bathroom. I keep putting them in there until they fill one drawer and I have to start on a second one.

Maybe they're part of the puzzle. Maybe they can tell me what happened to the kid from the pink room and the family that vanished and the house full of secrets that is now mine.

* * *

Emma and I are quiet as we walk home from the house on Friday. It's sort of a happy quiet, though, not the angry kind we used to have. I'm glad to have her matching me step for step as we walk across the street and onto our block.

I can hear the basketballs bouncing as we cross the street. I hear them—the boys from school—yelling at one another. We are going to have to walk past them.

I rub the little doll in my pocket.

It's going to be OK, I tell myself. *It's going to be like every other day this summer.*

We walk like always. No one has noticed me. My doll is working. I squeeze her harder, thanking her and begging her to keep it up.

But then I hear his voice. Just the sound of Andrew yelling "Hey!" makes my stomach turn.

He's back.

I start walking faster. I clutch the doll. But I'm not fast enough and she's not strong enough.

The boys all come to the fence and stare as we walk by. I cross the street even though the park is on the same side as our building. Emma follows me and doesn't ask why.

But their voices carry across the street.

One of them starts: "Swing, Swing!"

"Hey, Swing, I miss your skirt!" one says, and the rest of them fall into a fit of giggles.

"Hey, Swing, haven't you ever heard of shorts?" another calls.

I squeeze my doll. She seems to vibrate a bit in my hand. She's getting ready to protect me.

"Hey, Swing—"

"Hey, idiot!" Emma calls back, right at Andrew. "Haven't you figured out she's not interested? Get a clue."

"OOOOH!" the boys all shout. They stop looking at me and form a circle around Andrew, laughing. "She got you!"

They're still laughing at him when we get to our building. I loosen my grip on the doll. It worked. It made Emma brave. It still works. The magic in the house is strong. I have to find the strongest bit of magic so I can take it to school with me.

As we walk into the elevator, Emma mumbles something about boys being jerks. My heart is still pounding. I turn to smile at her. "Thanks," I say.

She shrugs. "Whatever. He's harmless."

For a second I had thought she understood. But Andrew isn't harmless to me.

I squeeze the doll in my pocket once again. Next week I'm going to take something stronger, something from the pink room. I'm going to be ready to face the boys by the time I get back to school.

The house is going to help me.

HOW TO PROTECT YOUR WEIRDO SELF
FROM THE WORLD

WHEN THE BOYS HAVE GONE DAYS and weeks without using your real name, when all you hear is "Swing! Swing!" every time you walk in a room, you'll look to your friends for help.

"I hate that nickname," you'll say.

But they'll laugh.

"I wish they'd start a nickname for me!" Miriam will say.

"I wish Andrew talked to me as much as he talks to you!" Diamond will say.

Andrew will pull your hair and pinch your sides.

Mona will say, "You're so lucky Andrew likes you!"

The boys will all laugh as Andrew doesn't stop when you try to walk away.

Diamond will say, "You're so lucky the boys all notice you."

So you'll try to like it. You'll try not to feel the disgusting bugs crawling under your skin when they use the terrible nickname. You'll try not to feel the bile climbing up your throat when they aim their mirror-straw invention at your knees.

Maybe the grown-ups can help, you'll think. But when you tell your teacher that you don't like the name, she'll just yell at the boys in a way that makes them say it even more and even louder.

And when your principal, Sister Janice, notices Andrew pulling your hair, she'll say, "Just ignore him. Ask God for help."

So when the world won't protect you, you'll turn to things outside the world.

Like God. But when he fails, you'll look for something stronger.

Like magic. But when it fails, you'll look for something stronger.

Like, maybe, the ghosts in your new house.

CHAPTER 6

SATURDAY NIGHT JEREMY IS AT OUR apartment for dinner for the third time in a row.

Mom, Emma, and I spent the day at the house. Mom was impressed with all the work I had done. I was sort of afraid she'd start on the pink room and be donating frilly dresses and teddy bears and other things I know I need to keep. But instead we spent the day in the junk room with the dark wooden door. The door to the pink room stayed fully closed. The junk room is half-empty now. I managed to put every toilet-paper roll into the bathroom drawer without Mom noticing.

While Mom and I cleaned, Emma sat in the hallway or on the front stoop and complained. But she finished one summer-reading book and started the next without Mom even asking. Or tricking her into it.

Now we're sitting around the fake kitchen table eating

homemade shrimp stir-fry and egg rolls. I'm starving and the dinner smells delicious, but Jeremy has clearly been cleaning floors in one of the buildings where he's a super. And the floor cleaner must be the same one my school uses. He smells like my school, like Andrew and the boys and their teasing, and the smell makes my stomach turn.

"Let's say grace!" Jeremy says.

He stretches his hands to either side and turns them palm up.

I shove my hand into my pocket and grab my doll.

I'm supposed to hold his hand.

Jeremy thinks that God wants me to hold his hand.

Maybe God does want me to hold his hand. Probably.

I should hold his hand.

I do not want to hold his hand.

I don't even realize how long I sit there staring at his hand before Mom says "Lydia!" like I'm causing trouble.

I look up. Emma's left hand is reaching toward my right.

I sigh and put my hand in hers. I slowly put my left hand in Jeremy's. I try to barely touch him but he grabs my palm tightly while I keep my fingers stiff so at least my fingertips aren't touching the back of his hand.

"Bless us, oh Lord," Jeremy begins. Mom and Emma join in. "And these thy gifts which we are about to receive from thy bounty. Through Christ our Lord. Amen."

Everyone else at the table does the sign of the cross. I don't.

I'm a little afraid Mom will say "Lydia!" again, but I also can't pretend to pray.

We only say grace if Jeremy's here. We only go to church if it's Christmas, Easter, or if he asks us to. We don't even talk about how weird this is when he's not around.

Once Mom said that she's mostly a Catholic because it connects her to her parents, who are both dead now. And to her grandparents and all her ancestors. She says we're Catholic because it's a part of what made us who we are, not because we believe every word and have to follow all the rules. She says we go to Catholic school because she can't afford private school and the public schools around us aren't any good.

I don't think Mom has ever explained any of that to Jeremy, though.

"It's just so wonderful for us all to be together!" Jeremy declares.

"I'm hungry," I say.

I dish some stir-fry and grab an egg roll. I douse soy sauce on it, hoping it will mask the smell of Catholic school floor soap. I take a bite. I know it was perfect the way Mom made it, but now it's too salty.

"Lydia," Mom says. "I need to talk to you about something." Her voice is flat and serious. She's sitting angled across the fake table from me, as far away as possible. Whatever she's about to say, she should say it when it's just her and me. When there aren't all these other people in the way, jamming themselves into our family.

I chew. I chew and chew and chew.

"Emma and I need to go on a little trip. We leave Monday."

I chew. The food won't go away.

Emma and Mom are going on a trip. The two of them. Without me.

I chew. I blink.

"Just for two nights."

I chew. I can't ask questions with all this food in my mouth, but it won't go anywhere. My throat is not accepting food right now. It's closed for business.

"We're going to see my dad!" Emma squeals, bouncing in her seat like she's four instead of eleven.

My eyes go wide. I feel both sicker and less sick at once.

Mom looks at Emma like she didn't want me to know where they are going. Even though I still don't know because no one tells me anything about my uncle, even where he lives. Somehow Emma is old enough to understand things I'm not, even though Emma is younger than me.

I finally swallow.

"Where will I be?"

If this were last year, I'd be sleeping over at Miriam's, playing pranks on her older brothers and enjoying the feasts of regular breakfast that her father whips up on weekend mornings. But it's not last year. Miriam should get back from her mom's house today, but I haven't talked to her all summer. It's impossible to talk to her when she's boy-crazy and I'm boy-scaredy. Even Mom has stopped asking about her.

Mom smiles and I know what she's going to say.

I cannot stay with Jeremy.

I cannot stay with Jeremy.

I cannot stay with Jeremy.

My heart beats out the phrase so hard I'm sure everyone at the table can hear what it's saying.

"That's why I arranged it for Monday and Tuesday," Mom says. "You'll stay with Dad one extra night. Jeremy will pick you up when Dad goes to work on Wednesday and I'll be home by the time you two get here on Wednesday."

I let out a long breath.

"We're going to see my dad!" Emma announces again, like she can't contain it.

I look at her. She really does look like a little kid, like a toddler who can't wait to go down a slide. She's brimming with happiness. It's overflowing out of her.

I don't understand it. Emma's dad is supposed to be unsafe. Adults actually call him unsafe. The same adults who act like the way boys tease us is nothing and don't say anything when men take our space at baseball games or hug us for too long. If all of that is safe, what could make Emma's dad unsafe?

It's a terrifying thought. But she looks so excited.

When Emma first moved in with us, she used to see her dad every week. But then he moved farther away for some reason and, I realize now, it's been a long, long time since she's seen him.

I smile at her. "I hope it's fun," I say.

And I do. I want her to have a good time with her dad. I just don't want her to have to borrow my mom to do it.

The next day Mom, Emma, and I go back to the house to work some more. Mom and I spend the morning in the living room and kitchen and junk room moving the garbage bags slowly out the door while Emma reads on the front porch. Mom has rented a dumpster that sits right in front of the house, taking up precious parking real estate.

"Lydia, don't you want to take off that sweater?" Mom says after a few minutes of rearranging garbage bags.

"If I wanted to take it off, I would," I snap back.

I lift a garbage bag and swing it onto my back.

"It's very hot," Mom says, "and I really need your help today. I don't want you complaining all day about how hot it is when you're wearing a heavy sweater."

"Do you hear me complaining?" I ask, and stomp out the door to swing the bag into the dumpster.

Mom follows me out with two garbage bags of her own. I turn from the dumpster so fast I almost knock into them.

"I wish you'd tell me what all these clothes are about, Lyddie," Mom says.

"And I wish you'd tell me why it's so important for me to help out but Emma can sit on the porch with a book!"

Emma stands and puts her hands out. "Fine!" she says. "I'm helping."

Mom and I look at her, stunned. She goes into the house

and comes out a second later with a half-full garbage bag.

Mom puts an arm around me. "I get that this is hard for you, Lyd. It isn't easy for any of us. But I promise I'm doing the best I can."

Is that true?

The rest of the day I pay attention to Mom. How she keeps switching bags with us to take the heaviest ones. How she keeps talking about how strong we are. How she keeps thanking us for our work even though we're working in what will be our own home.

Or at least my own home.

After a few hours Mom pulls some Popsicles out of the freezer and tells us to sit on the couch and eat them. She keeps working while Emma and I watch out the window.

Mom climbs up the corner of the dumpster with a garbage bag on her back, then jumps down into it to rearrange the bags so more will fit.

"She sort of looks like Santa going down a chimney," Emma says.

"Maybe a tiny Santa," I say, glad she's talking.

"With the most disgusting toys in the world!" Emma says, and dissolves into giggles.

Before I know it I'm laughing with her. We're laughing at the stupidest stuff. We're imagining a dumpster family who uses my mom and her garbage bags as a Christmas celebration. By the time my mom comes back inside we're a pile of giggles. We get up to join her.

"Aunt Molly is crazy," Emma says at the end of the day, when there are only a few bags left and we both watch my tiny mother carrying two huge ones on her back like she's an ant who can carry twice her body weight. "Your mom is crazy."

It's a sentence that would usually bother me. But the way Emma says it today is different. It's not competitive or whiny. It's like her tone acknowledges how much we both love my mom.

"Yeah," I say.

"But she's ours," Emma says, then hoists a garbage bag onto her own back and trudges out the front door toward the dumpster.

I watch her go. She's tall and lanky and black and looks nothing like my mom, but the way she walks and the fact that she's carrying garbage when she could totally opt out makes her seem more like my mom than I've ever noticed.

Suddenly my heart surges toward her. Maybe I don't mind my mom being *ours* in this house. Maybe this house is too big for just my mom and me anyway.

Emma might be right that she's not going to be here by the time we move in. But I've never really stopped to think about how I feel about that.

I think I hope she's wrong.

I think I hope she's here.

When Mom comes back through the front door, I snap back to work. Mom's phone is ringing. She looks at the screen and walks right past me without even seeing me.

"Hello," she says, hushed.

At first I think she must be talking to Jeremy and the hushed secret must be the house.

I'm on my way out the door when I hear her say, angry, "You cannot be doing this again."

Then I know it's not Jeremy. It's worse.

I let the screen door bounce open and closed so she'll think I'm outside. Then I squat behind my garbage bag to listen.

"You know I was counting on you this week. I have to take Emma upstate and—"

There's a pause. I watch out the window as Emma drops a garbage bag in the yard and then looks up, tracking the clouds as they cross the sky.

Stay out there, I beg her internally.

"I can do that but it's not what she wants, Phil."

It's him. It's Dad. I knew it.

"It's her last week of summer," Mom says.

She's laying it on thick. Dad does his best. That's what he always tells me: "Girlie, I do my best by you. Even if my best isn't everything, it's all I can do."

Mom nagging him never makes him any better.

But still. This doesn't feel very best.

"I can't believe you," Mom spits.

I can't take it anymore and Emma is almost back. I charge outside so fast I forget my garbage bag and have to go back for it.

64

"What's wrong with you?" Emma asks as the screen door crashes behind me.

"You're not the only one who has problems," I spit back.

"OK, then!" Emma says.

Like that, our day of being a real family is erased.

I don't say anything as we walk toward the Chinese restaurant. And Mom doesn't tell me until we're sitting at dinner at our booth.

"Your dad canceled for this week, Lydia," she says.

Jeremy isn't here but the booth gets ruined anyway. I think the frilly pink room in the new house might be the only not-ruined place in the world.

"Why?" I ask.

I keep my eyes on my brown rice. Whenever I get upset about Dad, Mom gets more upset about Dad. I hate it, and not just because I don't like seeing Mom upset. It's like she's stealing the emotion from me.

"I don't know," Mom says, getting more upset anyway. "He didn't really tell me."

"Why didn't he tell me himself?" I ask.

"I don't know," Mom says.

"Because he's a chicken, that's why," Emma says.

My eyes leave my brown rice and go right to her face. Mom is staring at her too.

"What, Aunt Molly?" Emma says. "That's what *you* say when she's away with him."

My heart is racing.

"I've never said he's a chicken," Mom says, looking at Emma but talking to me. "I don't call anyone names."

"Well, whatever you said, it meant the same thing," Emma says.

I can see my mom's ears get red. She's angry. At Emma. I think that must be against the rules of Emma staying with us or something, because Emma has done some messed-up stuff in the year she's been with us but I haven't seen Mom get angry once.

"So I'm coming with you guys, then?" I say.

Mom looks at me. She shakes her head as if to clear a thought. "What?" she says. "No. Absolutely not."

Why? Why is whatever they are doing OK for Emma to do but not for me?

"So I'm staying home alone?"

"No, Lyddie," Mom says. "I'll figure something out, but—"

Just then her phone buzzes. She turns it over, reads it, and breathes a sigh of relief. "Oh, thank goodness," she says.

"What?" I say. "Dad changed his mind?"

"No," she says. "Jeremy will stay with you."

"What?" I say

"He worked it out. He switched some work around. He'll be with you the whole two days." Mom's voice is pure joy. "Thank goodness for Jeremy."

"No," I say before I can stop myself. There's a desperation to my voice. The desperation to stay away from Jeremy that

Mom is never supposed to see or hear. "He doesn't need to do that," I say. "Mom, no. I can stay home alone."

"Lydia, you're twelve years old."

"So?" I say. "I know how to order pizza and how to get dressed and flush the toilet. What else is there?"

Mom looks at my jeans and long-sleeved tee. She swallows. I can tell she wants to say something about how I'm actually not that great at getting dressed for a twelve-year-old.

Instead she says, "You'll stay with Jeremy, OK, sweetheart? He's looking forward to it."

Mom never called me sweetheart until Jeremy started doing it. It makes my skin crawl.

"I . . . I don't want to burden him or whatever."

"I just said he's looking forward to it," Mom says. She might be angry at Emma but it's coming out directed toward me.

"Can I work in the house during the day? I'll come back at night so I'm not alone." Maybe I'll find something stronger. Something I can take to school. Something that would keep all boys—and men—away.

"No," Mom says. I wait for the reason but she makes me ask for it.

"Why?"

A huge smile crosses her face like she has just tasted the most delicious chocolate cake in the world.

"Because Jeremy doesn't know about the house yet," she says.

"So it's a secret?" I ask.

"No," Mom says through that huge smile. "It's a surprise."

"A surprise?" I ask. How can a new house for us be a surprise for Jeremy?

But then I figure it out. Right before she opens her mouth to say it, I've already figured it out.

"I'm going to wait until the house is all ready," she says. "And then I'm going to invite Jeremy to come and live with us in it."

And just like that, the pink frilly room is ruined too.

HOW TO EXPLAIN YOUR DIVORCE
TO YOUR DAUGHTER, PART 2

THEY BOTH REALLY LOVE ME.

That's usually all they will say.

CHAPTER 7

MONDAY I WAKE UP TO A house empty except for Jeremy. As planned, Mom and Emma left before the sun was up.

A day with Jeremy is a sugar fest. Mom saves dessert for celebratory occasions. She says sugar is the underage champagne. And then she only eats—and only lets us eat—decadent desserts. Flourless chocolate cake if we're out for our birthdays. Hand-dipped ice cream from Ample Hills on the first truly hot day of summer. No candy. No grocery-store-brand maple syrup. No frosting.

By the time Jeremy has been in charge for one hour I'm sure my teeth will fall out. I'm eating chocolate-chip pancakes covered in maple syrup while he sits across the table and stares at me. If Miriam's dad had made me this breakfast, I'd relish it. But Jeremy at the table makes it taste not as good.

I don't want to think about Miriam. She was supposed to be home two days ago. She still hasn't called me. I don't know how to talk to her anymore.

"So what do you want to do today, sweetheart?"

Other than a too-long hug the minute I woke up, there hasn't been too much touching. And I have house magic stowed in each pocket. I'm only slightly nervous.

"We could go anywhere," he offers.

He sounds almost like my dad, except my dad always has the adventure picked out for me.

I think about it. The only thing I really want to do is go to the house, but I can't say that because Jeremy doesn't even know about the house and the worst thing in the world would be to be in that house alone with Jeremy, which means the worst thing in the world is definitely going to happen because Jeremy is going to live in that house with us.

He's still looking at me. I need to pick something else to do.

"The movies?" he says. An afternoon of air-conditioning sounds amazing. But that would mean sitting next to Jeremy in the dark for hours.

"No," I say. "It's too sunny for the movies."

I need somewhere public.

I need somewhere bright.

"How about the beach?" I say. "I still have to finish my summer reading. I love to read on the beach."

"Riis Park?" Jeremy asks.

I nod.

I can tell he's not excited about that idea. I look down at my jeans. That makes two of us.

"Are you sure?" he asks, looking at me and my clothes.

This is the closest Jeremy has come to mentioning the strange way I'm dressing this summer. The fact that he says nothing about it scares me. It makes me wonder if he somehow maybe knows it's partly because of him.

"I'm sure," I say.

An hour later I sit in a beach chair, my covered legs in front of me, my book in my hand, my bare toes digging in the sand. I wish we had an umbrella. Sweat runs down my forehead and into the collar of my long-sleeved polo shirt.

Jeremy is lying on the towel next to me, shirtless, his big chest taking big breaths of salt air. I think he's sleeping.

Suddenly there are two shadows in front of me.

"Lydia?" I look up.

Mona and Diamond stand in front of me, dripping wet in two-piece bathing suits.

"Hi!" Mona says. "Is it really you?"

"I thought maybe you moved!" Diamond says.

"Hi, guys," I say. I wiggle in my chair, trying to hide my summer-reading book behind my back. Maybe it's not that cool to be doing summer reading on the beach when I could be swimming and eating potato chips with two of my friends from school.

"Are you OK?" Mona asks.

"Yeah, are you sick or something?" Diamond says.

"No," I say. "Why?"

"No one has heard from you all summer," Diamond says.

"And why are you wearing jeans on the beach?" Mona asks.

Suddenly I wish they would disappear.

I hate this. I hate what's happened to my brain and my life. I hate that I'm wishing my friends would disappear when they are being so warm and friendly after I've ignored them all summer.

Jeremy props himself up on an elbow. "Well, hello!" he says. "So nice to meet some of my Lydia's friends."

My face gets even hotter.

"Who are you?" Mona asks.

"Mona!" Diamond admonishes.

"My mom's boyfriend," I say at the same time Jeremy says, "I'm her stepfather."

Stepfather?

Step*father*?

The word makes all the syrup in my stomach start climbing up my esophagus.

But what else did I expect? It's going to happen. He's going to move into our new house. He's going to marry my mother. I can't do anything to stop it. I'm just a girl. And he hasn't done anything anyone except me would consider wrong.

But then I see it. I see him looking at my friends.

I see his blue eyes tracing the way Mona's bathing suit hugs her butt. I see him looking at Diamond's brown skin over her muscly arms and legs and stomach.

"Do you want to come to my umbrella?" Diamond asks.

"My mom was about to give us lunch. I know she has extra sandwiches in the cooler."

"Sure," I say quickly. I don't even look at Jeremy to ask him. I get up, leaving my book on the chair. I walk behind my friends, trying to take up as much space as possible, trying to use all my extra clothes to protect their almost-naked bodies from the eyes of my almost stepfather.

"Hi, Lydia!" Diamond's mom says as we get back to her umbrella. "How nice to see you here today! Would you like a sandwich?"

Diamond's mom reaches into the cooler next to her and pulls out three squares wrapped in wax paper.

"Thank you," I say, and sit down on the towels laid around their area. The only people over here are Mona, Diamond, and Diamond's mom and her two little toddler sisters. One of them crawls into my lap, and my whole body relaxes at a touch it enjoys.

"Sorry there's no meat," the little girl says as I unwrap my sandwich. "Mommy says we're still vegetarian even though I sometimes eat pepperonis at preschool."

We all laugh in the way that you laugh when an adorable kid says something that wouldn't be that funny if any other kind of person said it.

The sandwich is spinach, tomato, and hummus. It tastes glorious. It's so nice to be eating something healthy after a morning of sugar.

After we eat, Mona and Diamond go back in the ocean. I feel good enough to roll up my jeans and let the waves lap at my feet and ankles. They come out of the water and we practice turning cartwheels in the sand. None of us is very good at it, though, so we end up being a sandy, giggly mess. We dig a little hole and sit in it together.

I feel real or something. I feel like a part of myself that has been sleeping ever since Andrew first called me Swing is finally awake again.

"I know this is crazy but I can't wait for school to start again," Diamond says. "The end of summer is so boring!"

Mona rolls her eyes. "You just want to see Malik again," she says.

"Malik?" I say.

Images immediately flash in my mind.

Malik laughing as Andrew pulled my hair.

Malik grabbing the mirror-straw from Andrew and aiming it at me.

Malik calling me Swing as I walked past the boys at the basketball court just the other day.

The smile I've been wearing since Mona and Diamond found me a little bit ago starts to feel strained.

"She has such a crush on him!" Mona squeals.

"I do not!" Diamond says. She hides her face, though, so I can tell she's lying.

"Just admit it!" Mona says. "I admit I like Jorge."

Jorge poking my side.

Jorge whispering "Swing" when I walked past him in the cafeteria.

"Jorge is so short, though!" Diamond says.

Mona sighs happily. "I don't care," she says.

"Who's cuter, Lydia?" Diamond demands. "Jorge or Malik?"

"Or Jason? Or Andrew?" Mona adds.

Something makes this different. It's the sun baking my head or the fact that my feet are bare or the fact that we're all covered in sand together. Something makes me not afraid to be a weirdo.

"Um, none," I say. "They're all gross."

The words are true. But I don't mean them the way they come out. They come out sounding like I mean they're gross because we've known them so long we remember when they used to pick their noses and eat it.

But now those boys are gross in a whole new way.

Still, Diamond and Mona laugh. Their laughter lifts me up. If I can have this much fun wearing jeans at the beach, I can manage. I can do this. I can be a girl at school or at a Mets game or on the subway. I can be a girl in the world.

In the late afternoon, Jeremy and I trudge through the beach parking lot, hot and sandy and sweaty and dirty. We're carrying towels and chairs and a beach bag and a cooler, and all the stuff makes spaces between us that Jeremy can't reach through to try to do something creepy like hold my hand or put his fingers on the lower part of my back. I can tell he would rather be anywhere else. Anywhere dark and cool. I can tell he didn't like that I made him go to the beach and then left him all alone. I'm trying not to care that he seems mad at me.

"Hop in the front seat," he says when we reach the car. He doesn't ask.

Mom always makes me sit in the back. She says I'm not tall enough for the airbags yet and the front seat isn't as safe.

Jeremy has heard me beg to sit in the front so many times. There's nothing I can do.

I shove my hands into my pockets. I touch the tiny doll in one. I touch the 4 in the other.

I open the front door and slide into the steamy car. Jeremy starts the engine.

"We had a fun time, right?" he says, pulling out of the parking lot. Then he reaches over and puts a hand on my knee.

He leaves it there the entire ride home.

I never want to sit in the front seat again.

HOW TO STOP BEING BEST FRIENDS

WHEN YOU'RE HAVING A SLEEPOVER AT the end of the school year and all you feel is freedom and the lightness in your shoulders that you get a whole ten weeks away from boys . . .

when your friend says, "Let's call Jason" during the scariest scene in a movie . . .

when you know that last year the same friend would have been clutching your hands over the big bowl of kettle corn your mom made . . .

when your friend has sparkles in her eyes at the idea of calling a boy . . .

a boy who is the best friend of the boy who has been torturing you . . .

a boy who has been joining the torture himself . . .

when she sees you make a face and says, "Whatever, you don't need to call them—they all flirt with you anyway". . .

when you just can't tell her that the boy is scary . . .

because you can't tell her all the details of what the boys have been doing to you . . .

because you can't be the reason the sparkles fall out of her eyes . . .

when you both watch the rest of the scary movie without calling any boys . . .

and also without any hilariously fun screaming . . .

You'll probably realize that you aren't best friends anymore already.

You won't be able to respond to her text messages when she goes away for the summer. You'll let her emails build up in your inbox. You won't be able to talk to her because if you do you'll end up telling her that the boys are creepy, not funny. That the boys aren't flirting with you. They're scaring you.

Because if you say that, only one of two things could happen.

Either she'd decide you're too weird to be her best friend anyway.

Or she'd believe you . . . and you'd end up ruining the world for her.

You love her too much to do that. So instead you find a different way to break your friendship. You make sure she's good and mad at you before she returns for the school year.

You don't even think about what will happen if you need her again.

CHAPTER 8

WHEN I GET HOME, I GRAB a change of clothes and go straight into the shower without even asking if I can have the first one. I lock the door, then push the giant box full of bathroom supplies that we keep in there in front of it. All my protection items have stopped working. I need to find something else. I need a way to protect myself.

I shower fast. Before leaving the bathroom, I put on pajama pants, long socks, a long-sleeved pajama top, a sports bra, and a huge fluffy bathrobe. It still doesn't feel like enough clothes.

I walk into the kitchen and Jeremy is standing right there. He spreads his arms out.

"Looks like you could use a hug," he says.

I take a step backward.

"Actually, I'm not feeling too good," I say. "I think I'm just going to go to bed."

"What about dinner?" he says. "We can get whatever you like."

"No, thank you," I say.

I go into my room and lock the door.

When I hear the shower turn on a few minutes later, I sneak out. I grab the house phone off the wall, a box of peanut butter crackers, an apple, a cheese stick, and a granola bar. Then I rush back into my room and lock the door again. I won't come out until he's asleep in Mom's room. I won't.

There are three numbers I know by memory, in addition to 911. This is an emergency, but it's not a 911 emergency.

I eliminate Mom right away, even though she's who I want more than anyone. I want to be able to tell her how much the man in our shower scares me. I want her to listen to me and to hug me and to dump him.

I call Dad.

It rings and rings but finally he picks up. There's a lot of noise behind him. I hear screaming and whooping and a crowd before he even says hello. It sounds like he's at a party.

I shrink a few inches.

"Baby?" he says. "Everything OK?"

"Dad, can you come get me?" I ask.

"What?" he says. "Why? Isn't Jeremy there?"

"Yeah, but—"

I think about how to say it. If I say, *But he put his hand on my knee*, it sounds so small. It sounds like nothing when it's put into words, even though the feeling of it is bugs all over my body and being dipped in sewage over and over again. It makes me feel small and gross and ashamed.

I rub my knee through the layers and layers of fabric I'm wearing. It's still there. I try to rub it back into being mine.

"Did something happen?" Dad asks. "Or do you just miss me?"

Dad didn't do anything about it when a stranger kept rubbing his knee against mine. Why would he do something about Jeremy?

"I miss you," I say. "And—"

"Hold on, baby," Dad says. I try to keep talking but he doesn't hear. He must have taken the phone away from his ear. I hear him mumbling to a man and a woman. I hear music and chatter and a few loud cheers.

I am less important than this party.

"I gotta go, Lydia," Dad says. "I'll call you tomorrow, OK?"

Tomorrow it'll be too late. I know that. I can't spend another day and another night with Jeremy. Something bad could happen. Something worse.

I hear the shower turn off and the bathroom door open and close.

"I'll see you next week," Dad says.

"Next week there's school," I say, but I'm quiet. I'm quieter than the party.

"I love you," Dad says. He hangs up.

I'm down to one number. My hands are shaking as I dial.

She has so many reasons to say no. She has no reason to say yes. But if she says no . . .

"Hello?" she answers on the first ring.

"Miriam?" I say.

I hear her sigh. She's mad at me. Of course she is. I ignored her for the first nine weeks of summer. And it's not her fault she's fun and normal. It's not her fault I'm having such a hard time.

"What is it, Lydia?" she says.

I should say I'm sorry. I should try to explain it. I'm too scared to say anything more than "You have to invite me over tomorrow. For a sleepover. You have to have your dad pick me up first thing in the morning." I picture Jeremy standing outside my door, his ear pressed to the doorway, listening. "I can't . . . I can't say anything else right now."

"Can't?" Miriam says. "Like it's not safe?"

Could this really not be safe? Could Jeremy really be dangerous and I'm the only one who notices?

It doesn't matter. I have to get out of here.

"I don't know," I say.

"OK," she says. "We'll be there at eight."

And that's the thing about best friends. Nine weeks of not talking can disappear in an instant. Anger can dissolve faster than cotton candy.

As soon as we hang up Jeremy calls through my door. "Come on out, sweetheart. We can watch the Disney Channel."

I hear the sounds of *Phineas and Ferb* through the door.

"I'm going to bed," I yell back.

I make sure my door is locked; then I get in the bed and cover my entire clothed body with extra covers.

After a long time I pull my Stephen King novel from under my bed. I put it under the covers and read with a flashlight about monsters and zombies, but nothing in the book is scarier than the man outside my bedroom door.

Twenty-four hours later, Miriam's dad puts a perfect triangular slice of vanilla cake with chocolate icing in front of me. It turns out it was Miriam's oldest brother's birthday today, but they still let me come and sleep over. I'm not sure what Miriam told her dad.

The day has been perfect. Miriam and I starting giggling as soon as her dad came to pick me up this morning and we haven't stopped all day. We spent the morning watching an old movie and the afternoon playing touch football with all four of her older brothers and her dad.

After cake, Miriam and I go to her room to get ready for bed. I'm pulling on my snowmen pajama pants when she says, "Are ever you going to tell me?"

I freeze, not sure what she means. She could mean am I ever going to tell her why I didn't return her calls all summer. Or she could mean am I ever going to tell her why I'm wearing all these clothes all the time.

Either way, I don't want to tell her.

"Tell you what?" I ask. Maybe I could just ask her for a pair of boxers. I could pretend I packed these by mistake. I feel pretty safe in this house.

But I feel safer with my legs covered.

"Are you ever going to tell me what wasn't safe?" Miriam asks. "Why you had to come here today?"

"Oh," I say. I sigh and plop down on the sleeping bag I spread out in Miriam's room. "It's a long story."

Miriam sits next to me on my sleeping bag. "We have time," she says.

We do. And she's my best friend. I should be able to tell her about Jeremy and Andrew and how scared I am to go back to school or to live with that man, but I'm happy and safe and I don't want to ruin the moment. For either of us.

"I have something even better to tell you," I say. "My mom bought a house."

Her face falls. "You're moving away?" she says.

"No," I say. "Not really. It's only a few blocks from our apartment."

"Whew!" Miriam says.

I pause for a second. She sounds so relieved I'm not moving away. Even though we spent the entire summer without each other.

That's what we really should be talking about. That's what she really should be asking about. But I'm glad she's not.

I recover and keep talking. "But listen to this: Emma and I think it might be haunted."

Miriam's eyes go wide. "Really?" she says. "Tell me!" We

spend the rest of the night talking about the creepy house until we're both asleep across my sleeping bag.

The next morning, Miriam and I link elbows as we walk down my block from the subway toward my apartment building. Her dad is walking several sidewalk squares behind us. Close enough to see us but far enough so that we have our privacy.

I'm not even thinking about the cargo pants I have on that fall baggy over my legs or the long-sleeved tee that's resting in Miriam's bare arm.

It feels so good to have a friend again.

I feel so normal.

A taxi pulls up right in front of our building just as Miriam and I reach the side of it. I see the door open and Mom and Emma hop out.

My heart pulls toward my mother. I want to hug her. I want her to fix everything.

"Mom!" I call out.

She turns with a big smile, which splits into an even bigger smile as soon as she sees the two of us together.

"Miriam!" she says. She abandons her luggage with Emma on the curb and rushes over to us. I have my mom and my best friend within reach. It's the best I've felt in a long time.

Miriam breaks away from me to give my mom a quick hug.

"It's so good to see you!" Mom says. "We've missed you around here."

Miriam's shoulders get wiggly under Mom's hands.

I try to shoot Mom a look. *We don't talk about it. We act like everything is normal.*

It doesn't work.

Mom grabs for me so that Miriam and I are each nestled under one of her arms. "I'm so glad to see you two made up."

There are smiles everywhere except for Emma, who is staring daggers at the three of us. Still I'm jittery under Mom's arm. I don't think it's over yet. I don't think Miriam and I can really be normal yet. Or maybe ever. Because in order for Miriam and me to be normal, I'd have to be normal my own self first.

Mom has me stuck in a hug, so I don't see Jeremy walk out of the building before I hear him say, "Look what we have here!" He's using his jolly voice.

My mom turns to him with a smile so huge it looks ridiculous, like a cartoon. She doesn't look back at Miriam and me. It's like she thinks he somehow magicked us into friends again. It's like she gives him credit.

He turns to us. "Your mom has been so worried about you guys," he says.

Mom plants a kiss right on Jeremy's mouth right in front of us.

Miriam's face turns red. I squirm.

"What would I do without you?" Mom says.

I hate that she keeps saying that. But it's sort of also right. What would she have done with me? My dad flaked, I was in a fight with Miriam, and I couldn't go wherever Mom and

Emma were going. Jeremy always shows up for my mom. Even if I don't like him, my mom sort of needs him.

But then she turns to pick up her luggage.

When Mom's not looking I watch as his eyes go to Miriam's ankles and then take in every inch of skin between them and the hem of her shorts. I watch his eyes linger for too long on her waist and chest. I stare at my mom, but he looks back to her before she turns around.

I feel my breakfast sloshing in my stomach.

Mom looks at Miriam. "So will we be seeing you on Saturday for the last-day-of-summer sleepover?"

I fidget with my fingers.

We've done that the past two years: Miriam has come to sleep over the night before the night before school. Last year Mom even gave us her room since Emma was in mine. Mom makes a huge pot of kettle corn and we watch horror movies and scare ourselves into being awake all night long. It's the best night of summer.

But there was never a man with creepy, wandering eyes in our house before.

"Sure!" Miriam says.

"Yay!" I say. I smile back at her. I pretend it's going to happen.

It isn't.

It can't.

CHAPTER 9

I SET DOWN MY OVERNIGHT BAG and run to the bed to check the box with my notebook in it. Everything is here. The box hasn't moved. I hope Jeremy didn't come in our room at all.

Emma has just collapsed on her bed when Mom says, "Come on, girls, I have the day off! Let's go to the house."

I look at my cousin, certain she's going to complain or refuse. She rolls onto her back. Her face looks ashen. Her hair is puffier than I've ever seen it. Her eyes are red.

She looks how I felt after that one day with Jeremy.

I wonder what her dad said. Or did. Or if he's as bad. Or worse.

She stands, slides into her flip-flops, and walks out of the room without objecting.

She hasn't said a word since she and Mom got back.

I catch up to her in the living room, letting my shoulder hit hers gently. "Hey," I say. "Are you OK?"

When she looks at me, her eyes are angry.

"Do you see my dad here?" she says. "No. He's still in that place and I'm still here with you two. So how do you think I feel?"

I bite my lip. "Sorry," I mumble. I try to think of something else to say. Something that can make it better. But how can missing your dad ever be better?

When we get to the house, Mom doesn't put us right to work. Instead she opens the door and gestures for us to follow her through the living room, past the old couch, and into the kitchen. Emma stands beside me, and my mom turns to us.

"Emma," she says.

Mom doesn't speak loudly, but Emma startles beside me, like she wasn't expecting to hear the sound of her own name.

"Huh?" she says.

I've never seen her like this. Dazed.

"I have something to show you."

Emma doesn't say anything. Mom walks toward the refrigerator, opens the cabinet next to it, then takes out a ring of keys. She turns and looks at my cousin, her eyes sparkling. She hands the keys to Emma, a gold one sticking up at the top. "Here," she says. "Unlock the door."

It reminds me of how Mom gave me the key to the house on the first day. And somehow I don't feel jealous. Emma looks too broken for me to feel jealous.

There is a red door next to the refrigerator. I guess I always thought it just went to the yard outside. Maybe there's something special out there.

Emma takes the keys from Mom slowly. She walks toward the door and looks back at my mom like she doesn't know what to think. "Go ahead," Mom says. "Open it."

Emma turns the key and the door creaks open. "Oh," she says.

I go on my tiptoes to peer over her shoulder. It's dark and all I see is a set of stairs.

"There's a basement?" I ask my mom. For some reason she's showing this to Emma and not to me, but Emma isn't saying anything so I sort of feel like I have to.

"There's a basement *apartment*," Mom says, flicking on the light. She reveals a set of wooden stairs with green carpeting mostly covering them. They are as filthy as the rest of the house used to be. The carpet is stained all over the place with who knows what. There are empty Coke cans and broken parts of toys and bottle caps and clumps of human hair and dog hair covering every stair.

"Ew," Emma says.

"Well, we'll do the same thing," Mom says. "We'll clean up down here as much as we can." She starts walking down the stairs. Emma and I follow. "Then we'll get some help. We'll have a contractor here to reinforce the stairs. And we'll tear out that carpeting, of course, and we'll put in something cheerful. Or, you know, whatever you want."

"Whatever I want?" Emma says.

Mom smiles. "Yes, Emma. Whatever color carpeting you want."

"Why?" Emma says. "I won't even be living here."

I wait for my mom to say *we'll see* like always. She doesn't.

Mom reaches the bottom of the stairs and Emma and I follow her into a big room that seems like it must be the whole apartment. There's another old beat-up couch in the middle, and along the wall is everything that would usually be in a kitchen—oven, stove, microwave, tiny fridge—except it looks like it's right in the middle of the living room. Of course, the whole room is covered in stuff—boxes, bags, dirt. All the stuff we're getting used to seeing every time we open a new door.

Mom turns to look at Emma. "When people are recovering, like your dad is," she says, "they often need a little help on the other end. I know you're eager to live with your dad again, and I really want to make that happen for you. But I'd hate for your dad to take on too much too soon and then be unable to sustain it, you know?"

Emma nods like this makes perfect sense, but I have no idea what my mom is talking about. Maybe because no one has ever given me any details about my uncle since Emma moved in.

"So I thought this might be a way to help you guys stay together."

"What way?" Emma asks.

"This apartment!" Mom says. "When your dad is ready to come home, you guys can live here. Rent-free. I'll still be able to help him out when he needs it so he can get a job. He can start to save some money. But you'll be able to live with him in your own space."

Mom is beaming. Emma is supposed to jump up and down and say *Thank you, Aunt Molly* and drown my mom in a hug.

Instead she stares at her for a long time, then looks around and says, "It's sort of gross."

No one notices me. This isn't about me. It doesn't matter that I'm frozen in terror. It doesn't matter that I barely know my uncle. That the only thing I know about him is that he's unsafe and now the only other thing I know is that I'm going to have to live with him.

And Jeremy.

Under the same roof.

Two men in my house.

Neither one my dad.

"Let's get cleaning," Mom says.

I can't, though. I'm frozen.

I look around for any sign of ghosts. I feel for goose bumps on my skin. All I have is sweat. I need to find more magic.

Mom sends Emma and me back to the house the next day and again the next day until we've spent most of our last week of summer cleaning the bedroom apartment for Emma and her dad to live in. Emma actually cleans the basement with me, maybe because she knows she's going to live here for real now. I keep wearing my long pants and long sleeves despite the musty, sweaty apartment that only my silent cousin can see me in. People stop mentioning it, though. It's the last week of summer and my mom has finally gotten used to the way I'm dressing.

In the evenings, I text with Miriam on my mom's phone, planning the last-night-of-summer sleepover. What we'll eat. What kind of matching T-shirts we can make. What movies we can watch. I pretend to plan it with her while my brain races for ways to move it to her house or anywhere that Jeremy won't be able to put his hand on her knee.

When there are three days left of summer, only one day left until the sleepover that's not going to happen, Mom takes the day off from work because she's arranged for men to come and pick up the old dirty couches to be donated. Emma asks if she can skip cleaning to finish her summer-reading book, and when Mom agrees, she heads upstairs and I know she's going to lie in the pink teddy-bear bed and read. I try to figure out a way to get up there with her, but I've finished my summer reading and I can't think of anything. Besides, I want to be up there alone. I want to find the most powerful magic in the house. Something stronger than my 4 and my little doll and a pile of toilet-paper rolls. I want to find something to take to school to keep Andrew and Jason and the rest of the boys away. I want to find something to hide in my new room that will make sure Jeremy and my uncle stay out of it.

Mom and I go down to the basement. It's mostly cleaned out now, and when the donation guys come to take the couch and boxes it'll be practically empty except for the stained green carpet.

"You need to stay out of the way," Mom says. "They'll be here any minute."

I breathe a sigh of relief. The last thing I want to do is see some enormous men who can lift a couch and have them ask in some half-teasing way why I'm wearing so many clothes.

"Why don't you start cleaning the office?"

"Office?" I say.

Mom points to the door at the back of the basement. "In there," she says. "It's a small room, but it's full of stuff, as you may imagine by now. I think it'll become your cousin's bedroom. Uncle Jack will have to sleep in the living room." She doesn't look like she's talking to me, but then she shakes her head and reaches out so her hand is on my shoulder. "Thank you, Lydia," she says. "You've been such an enormous help. I hope you're going to love living here. . . . Are you excited?"

My face burns and I look down at my sneakers.

"I know moving is hard. As excited as I am, I'll miss our old place too."

I nod like that's the issue and head toward the door in the back of the basement.

I open it and gasp so loud Mom calls out behind me. "Everything OK, Lyddie?"

I slam the door shut and call through it, "Yeah!" I think of a lie, quick. "I just saw a spider. I killed it."

I lean against the door to the little office and breathe in the scent of it. It's fresh wood mixed with fruit and flowers and a little bit of peppermint. It's the smell of magic. Of ghosts. Of hope. This tiny room is filled with even more magic than the pink room upstairs.

I look around in awe. The room is full of stuff, like the rest of the house. But it's different. It's organized.

Directly opposite the door is a big wooden desk, dark and stately. And above it are shelves and shelves with little glass bottles lining them, each with a carefully printed label. I tip-toe across the room. I feel like I've barged into the most secret spot in someone else's brain. I climb onto the desk and pick up one of the vials. I read the label: *Lemon Extract*.

I look at the other vials. There's peppermint extract.

Lavender extract.

Dried ginger.

Dried eucalyptus leaves.

Dried honeysuckle.

It's like a science lab except there's no science.

The magic is real after all.

The answer isn't up in the pink room. It's here, in this tiny room among these tiny jars and bottles. I start reading more labels, trying to make a list to remember them in my head. I'll go home and google them. I'll figure out what they are doing here. What the house is trying to tell me.

There's a pen on top of the desk. I find a box full of books and start to dig through it, looking for a notebook so I can write down everything I'm finding.

Men's voices bang through the door behind me. My stomach growls, so I know it's almost lunchtime. I only have a few more minutes alone. My heart is racing I'm so excited. The only thing that could make this better would be if Miriam were here with me.

My hand brushes against something leather. A notebook! I pull it from the box.

The cover is brown leather and someone has written on it in gold Sharpie. I read the words and my heart stops.

This is too good to write in.

This is too good to keep to myself.

Just the words on the cover make me believe in the power of the house again: *Pan's Personal Book of Spells.*

"Lydia," my mom calls from upstairs. "Come up for lunch."

I have to figure all this out later.

I stash the book in the waist of my pants and turn to leave the room. As I'm walking out of the little office, though, there's a crash behind me. I jump and turn to find that several of the little vials have fallen from the shelves.

"How did that happen?" I whisper to myself. I hope there's not a mouse or something else gross and very un-magical knocking things over in here.

I rush back to replace the little bottles, then turn to leave again.

My foot barely crosses the doorway when there's a crash behind me again.

Slowly, I turn. Four of the vials are off the shelf, rolling across the desk. One is rolling on the floor. Even though they're glass, none of them has broken.

My eyes go wide and I turn back and slowly take another step.

Crash!

Three more vials fall.

I walk all the way back into the little room and put them back on the shelves. My hands are shaking now. I can't stop thinking about what my principal, Sister Janice, says: *All magic comes from the devil.*

I don't believe in the devil. I also don't think I fully believed in real magic until this moment, either. If the nuns are so afraid of it, though, there must really be something to be afraid of.

Slowly I place *Pan's Personal Book of Spells* back on the big wooden desk. Then I whisper, "Do you want me to keep this here?"

Nothing happens.

I slowly walk backward out of the room. When my feet cross the doorway, a few of the vials vibrate like they might fall, but they don't.

The message is clear.

The book belongs here. I can't take it with me.

I have to get back to this room as soon as I possibly can. And I need to bring Miriam with me.

HOW TO RESCUE A FRIENDSHIP

I CAN'T QUITE TELL HER THE truth.

So instead of truth, I'll use secrets.

I'll hide the biggest secret I have until we can be alone. And then I'll share it with only her.

We'll find the perfect spell for protection.

We'll perform the spell together.

We'll be bonded forever by *Pan's Personal Book of Spells*.

CHAPTER 10

MY NEWEST, BIGGEST, BEST PROTECTION ITEM hasn't even been with me for five minutes before its magic starts working. We're sitting on the new house's stoop munching on the tomato and pesto sandwiches Mom made for us. The sun is beating down on my head in a way I would have loved last summer, but this summer it makes the skin inside my turtleneck itchy with sweat.

"Lyddie," Mom says. "I had an idea. . . ."

I turn to look up at her. Emma is sitting beside me, quiet and pensive like she has been all day. Mom is on the step behind us.

"If you don't like it, just say so . . . I won't be offended. But I was thinking perhaps you'd like to have your end-of-summer sleepover with Miriam . . . here?"

My eyebrows bounce on my head. My heart speeds up.

"Here!" I say. "Really?"

"Maybe," Mom says. "If you want. Pretty soon the contractors are going to be here to finish up all the work, paint and all that. I think we should spend a night here before we have to go months without coming back. And it would be sort of special if the first time we sleep in this new house is to continue the tradition. Don't you think?"

"And Jeremy doesn't know about the house yet?" I'm so excited I blurt the words before I can even think about how they're going to sound to Mom.

I squint to see her in the sun. She lowers her eyebrows at me. She takes a second and looks me over like she's just now noticing my outfit for the day.

My heart is racing. I don't want to think about Jeremy right now. I can't answer questions about him. They are even more complicated than questions about my outfit.

Before Mom says anything Emma whines, "I don't want to sleep here! It's creepy!"

But when I look at her she's smiling. Almost like she said that for me.

"You still think it's creepy?" Mom asks, disappointed.

"That's the best thing about it!" I say. "Our end-of-summer sleepover is all about scary stories and creepy things. This is the perfect place."

Emma sighs.

"If you don't want to sleep here," Mom says, "I can ask Jeremy if he'll stay with you back in the apartment. But I'm not going to interrupt Lydia and Miriam's sleepover."

I freeze. This is Mom taking my side. This is one of the only times in the year since Emma moved in that I've felt my mom choose *me* so clearly. But I can't enjoy it. I can't let Emma be alone with Jeremy for a whole night.

"No," Emma says, quickly and loudly. "I guess . . . I guess Lydia's right. The creepiness is part of the fun."

Now I stare at her. She is smiling at me like I'm in on the same secret. But I'm not sure what the secret is. She said no so quickly. Does she also think that Jeremy is creepier than the house? Are we together in some sort of creepy secret? But if we are, why is she smiling? If she thinks he's creepy, why does she let him give her bear hugs? Why does she eat his candy?

How can I ask her about any of this when she acts like he's so normal?

"It's settled, then!" Mom says. "We'll have our first night here tomorrow night! Lydia, you'd better call Miriam as soon as we get home. Or, to our other home."

I beam.

For the next twenty-four hours all I do is imagine what is inside Pan's book. I imagine the perfect spell to protect myself from Jeremy and my uncle and Andrew and Jason and Malik and everyone. And before I know it, Miriam is at my new house.

The first thing I want to do when she arrives is pull her into the little basement office and show her my book. Alone. I can't risk anyone finding it first, so I've stolen the key to downstairs. The sweatpants I'm wearing today don't have pockets, so I've hidden it in my backpack and I won't take the backpack off until I can show Miriam the book.

But Miriam wants a tour of the whole house, so that means dragging my heavy backpack through every room. Emma follows us as we traipse through the living room and kitchen, up the stairs into the dark room that's still full of stuff and the sparse room with the big bed and the pink frilly room.

Miriam hops on the pink teddy-bear bed. Emma sits next to her as if Miriam is her friend as much as she is mine.

"You guys are going to live here?" Miriam asks, like she can't believe it. She lies back on the bed so her dark curly hair covers up several of the teddy bears.

"I know! It's creepy, right?" Emma says. I look at her. She forgot her line. Usually she says she's not going to live here.

"It used to be a lot creepier," I say. "We've been cleaning it up for weeks now."

Miriam sits up to look at me where I'm leaning against the wall next to the closet. "*That's* what you've been doing all summer? That's why you were too busy to ever talk to me?"

It's like she punched me in the heart. Emma sits up too, to look at me and see what I'm going to say back. Words don't come and it's silent for too long.

Finally Miriam says, "I don't really think it's a creepy house. I think it's huge."

She's right, I realize. Three bedrooms, a separate kitchen big enough for a kitchen table. By Brooklyn standards it's enormous.

"I guess I didn't notice," I say. "It was so dirty!"

"It was so gross!" Emma echoes, laughing. "You wouldn't believe the stuff her mom made us clean up. Toilet-paper rolls everywhere. Clumps of hair. Sticky soda cans that had been sticky for like a million years . . . All Lydia has wanted to do is pick up gross stuff."

"Ew," Miriam says, dissolving into giggles with my cousin.

I shift against my backpack. This doesn't feel right. The last-day-of-summer sleepover is supposed to be about Miriam and me. The two of us.

"I liked it because it was creepy. It felt like something out of a horror movie," I say.

I have to get Miriam downstairs to the little office so she can see. I have to find a way to ditch Emma. It's hard to think of anything, though, with them giggling together.

"Lyd," Miriam says. "Dirty and creepy are not the same thing." She and Emma become a pile of giggles all over again.

"Emma, did my mom finish setting up the TV yet?" I ask. The house doesn't have cable or Wi-Fi yet, but my mom found some old DVDs she swears are scary and said she'd bring over the little TV and set it up in the living room.

Emma looks at me like I have three heads. "I don't know," she says. "How should I know?"

"Well, could you *check*?" I ask, letting the annoyance I feel slide into my voice.

Emma sits straight up and stares me in the eyes. "If you care, you check," she says.

Miriam looks back and forth at us, then sighs and stands. "Let's all go check," she says. She finally takes a step away from Emma.

Except I don't really care about the TV.

It turns out I don't get Miriam alone all day. We help my mom figure out how to hook up the TV and DVD player. We order pizza. We make brownies to christen the new oven, as my mom says. We pop popcorn and watch one of Mom's old DVDs, which has effects so fake it isn't scary at all. We get into pajamas in the pink frilly room.

The entire time I wear my backpack. I can't let Emma find the key to her downstairs apartment. I can't let her find *Pan's Personal Book of Spells* even if it is in her future bedroom. Miriam is the only person in the world who would get as excited as I am about a book of spells. I need to save it for her.

"Why are you wearing that anyway?" Emma asks as I pull my backpack on over the soft long-sleeved T-shirt I have for sleeping tonight. "Is that going to be the next weird thing? After all the clothes, now you need a backpack, too?"

I expect them both to start laughing again like they have all day, but this time they don't. They stare at me.

"No," I say. "It's just . . . just for today."

Emma shrugs. "Whatever you say," she says.

But Miriam tilts her head at me. "Why are you wearing long sleeves and jeans in summer, though?" she asks.

The words climb up my throat.

To protect myself.

Because I don't want everyone touching my bare skin.

Because I don't know how else to keep my body for myself.

. . . But, Miriam, even this isn't really working.

I want to say them so badly. But I look at Miriam jumping into a pair of black boxers with emojis printed on them. Her legs jiggle underneath the yellow faces, at least four-fifths of each of them exposed. Her shoulder skin is smooth, peeking out on each side of her tank top. I used to dress like that. I miss being that girl. The one who didn't know.

Miriam gives me a half smile like her face is trying to coax the words out of me.

She's my best friend.

I love her too much.

I can't ruin the world for her.

"Let's go watch another fake-scary movie," I say. They both sigh like they were really hoping I'd tell them. But they follow me and my backpack back downstairs to the living room, where we three crawl into sleeping bags and fall asleep to the sounds of Alfred Hitchcock's *The Birds*.

CHAPTER 11

SOMETHING WAKES ME UP IN THE middle of the night.

Or someone.

Or maybe it's the house that wakes me up. I lie still and I can feel the ghosts working harder in the dark.

When my eyes open, I'm face-to-face with Miriam, who is also awake. Emma is snoring on my other side.

"Hey," Miriam whispers.

My eyes go wide. "What time is it?" I ask.

"Three in the morning," Miriam whispers. "I don't know why I'm awake."

"I do," I say, sitting up fast and shoving my sleeping bag down to my waist. "The house woke you up."

I wiggle into my backpack, which has been sleeping between my hip and Miriam's.

"What?" Miriam says.

"It woke me up too," I say.

I'm out of my sleeping bag now, tiptoeing around Miriam, who half sits and twists to watch me.

I gesture to her with my hand. "Come on," I say.

She seems unsure. "Where are we going?" she whispers.

I smile. "It's a surprise."

I can tell she doesn't really feel like getting out of her warm sleeping bag and letting the chilly air-conditioning blow on her mostly bare skin. But she's my best friend, so she follows me.

I turn to encourage her. "Wait until you see what I have to show you."

A little smile plays on Miriam's lips. "Something that cool?"

I don't say anything else. I reach into my backpack and take out the keys. I pause for a second to listen for the sound of Emma snoring, and sure enough she still is. I know my mom is asleep in the bedroom upstairs. I unlock the door and flip the light so that the gross green carpeting appears before us. I probably should have told Miriam to put socks on for this mission, but there's no time now.

"Whoa," Miriam says, peering around my shoulder. "There's even more of this house?"

"Sort of," I say, shutting the door behind us so we can talk. "This is technically a separate apartment where Em—well, never mind," I say. I don't want to get into Emma's dad or the fact that he will be living under the same roof as me. I want to talk about spells.

108

"Come on!"

Miriam follows me down the stairs, through the room that is a living room/kitchen/bedroom all in one, and to the little plywood door at the very back of the basement.

"Ready?" I say with my hand on the doorknob.

"Ready for what?" Miriam asks.

"This!" I say. I swing open the door dramatically and it bounces against the wall behind it with a bang.

"A desk?" Miriam says, walking inside. She runs her hand along the wood.

"Look above the desk. On the shelf," I say.

Miriam looks up at the vials on the shelf, leans over, and picks up one of the little jars to study it. "Cool! Is this, like, a perfume lab or something? We can make our own scents?"

"Better," I say. "Look at the book on the desk."

I watch Miriam's eyes closely as she bends over and reads the cover.

"*Pan's Personal Book of Spells*? No way!" she says. "Is this real?" She runs her fingers over the gold Sharpied letters like she needs to touch them to understand the meaning. "Who is Pan? Where did you find this?"

"Right here!" I say. "In this room!"

"Wow," Miriam whispers. She picks up the book and it looks like she's going to open it.

"Wait!"

"Wait?" she asks. "Why?"

"I found the book yesterday, but I've been waiting for you

to open it. Let's open it together," I say. "I've been dying to tell you about this all day. I couldn't get you by yourself for a single second."

Miriam lets her hands and the book fall to her lap. "You mean Emma doesn't know about all this?" she asks.

My face burns and I shrug. Maybe I should have shown Emma. Maybe I should have given all of this to Emma. I did find it in what's going to be her bedroom.

"You wanted to do the spells with me and not Emma?" she says.

I lower my eyebrows. "Of course," I say. "You're my best friend."

"But you love Emma," Miriam says.

"Yeah," I say. "I guess . . . she's my cousin. It's just . . . It's been complicated." I sit beside Miriam and put my hand on the book. "Ready?" I say.

"No," she says. "I'm confused. I thought you'd been off having some amazing summer with a perfect twin-sister-cousin-new-best-friend hybrid. I thought that's why you couldn't find a minute to message me or email me or call me the whole time I was bored out of my mind at my mom's."

Images from my summer run through my head. My mom giving Emma the first shower. My mom asking me about the clothes. My dad not showing up. Jeremy's hand on my knee.

"Um, no," I say. "Not at all."

Miriam shakes her head. "But then . . . that's almost worse. I mean, where have you been?"

She stares right at me like she's trying to read the truth straight from my brain. I think about last June, before school let out. I think about Miriam leaning close to my ear, whispering about how lucky I was because Andrew Quinn was flirting with me.

"Miri," I say. "I can't—"

"I've missed you all summer," she says. "And it turns out you've just spent it cleaning a dirty house?"

"No," I say. "I didn't even know about the house until a couple of weeks ago."

"Then what have you been *doing*?" Miriam demands. "Why were you ignoring me? What did I do?"

"You didn't do anything, Miri," I say. That's exactly the problem. I was being tortured at school daily and she did nothing. She couldn't see it. She thought it was good to have boys divide me up so that instead of being a person I was a list of body parts: legs, chest, neck. I can't tell her how dangerous that attention felt. I want her to be happy. I want her to love nicknames. I don't want her to feel the feeling I do when the boys call me Swing.

I have her alone. I've been waiting for this moment all day and now that it's here I'm almost crying.

I look at her hand on the book.

I feel for the ghosts around me. I ask them for help.

"It's so complicated," I say.

"Tell me."

"I haven't been . . . I've been bored too. There was nothing to say and I . . . I just didn't feel like talking. It wasn't you. It was me."

I'm the weird one.

I point at the book. "But we're together now. Here. We can only do this now. Tonight. When we're really alone."

She chews her cheek. "That doesn't seem like a good enough excuse to ignore your best friend all summer."

"I know," I say. "I missed you too. Let's . . . let's do something together. Let's use this secret to make us best friends again."

She pauses. For a moment I think she's going to leave me here. I think she's going to give up on us right now like I gave up on us all summer.

"I missed you like crazy," I say. "I don't know how to explain it. But I really want to do this with you. Please?" I beg.

She takes another second but I see something shift in her eyes.

"OK," she says. Then she smiles in a way that fills my whole body up with identical smiles. "Let's do it."

We sit together on the one desk chair and each use our right index finger to open the front cover. The first page is a handwritten list.

A Spell for Charm
A Spell for Love
A Spell for Fortune
A Spell for Revenge

A Spell for Protection

There are several more listed but that's as far as I get before Miriam turns to me and whispers, "Fortune!"

That's when I realize I didn't think this through. I should have looked for a spell by myself. I can't do the spell for protection without explaining what I need protecting from.

"Really?" I say. "That's the one you want to do?"

"Which one did you want to do first?" Miriam asks. "Love? Do you have a crush on someone?"

"No," I say. "Why, do you?"

Miriam's face turns red.

"You do!" I say.

She shakes her head. "I'm not telling you. Not yet. We need to be best friends again first."

It stings but I pretend it doesn't.

I don't want to know who her crush is anyway. What if it's Andrew?

"Of course you don't care about the fortune spell," she says. "Look at this huge house."

I don't bother to point out that this huge house was full of garbage and stuff and is falling apart with a broken banister and missing shutters and a bathroom sink that has no water.

"Let's do fortune," I say. "You're right."

Miriam flips pages until she finds it.

It's written in red ink and in what looks like someone else's handwriting altogether.

"I wonder which spells Pan wrote," I say.

"I wonder who he was," Miriam says.

"You mean she?" I say.

"No," Miriam says. "Pan, like Peter Pan."

"I was thinking Pan like *Pan's Labyrinth*."

"Even more to wonder," Miriam says. She starts reading the spell.

"'As with all spells, the cylinder shape is essential to the success. Season the inside of your cylinder with bayberry and cedar. Cover the outside in green and gold. Inside, fasten the petal of one daffodil (dried or fresh). Be sure the cylinder is touching you at least twenty-three hours a day. *Do not* let the cylinder touch another mortal or the spell will be reversed and financial devastation will be imminent.'"

Miriam looks up. "Do you understand any of this?" she asks.

My eyes are wide. My jaw has dropped.

"You do," she whispers.

I thought we'd never understand anything about what happened in this house before we got here, but at least one puzzle piece has come together.

"Stay here," I say. "I'll be right back!"

Before Miriam can object, I run out the door, up the stairs, and back into the kitchen. I tiptoe past my sleeping cousin, up the next set of stairs, past the room where my mom is sleeping, and into the back bathroom.

This house is going to protect me after all.

It had all the answers the whole time.

I open the drawer beneath the sink and survey the hundreds

of toilet-paper rolls I've stashed in it. I find two that are pretty much still perfect, no tears or folds or bumps. Then I sneak back to Miriam.

"That was not cool," she says as soon as she sees me. She's clutching the book, her lips pressed together. I realize she was scared. She's still not used to this maybe-haunted-maybe-not-quite-haunted-but-somehow-spooky house.

"I'm sorry," I say. "I just thought that if we both went we might wake them up."

"Went where?" Miriam says.

I smile and pull the toilet-paper rolls from behind my back. "Here," I say, extending one to Miriam.

She tilts her head at me. "Garbage?"

"Look at them," I say. "Look at the shape."

Miriam's eyebrows jump. "Cylinders!" she says.

"They were all over this house!" I say. "They were everywhere as we were cleaning. Something told me I had to keep them."

Miriam turns one over in her hand. "Maybe we shouldn't do this," she says. "I mean, this is real, right? This isn't like a movie or a book."

I nod. I understand why she's scared. At school we learn all about how powerful and dangerous magic is. I'm a little scared too, but that's adding to my excitement.

"This is, like, real magic," Miriam says. "The kind Sister Janice is always warning us about. . . . What if it's, like, from the devil?"

But if the devil is magic, maybe I need the devil.

Maybe if Sister Janice had done something when she saw Andrew pull my hair. Maybe if she'd told him to stop. Maybe if she'd told him to wait and see if I was OK with it before calling me the same nickname over and over. Maybe if she and the teachers took away those stupid mirror-straws. Maybe then I wouldn't need magic.

"I think it's from the girl who had all those pink teddy bears. Do you think she could have been the devil?"

Miriam half smiles. "No . . . no way. Devils don't have pink teddy bears."

I sink into the desk chair. "I get it," I say. "We don't have to if you don't want to." I don't want to scare her. And now that we've found so much, I can do the protection spell tomorrow after Miriam leaves. That's the one I really want to do. Still, it would be good to have a practice round.

"But it's just toilet-paper rolls and a flower petal," I say. "Do you really think it could be dangerous?"

Miriam laughs. "Good point." She looks at the roll in her hand. "I guess if it's just for fun, right?"

"Right," I say. Then I giggle, sort of on purpose. "Unless it works."

Miriam giggles back. I know she can't resist my giggle. Even after a summer of me being the worst friend in the world.

"OK," she says. She climbs onto the desk to look at the jars and vials more closely. "I'll search through these for bayberry, cedar, and daffodil. How do we cover them in green and gold?"

"There has to be something," I say. I open the top desk

drawer and find a stack of multicolored tissue paper and Elmer's glue.

"That was creepy," Miriam says.

"I told you," I say. "It's the house. It has all the answers."

Miriam shivers. "And you're going to live here," she says, like I'm doomed. Except I'm already doomed by having to live with Jeremy. Somehow a spooky, kinda-haunted house makes me safer.

I get to work pulling out the shiny gold and kelly-green tissue paper and carefully covering our cylinders in glue. Miriam shuffles through the box of jars and vials.

"Found bayberry," Miriam says. A few minutes later she says, "And cedar. We should alphabetize these."

"Good idea," I say, even though I doubt haunted houses love organization. But if she wants to alphabetize, maybe that means she'll do more spells with me.

I hand over the cylinders to Miriam. The top of each is covered in gold and the bottom in green.

"What do you think it means by 'season'?"

"She," I say.

"Huh?" Miriam says.

"Or he," I concede. "You mean Pan, not it."

"OK, what do you think Pan means by 'season'?"

"Probably like cooking, right? Like when I cook with my mom and a cookbook says 'season the chicken with salt and pepper' or whatever, it means just sprinkle some on so you can taste it."

Miriam lowers her eyebrows. "I hope I do this right," she says.

She squints to concentrate and sprinkles two drops of bayberry on each cylinder, then two drops of cedar. "Whoo!" she says as the small room fills with the smell of days-old fruit and burning wood.

"Did you find the daffodil petals?" I ask.

"Yeah, dried," Miriam says. She hands me one so delicate I'm afraid the gentlest touch will turn it to ash. You can tell that it used to be yellow, but it's faded beyond white to almost see-through.

I put a dot of glue in each cylinder, then hand one to Miriam. "You better do yours," I say. "Once it's done, I'm not allowed to touch it."

"Right," Miriam says.

She holds the cylinder in one hand, the daffodil petal in the other. I mirror her.

We've covered the toilet-paper rolls in green and gold. We've put in the right scents. Once we do this step the spell will be complete.

"Ready?" she says. "On three."

"Ready," I say.

"One, two, three!" she says.

We fix the daffodil petals to the insides of our toilet-paper rolls at the exact same moment. Then we hold our breath.

I sort of thought gold would start falling from the sky.

I sort of thought the pocket of my pajama pants would

suddenly be thick with dollar bills.

But nothing happens.

"Twenty-three hours a day," Miriam says. "Remember."

"Right," I say. I look back at the book. There is some even smaller handwriting at the bottom of the page.

"Look," I say. "It says it works in one to three days."

"I have to be touching this thing for twenty-three hours a day for three days?" Miriam says. "That's like sixty-nine hours!"

I shrug. "Tuck it into your clothes," I say. "Somewhere no one can see."

Miriam looks at me like she wants to say that that's easy for someone who dresses like I do all the time but harder for someone who actually wears seasonally appropriate clothes in the summer.

Instead she says, "Let's clean up."

We work one-handed—the cylinders snug in each of our left hands—to hide the glue and the tissue paper and the vials.

By the time we get back to the living room it's five a.m. and the birds are already cheeping outside the front windows. I watch Miriam wiggle her way into her sleeping bag and arrange her cylinder so it's touching her bare shoulder. I push into my own sleeping bag and then shove mine inside my pant leg so that it's pressed against my knee. I'm careful not to crush it.

If this spell works, then the protection spell will work. If this spell works, I will finally have an answer. An answer *and* a best friend.

A few hours later we wake up to banging and crashing coming from behind our heads. I jolt awake, then feel for my cylinder. It's still touching my knee.

Beside me Emma pulls her sleeping bag over her head. On my other side Miriam rubs her eyes.

There's another crash and a *flump* that comes from the kitchen.

"What time is it?" Miriam asks.

"Mom," I call over my shoulder. "What are you doing?"

Emma buries herself deeper in her sleeping bag. I watch her and a rush of sadness runs over me. When we were little and we used to have cousin sleepovers, she always wanted to sleep later than I did. I'd stand over her bed whispering that she should get up and play and she'd dig herself deeper and deeper under the covers. I'd be so impatient, so desperate for her company. She buries herself the same way now but I forgot all about that. I spent all of yesterday trying to get rid of her.

"Sorry, girlies," Mom calls back cheerfully. "I was just downstairs cleaning."

Miriam and I sit up straight and stare at each other. Did she find the vials? Did she find the book of spells?

"I found all these bags of junk in the basement closet,"

Mom says. "I thought I'd just bring them straight up to the dumpster. I didn't mean to wake you guys."

"Wait!" Miriam says, too loudly. On my other side, Emma groans.

I lower my eyebrows at Miriam and she holds her cylinder out to me. Then I nod, knowing what she means. There could be more stuff in those bags. More extracts and dried herbs. More spells.

"Yeah, wait, Mom," I say, trying to be casual. "What if there's something in them?"

"Something like what?" Mom says. I hear her shifting the bags around in the kitchen. There's a lot of crashing and banging.

I carefully put the cylinder in my sock and watch as Miriam wiggles hers into the waistband of her boxers.

"I don't know," I say slowly. I get up and walk into the kitchen. I have to say something my mom wouldn't be too interested in. Something Emma wouldn't be too interested in (because I know she's listening even if she's pretending to be asleep). But something that sounds like I would be. "Like, a clue?"

"A clue to what?"

"A clue to where the people are," Miriam says. "Whoever owned this house."

"The bank owned it before us," Mom says, trying to drag a heavy black garbage bag across the yellow kitchen floor.

"The bank didn't fill it with junk," I say. "That's what I mean. I want to know what happened. Like . . . did somebody die here?"

"UGH! Why would you even want to know that?" Emma's voice comes from behind me. She's up so suddenly I'm startled.

"Yeah," Mom says. "I'm with Emma on this one. If you do find out someone died here, keep it to yourself."

I giggle. "OK," I say. I walk over to a bag and untie it.

Then I see them. Things so wonderful it's terrifying. I gasp before I can help it.

"What?" Emma says. Then: "Never mind. If I have to live here I don't want to know."

"Tell you what," Mom says, walking to the kitchen sink to wash her hands. "I'm going to the store to get some bagels."

Bagels and cream cheese are the only normal-person breakfast food I ever see my mom eat. And even then it's only fancy New York bagels with deliciously flavored cream cheeses.

"When I get back," Mom says, "we're all taking these bags to the garbage. So you have about half an hour to look for clues if you really want to."

"OK!" I say. I try to gather the black plastic into one hand so that no one else can see in the bag.

"Do I really have to carry out garbage, Aunt Molly?" Emma whines. "I'm not the one who wants to rummage through it."

"Get dressed," Mom says to Emma. "You come help me carry bagels and you'll be officially excused from garbage duty."

"OK!" Emma says, sounding surprised even though she should be used to getting her way by now.

But this time I don't mind.

I keep my hand on the plastic and lean against the kitchen counter like it's the most casual thing in the world until Mom and Emma are out the front door; then I rip it open.

"Miriam!" I say. "Look!"

I reach into the bag. It is mostly just garbage, so my hand rubs against an old banana peel and something way too sticky, but it's OK. It's worth it.

I pull out two perfectly crisp, impossibly clean hundred-dollar bills.

"Whoa!" Miriam says, rushing across the room to grab the one out of my left hand. "This was in the bag?"

I nod, my wide eyes matching hers.

Who knew a hundred-dollar bill could be creepy? Our hands are shaking a little bit.

Miriam pulls her bill straight in both hands and stares at it.

"It's . . . it's incredible," Miriam says.

"No," I say. "It's fortune."

After another moment in mystified silence, we're screaming and squealing like we used to. We run at each other and hug even though my hands are covered in sticky stuff now and Miriam's arms are bare.

We are best friends again. That's my real fortune.

HOW TO DECIDE WHAT'S SCARY

LISTEN TO YOUR MOM SAY MOTORCYCLES are dangerous.

Listen to your principal and all the nuns at your school say magic comes from the devil.

Listen to your dad when he tells you where to sit at a Mets game.

Listen to the grown-ups for eleven years.

As soon as you turn twelve you'll be scared every single day anyway.

CHAPTER 12

I WAS HOPING WE'D SPEND THE whole day in the house but instead, as soon as Miriam's dad comes to pick her up, Mom takes us back to our apartment to shower and then we go to Target. Tomorrow is the first day of school and she says we need new stuff.

I'm ready for some new stuff. I need more sets of tights to wear under my uniform skirt and a new sports bra that matches my skin so it won't show beneath my white button-down. I'm feeling OK about going back to school now that I know I can use Pan's protection spell, but the extra clothes make me feel even better.

Once we're showered and dressed, Mom rushes Emma and me onto the subway with her cell phone glued to her left hand. She is texting constantly. That almost never happens, and whenever it does it's always bad news for Mom. And for me. So I don't try to bargain for a chance to get back to the house later today so I can do the protection spell. I'll just wear my winter uniform and be the weird girl who avoids boys tomorrow. I'll find a way to get back to the house after school tomorrow. After I see Dad tomorrow, if he manages to show up. I'll do the protection spell then.

In Target we walk up and down the school-supply aisles, filling our cart with binders and loose-leaf paper and pencils and pens.

The whole time Mom is distracted and texting.

Then we walk to the clothing section. Mom parks the cart. "You each need new navy sweatpants for gym days and . . ."

She trails off as her phone buzzes.

Emma and I wait, looking at her.

Finally Emma says, "And what, Aunt Molly?"

Mom shakes her head and looks up at us again. "And new socks, underwear, bras. That sort of thing. Go pick out some you like."

She's looking at her phone again.

As soon as Emma and I disappear between the racks, Emma leans over and whispers, "Who's she texting?"

I shrug. "How should I know?" I say.

Even though I do know. It's my dad. I'm sure of it.

A few minutes later, we return to the cart with our hands full of clothes.

"Let's go try them on," Mom says.

"Try them on?" Emma says.

I want to say the same thing. Who tries on sweatpants and

tights and bras? But I just walk toward the dressing room. Mom doesn't answer Emma and they both follow me. Mom walks into the actual dressing room with me like I'm a little kid, but I don't object. She doesn't even look up from her phone as I put on the pair of navy sweats.

"I have the pants on, Aunt Molly!" Emma calls from the dressing room across from mine.

"OK," Mom says. She gets up and opens the door just as I'm about to take off my T-shirt to put on a bra.

I quickly pull the shirt down as far as it'll go as the door opens.

When the door is closed, I lock it. Then I pull my shirt off and hear a buzz. She left her phone. It's facedown on her purse so I know I'm not supposed to look. But I do anyway. Just to confirm my suspicions.

Sure enough, my dad's name appears in bold at the top, his message underneath it.

Phil

Come on, Molly. Be reasonable.

I put the phone down and pull my T-shirt up to my eyes to catch any tears that might escape. That means he's either late on the child support or canceling another visit.

Next door, I hear Mom and Emma arguing about whether her sweatpants are too tight.

Mom says, "Fine!" and knocks on the door just as I'm pulling a new sports bra over my head.

I stand behind the door and open it for her to enter.

She looks at me and says, "No, Lydia. Absolutely not."

"What?" I say, looking down at my sweatpants. They're not too tight. They aren't super loose either. They actually look completely normal.

"You're not going to spend the entire school year in a sports bra," Mom says. "That's over. I let you dress how you wanted to this summer. But that's it. I'm tired of it."

"Why do you care about my bra?" I say. My voice comes out high and demanding.

"You need to wear some normal bras," Mom says. "You're going to have to get used to it. You'll have to wear one the rest of your life."

"Why?" I say. "Why can't I wear the kind of bras I want to wear?"

Mom shakes her head. She picks up the pair of navy tights I had put on the dressing room stool. "I'm not buying these, either. Not until it's cold outside."

"What?" I say "Why? I have to wear tights tomorrow."

"You don't have to wear tights tomorrow. It's going to be eighty-five degrees."

"But—"

"You haven't wanted to have this conversation all summer. I tried it nicely. But I'm done. Lydia, I'm done. You're going to dress normally for school. I'm going out into that store to pick out a normal, traditional bra and that's what you're wearing tomorrow."

I think about the bras Miriam wears under her uniform.

They're silky and lacy and have wires and other things that look like they poke or itch. I don't understand the point of putting something silky and lacy where no one is ever going to see it. Unless maybe it's designed so that someone *can* see it. I don't want to think about that.

Mom keeps talking. "Summer is over and we're done with the weirdness. Now."

But I can't do that. I can't go to school with my skin exposed. I haven't even gotten to do the protection spell yet!

"Mom," I say. "I need—"

Her phone buzzes. Out of instinct I wait for her to reach for it but she doesn't. She stares at me, waiting. She's ready for me to say something. She thinks I'm finally going to tell her why I dress the way I do. She thinks forcing a regular bra on me will make me talk.

But I can't talk. I don't have the words.

"You need what?" she demands.

I have to say something. If I don't I'm afraid I'll be going to school tomorrow in bare legs and with bare arms and a normal bra under my white uniform shirt.

Andrew and his friends will all follow me around calling me Swing while they watch my skirt swinging on my legs and my legs will be bare and the back of my bra will show through my shirt and . . .

"I don't . . . feel right . . . without extra clothes on," I manage. I open my mouth to say more. Something about how it feels when boys look at my legs. Something about how men press up against me in the subway. Something about Jeremy without saying his name. But I can't find the words for any of it.

"Well, you don't look right with them," Mom says. Her phone buzzes again. She picks it up this time and opens the door even though I'm standing there in nothing but pants and a sports bra. She glances back at me. "The pants are fine," she says.

She shuts the door and I'm alone so I crumple in on myself. I hug my knees to my chest in the corner of the dressing room, waiting for her to return with the traditional bra, whatever that means. And maybe I am tired of wearing all these clothes. Maybe I do want to feel OK in my skin without it covered all the time. But I want to find something else to protect me before I dress normally again. I would have started small. Just capri pants with my ankles showing for the first day, maybe. Or a three-quarter-sleeved shirt.

No matter what, I don't want my mom to decide how much of my body gets to show and which parts I'm allowed to hide. I want to decide for myself.

When she's not back after a few minutes, I stand and take my pants off. I face the dressing-room mirror and look at myself in just a sports bra and underwear.

I reach down and, starting at my toes, I try to touch all of my skin, every cell of it. I try to touch it into being mine. If I'm not allowed to dress it and I'm not allowed to say who touches it, what really makes it mine?

130

* * *

That night I lie in bed listening to Emma snore. It's impossible to sleep. I don't reach for the Stephen King under my mattress. Even scary stories can't comfort me now.

Why didn't I fight harder with Miriam? Why didn't I make her do the protection spell? How long will I have to walk around in my summer uniform, skin exposed, no spell to protect me? How long until I can get back to the house?

I roll on my side and look at my desk chair. The moonlight illuminates my room just enough for me to see the clothes hanging off the back, ready for tomorrow.

Brown loafers. White ankle socks. Blue, green, and gold plaid skirt. Tiny blue shorts to go under my skirt. White short-sleeved button-down blouse. White underpants. White "traditional" bra.

Ever since I saw that bra in Target I've been praying for a freak September snowstorm, but I checked the weather on Mom's phone before bed and it isn't going to happen. Tomorrow I will have to go to school with my legs bare and my arms bare. All day long the boys at school will be able to see my skin. And all the men on the subway ride. If Mom makes me sit next to a stranger like Hairy Kneecaps from the Mets game, he'll push his leg into mine and all the hair will curl around my thigh and into the hem of my skirt. The thought makes me pull the covers tighter on top of me even though it's warm in our apartment tonight.

After school Dad will flake. Jeremy will finish work early

and be here. He'll reach to hug me. Mom won't be watching. His palms will touch my elbows and forearms. He'll put a hand on my knee and there will be no fabric between his flesh and mine.

I roll toward the wall and tell myself to go to sleep. I'll have to survive a few days without the spell. Unless I can find a way to do it tonight. . . . I stand and reach under my bed. I take out the box with my notebook. I pick up the toilet-paper roll and put it into the front pocket of my sweatshirt. Then I tiptoe into the living room. I listen at Mom's door for a while. No sounds.

My hands are shaking. My knees are shaking.

Mom will be so mad at me if she ever finds out what I'm going to do. She'll say it's the worst thing I've ever done. The most unsafe.

But she doesn't understand how unsafe I feel every minute of every day.

I go to the hook next to the kitchen sink where she hangs her keys. I say a quick prayer, which is something I haven't done since God stopped protecting me at the end of last school year, but I need something and there are no ghosts in this apartment.

Then I tiptoe over to the coat closet. I put on my huge winter coat, tying the hood so that I won't look like a kid or a girl. Then I slip on my sneakers and open the front door. I turn and look at the empty moonlit living room. "I love you, Mom," I whisper. Because I do. That's the hardest thing about all of this. I love my mom and I know she loves me, but she can't help me. She can't change the entire world for me.

Then I close the door behind me, go down the elevator, and rush out the front door and into the hot September night.

During the day, with Emma or with my mom, the walk to the house usually feels quick. Tonight it takes forever. Almost no one is on the street at two in the morning, but whenever I see someone, I pull the hood of my winter coat even tighter around my face so that they don't call the police to report a kid runaway or something.

But I make it. Soon I'm unlocking the front door. Then I'm inside. It's even creepier than usual. The AC isn't on and I miss its background buzzing. I drop my coat inside the front door and despite my long pajama pants and sweatshirt, I'm immediately covered in goose bumps. "Hi," I whisper to the ghosts, whoever they are. This would be so much better if Miriam were here. Or even Emma. But no, this is something I have to do alone.

The problem is mine. I am the weirdo.

I walk my goose-bumped limbs through the living room and kitchen. I open the kitchen cabinet, find the keys, and unlock the red door to the basement. Then I tiptoe down the green steps. I'm trying to be as quiet as possible even though no one is here. It really feels like I'm not alone.

I don't relax until I'm in the little office inhaling the aroma of Pan's magical ingredients.

Suddenly, I'm tired. I want to curl up under the little desk and sleep here in this wonderfully fragrant room in this creepy house where I feel safe.

Safe, for now, at least. Safe, until I have to share this house with two men.

But I have to be quick and get back to the apartment before anyone knows I was missing.

I open the drawer and pull out *Pan's Personal Book of Spells*. Quickly, I find the one I'm looking for.

It begins like the fortune spell.

> *As with all spells, the cylinder shape is essential to*
> *success.*

I pull the toilet-paper roll out of my pocket. Because it's been in the box under my bed instead of shoved in a bath-room drawer with all the rest of the toilet-paper rolls, it's an even more perfect cylinder than the ones Miriam and I used for the fortune spell. I know now that this spell, right here, is why the house gave it to me.

> *Season the inside of your cylinder with cedar and*
> *frankincense. Cover the outside in perfectly even stripes*
> *of black and peach.*

I pause, nervous that all the ingredients won't be here. But they are. I find black and peach tissue paper in the left-hand drawer. I already know we have the cedar. I find the frankincense essential oil too. The directions here are more specific than the last spell. I have to use perfectly even stripes of tissue paper. I search all the desk drawers for a ruler but I don't find one. I decide to use the first segment of my index finger to keep the stripes even. I cut three black and three peach stripes and glue them carefully to the outside of my cylinder. I brush the frankincense oil all along the inside and sprinkle the cedar flakes over that.

Inside, fasten exactly three alyssum flowers so that they form a triangle. Fresh or dried will do. Make sure they are in good shape, not missing any petals or torn in the middle. Then take a fourth flower and fasten it directly to your right hip. Be sure the cylinder is touching your left hip at least twenty-three hours a day. DO NOT let the cylinder touch another mortal or the spell will be reversed and danger will be imminent for both of you. You will both be doomed.

I shudder reading that. But as long as it's pressed against my hip, it shouldn't be a problem. Even my mom understands that part of my body needs to be covered in clothes.

I find the alyssum flowers. They're tiny, not even the size of the tip of my pinky. It takes a while to study them, to be sure they aren't torn and they have each of the five petals they need in order to be symmetrical. I find a blue one and two white ones and glue them like a triangle to the inside of my cylinder.

I find a fourth one—yellow—and use Scotch tape from the top desk drawer to tape it to my right hip.

I secure the cylinder inside the left-side waistband of my underpants. It feels sturdy there.

My heart feels lighter already.

I read the end of the spell.

This spell should work immediately. It will last five days. Be sure to change the alyssum flower each twenty-four-hour period.

If results are mixed, try doubling or tripling the spell to make it more potent.

"The spell should work immediately," I say out loud to the ghosts. I make sure they know that means I need to be safe outside this house the same way I am inside. I stick the little vial of alyssum flowers into my sweatshirt pocket so I'll have a new one ready every twenty-four hours. Then I leave. The house lets me take the vial out of the room.

I lock the red door and the front door. I put my coat back on but don't bother to pull the hood too tight. I feel much lighter on the way home, relief dancing like helium in my lungs.

I'm protected.

Finally.

When I'm home with my coat hung up and the keys back on the hook and the front door locked and my protection items stored back under my bed, I put my head on my pillow and I'm immediately, finally, blissfully asleep.

CHAPTER 13

IN THE MORNING, I WAIT UNTIL Emma is in the bathroom to get out of bed. Then I get dressed as quickly as I can. I hold the cylinder to my hip with my left hand as I change my underwear with my right. Then I quickly pull on my skirt, shorts, and uniform shirt.

I can't let Emma see the cylinder. If she sees it, she might touch it. Then we'd both be doomed.

Even with my spell secure against both hips, and even though I'm forcing myself to believe in it completely, I still feel uncomfortable in my school uniform with so much skin out in the open.

I walk over to the full-length mirror next to Emma's bed. For a second I'm startled to see myself. I've spent the summer avoiding my reflection. Anytime I had to see it, I always looked so out of place and freaked out.

Today, though, I look . . . normal. My hair isn't done yet

but it sits flat on my head, no crazy bed head today. My arms hang out of my sleeves. My legs hold me up under my skirt. I smile at the girl in the mirror and run my fingers through her short brown hair, straightening it out. Looking normal feels nice, actually. There's a lightness to my shoulders. It almost feels like my arms may float away.

How can something that feels this nice also make me so nervous?

I decide to do what I did in Target yesterday.

I bend and put my fingers around my ankles, just above the edge of my socks. Then I run my hands all the way up my legs until they reach the hem of my skirt.

This is your skin, I tell myself. *You control who can touch it. Who can see it. Who can talk about it.*

I stand straight and clasp my hands in front of my face. Then I do the same, running my right fingers all the way to my left sleeve and vice versa.

Even if the world doesn't like it. Even if every other girl in the world is able to follow the same weird rules that let other people touch her. . . .

I move my fingers to my collarbone and run them up my neck and the sides of my face until they meet at the top of my head.

This is your skin. You decide about your own skin.

Then I take a deep, clean breath. I can do this. My cylinder and I can do this.

"*What* are you doing?" Emma demands.

I jump and spin to face her, the underwire of my "traditional" bra scraping horribly against my ribs as I do.

"What was that?" Emma asks. She's still in her tiny silk pajamas. She tilts her head to one side and juts out one of her hips.

I can't tell if she's being sort of mean or genuinely confused.

I open my mouth. "Ah, you know . . . stretching." I pick up my socked foot and hold it in my hands behind me in a quadricep stretch. "Don't you get all stiff when you sleep?"

Emma shakes her head but comes into the room. "It looked like some weird hippie stuff or something," she says.

That works too. I put my foot down and shrug. "So what if it was?"

She sort of laughs out her nose and shakes her head. I can't tell if she's making fun of me or enjoying me. I feel my cylinder digging into the skin above my underwear. I decide not to care.

"Your mom made spaghetti and meatballs. For breakfast," Emma says.

"Yum!" I say. "Garlic bread, too?"

"Yes." Emma shakes her head again. "I'm never going to get used to it here." She walks over to where her own uniform is hanging on her own desk chair and I leave to give her some privacy.

When I get to the kitchen my mom looks up from where she was working by the stove. She stares at me.

"Good morning, Lydia," she says. I see her face get a little pinker than usual. I wonder if she's feeling bad for the way she spoke to me in the dressing room yesterday. I wonder if she's going to say something about it. Something about how it's my body and I can dress it how I want to. Something close to an apology. I wonder if she's finally going to tell me what the texting was about yesterday. If she's going to tell me now how my dad is planning to disappoint me on the first day of school the same way he did on the last week of summer. How I have to go two full weeks without seeing the one safe man in the world.

She pauses and looks at me for way more that usual but then she says, "Sit down, honey. Have some breakfast. I'll do your hair."

She does my hair. She gives me a nice first-day-of-seventh-grade hug. But she doesn't tell me anything.

Mom always takes us to school because school starts before work. We have to ride home on our own. On the subway ride I sit between Emma and my mom so even though it's rush hour and the train car holds a bunch of strangers squished together like gummy bears that have been in Jeremy's pocket all day, it's only Emma's bare thigh pressed against mine and only Mom's elbow bouncing against my shoulder. I notice a man almost fall into Mom's lap as the train makes a sudden stop, but she laughs and says it's OK.

I'm supposed to be able to do that.

But today I don't have to try. The spell is working.

As soon as I walk onto the playground where the teachers

keep us until it's time for school to start, several people call my name. My real name. "Lydia!" Diamond, Mona, and Miriam run over to me. We all hug like we haven't seen each other in ages even though it's only been days.

It is different, though. Now we get to see each other almost every day. I forgot to like that about school. I don't have to be nearly as lonely. With my spell, I can fit in.

I see Andrew and a bunch of the other boys hanging out by the swing set. I notice Miriam following my gaze over to them and for a second I'm nervous that we're going to have to talk about which boys are cutest again. But instead Miriam says, "Guess what! When I was in New Mexico with my mom, I rode a horse! She said she couldn't believe I'd never ridden one before, and when she comes to visit at Christmastime she's going to find a way to take us all horseback riding!"

We all squeal and talk about that until it's time to go inside.

Ms. Banneker is the seventh-grade teacher. I focus on the feeling of my cylinder against my hip as she goes through our assigned seats.

"Lydia, please sit by the windows next to Melina," she says. Then she puts Megan behind me. I'm safe at least until recess.

And at recess, everything is still fine. The boys all run off with a basketball. Miriam and Diamond and Mona pull me to the side of the playground, where we stand in a tight circle.

"I've been working on a rap!" Diamond announces. "Someone give me a beat."

Miriam starts making beat noises with her mouth and we

all listen and bop along as Diamond raps about how kids should be allowed to drive.

No Swing.

No footballs.

Nothing that makes me feel dirty and disgusting and exposed.

Except for the pile of homework Ms. Banneker assigns, the entire day is perfect.

HOW TO BE SAFE AT SCHOOL

TURN INTO A BAD GIRL.
Break all the rules.
Tell no one.

CHAPTER 14

AFTER SCHOOL, EMMA AND I GET off the subway at our stop and walk the three blocks to our apartment. As we turn the corner, I hear shouting. Not just any two people in Brooklyn shouting over a parking spot or a basketball game or something.

I hear familiar shouting.

Mom.

And Dad.

Dad is here.

Dad didn't flake.

They're standing outside our apartment building, facing each other. Mom is leaning in toward Dad. Dad is leaning back on something in the street. All of this is weird because (a) I totally forgot today is Monday, which means Dad is supposed to come after school. Or maybe I didn't forget. Maybe I just didn't let myself think about it because after that text fight I was afraid he wouldn't show up. And (b) Mom is not supposed to be home from work yet.

They stop as soon as they see us, of course. It's as if they think that if I never see them fighting it erases all the times I hear them fighting.

I don't know what they could be fighting about. Is it the same fight they were having over text yesterday? The divorce didn't solve everything, but it does seem to mean that when they fight it doesn't last as long.

"Lyddie!" Dad calls out, and holds out his arms to me. He stands up straight and I see that he's been leaning on someone's parked motorcycle.

There are a million reasons I should be mad at him. But this isn't his voice on the phone. This is him, my real dad, in front of me. My dad who I haven't seen in thirteen days. I can't help it. I run to him.

He puts his arms around me, lifts me, spins me around, and then puts me down in a perfectly timed hug.

"How was the first day, kiddo?" he asks, his left hand on the right side of my head.

"Don't mess up her hair," Mom says. Even though this was a touch I was totally fine with. I glare at her.

Emma wanders up to us and stands next to Mom.

"I don't think messed-up hair is going to matter much," Dad says. "I have something for you, Lyddie."

"Phil, no," Mom says.

"Molly, yes," Dad says.

"Emma, hello," Mom says, almost like she's startled to

see her there. Mom puts her arm around Emma's shoulders. "How was your first day?"

"Awful," Emma says at the same time as Dad hands me a heavy paper bag. The top of it is stapled shut, as if he sort of thought that a brown paper bag and staples counted as wrapping paper.

"Phil, we discussed this," Mom says. "Lydia, don't open that."

Dad looks at his watch. "Molly, right now it's four p.m. on a Monday, which I believe is Dad time no matter what season of the year it is. Which means it is completely my right to give this *perfectly legal* gift to my daughter." He looks at me. "You don't have to open it if you don't want to. But it is for you if you'd like to open it."

"Perfectly legal?" I say.

"Phil!" Mom says. She's close to shouting at him even though I can see them both right now.

Emma stares at me with her mouth open. It's like she never realized my family ever had any problems just because her family always had more.

Then Mom and Dad stare at me. Everyone stares at me and I hate that I have to make the decision to disappoint one of my parents or the other. They try not to put me in the middle. At least they always tell me that after they do.

I hold the package. It's heavy for my fingers but I let it dangle next to my knee. No one says anything. No one's eyes move. Finally I say, "Dad, you didn't say hi to Emma."

147

"Oh." Dad looks embarrassed.

"And, Mom, Emma said her first day of school was 'awful.'"

Mom looks broken. "Emma, sweetie," she says. "Lydia's right. I'm sorry. What happened?"

"I'm OK," Emma mumbles.

But while Mom has turned to look at her, I wiggle one staple on the paper bag loose and glance inside.

It's purple and sparkly and round and smooth, like the top of a bowling ball. Except it's even heavier. And it has a thick chin strap at the bottom. My mouth drops open and I almost drop the package.

I point to the motorcycle Dad has been leaning on. "That's *yours*?"

Dad nods, proud. "I bought it for you, baby girl. I wanted to find a way for the adventures to continue all year," he says. "I've been saving up for it. Working extra shifts. That's what I was doing last week when I couldn't see you."

My eyes go wide. He wasn't at a party. He was working. He was working so that he could see me more.

"This way I never have to miss a Monday or a Tuesday," Dad announces.

"Wow," I say. I walk over to the motorcycle and touch it. It's black and silver. It looks powerful and dangerous but in an exciting kind of way.

"Lucky," Emma mumbles.

I look up at her. I don't want her to think I'm lucky. I don't want her to think having a dad who figures out how to show up consistently after two whole years is lucky. I don't want her to think having parents who fight in the middle of the street for the whole block to hear is lucky.

"Maybe you can take a ride too," I offer.

Mom steps in front of Emma. "No way," she says.

"See?" Emma says. "Lucky."

"Come on, Lyddie," Dad says. "Try on that helmet. Let's go on an adventure."

"Phil," Mom says in her no-nonsense voice. "I am very, *very* uncomfortable with this."

I expect my dad to spit back fighting words. Something about a lawyer. Or his parental rights. Instead he slumps over a little.

"I'm just trying to figure out a way to see my daughter more, Molly," he says. "I can't afford a car and parking and all of that. And last year I spent most of my time on the subway. I can get here almost an hour faster now."

But the motorcycle means even more than that to me. It means two guaranteed afternoons a week with my dad, which also means two guaranteed afternoons a week away from Jeremy. My heart is swelling with love and gratefulness, but I'm not sure if it's directed at my dad or my spell.

"I don't care how you get here but Lydia is not riding on that," Mom says.

"I think she is," Dad says. "That's how we bond, right, Lyddie? Adventures?"

Then she looks at me. "I'm sorry, Lydia. I didn't want to

have this conversation in front of you. Or you, Emma."

"Neither of us did," Dad says, a little forcefully.

"I know," I say. Because of course I know that. Because they usually hide every bit of their conversations from me so I never know why things are happening the way they are. I wish they'd have conversations in front of me more often, even the ones that are almost fights.

"It's up to you," Dad says to me. "You don't have to ride with me if you're not comfortable. But I took lessons and learned how to operate a motorcycle safely. I had to get a special license to drive it and I did that. And of course with you as my precious cargo I'll be even more careful. And it's perfectly legal to have a child as a passenger."

Mom sighs but doesn't say anything else. Dad sounds way more responsible than usual. I don't know what she could say.

I look back at her.

"So what do you say?" Dad asks. "A little adventure for today?"

I pretend it's hard to decide. And it sort of is, even though I have goose bumps up and down my neck I'm so excited. I'm imagining what it will feel like to have the wind in my face and the motor running under me. No crowded subways home with dad after dinner where men can stand too close to me and make me want to burst out of my skin. But also I know what my mom is feeling. I know what it feels like to think something should be wrong even when the world is telling you it isn't.

I look back at my mom again. "He's right, Lydia," she says. "It's up to you. It makes me very uncomfortable, but he is your dad, and ultimately I cannot make this decision."

Then she turns around like she's going to go inside but she doesn't take a step.

Dad takes the brown paper package from me and opens it. He holds the helmet out to me. "Adventure?" he says.

My backpack weighs heavy on my shoulders. It's the perfect thing to say, the thing that does not choose either of them. "Um, I have a lot of homework."

"Oh," Dad says. He smiles at me, then at my mom. "We'll start off slow, then. How about we just take this beauty to the library. And after homework we can get some pizza across the street."

The library is three blocks away. I look up at my mom. She's not smiling or anything but I can see her face relax a little bit when she knows we're only going three blocks.

I reach out and take the helmet from my dad. He clips it around my chin and my mom double-checks to make sure it's on the right way. Then I climb on behind him and he starts the engine.

For the next three blocks I'm glad I'm in a skirt and short-sleeved shirt.

Other people's fingers on my skin are awful.

But the wind on my skin is the feeling of pure freedom.

My cylinder—Pan's spell—has freed me.

* * *

When I get home that night Mom sits me down at the kitchen counter. It's just the two of us. The shower is on so I know Emma is in the bathroom and can't hear what we're saying. It's good to have my mom to myself for a minute.

"I'm sorry," I say. "I didn't know what to do."

Mom nods. "I understand," she says. "I wish we didn't put you in that position. I just couldn't help imagining you falling off that crazy thing with your brain splattered all across the road."

"But I was wearing a helmet!" I say.

Mom nods. "I know but—"

"And Dad was very careful. He doesn't want my brain splattered either."

"I didn't mean to imply that he did," Mom says. She's shifting in her seat. She almost looks like she'll cry. "I just didn't think—"

"I'm sorry, Mom," I say. "I won't ride it again."

She shakes her head. "That's not what I'm trying to say. That's not how I wanted this conversation to go. You need to . . . Your dad is your parent too. If he says it's OK, I need to respect that for your sake . . . even if it makes me uncomfortable. I'm sure he's not comfortable with . . . everything . . . I can't . . ."

"Huh?" I say.

Mom breathes deeply. "Don't worry about me," she says. "I will need to find a way to deal with the fact that your dad does things differently."

152

The shower turns off.

"So I can ride the motorcycle?" I ask.

"I guess that's sort of what I said." Mom smiles but I can tell she's forcing it.

"What motorcycle?" a big, male voice says behind us.

I jump about seven feet in the air. It's Jeremy. He was the one in the shower. Which means Emma is in our room with the door open and could hear everything. I'm still trying to process all of this when I hear my mom say, "Lydia's father decided it's a good idea to have her ride a motorcycle." She adds a sarcasm to her voice that wasn't there when she was just talking to me.

I pause and look at her.

She's so concerned for my safety, but she's making my own house feel so unsafe.

"The shower's free if you want it," Mom says to me.

I walk past Jeremy into my room to grab my pajamas. I sneak the little vial full of alyssum flowers and a roll of Scotch tape with me into the bathroom.

I take off my uniform and shake out my hair. My clothes and hair and skin all smell like gasoline and the smell is delicious. My stomach is settled with the pizza and chips and candy Dad bought me for dinner and my blood is still skipping happily from the Coke he said I could have to go with it. My cheeks are starting to hurt from smiling so much. I didn't know cheeks could get out of shape but apparently mine did this summer.

I check my watch to be sure I know exactly what time it is when I take off my cylinder because it cannot be off me for more than one hour or else it'll stop working.

I'm about to peel off the Scotch tape and flower from the other hip when I remember that the spell didn't say anything about twenty-three hours a day for the extra flower. I squeeze my eyes shut and try to remember exactly what Pan said about the extra flower. I see the handwriting behind my eyelids.

Be sure to change the alyssum flower each twenty-four-hour period.

So I have to shower with my flower on. I have to change it at exactly 2:47 a.m., the time I first taped it on last night. How am I going to make sure I wake up at 2:47 a.m. every night?

I decide to set the alarm on my watch and sleep with it under my pillow. All it does is beep, not nearly as loud as our regular alarm clock. Hopefully it won't wake up Emma.

I shower (careful not to get the tape and flower wet), reapply my cylinder, and put on winter pj's and a robe for my walk back to my room. Yes, I trust the spell now. But still, I'm not taking any chances with Jeremy sleeping here tonight.

When I walk out into the kitchen, Jeremy is in there alone with a spoon and a pint of ice cream. We both freeze. My knee starts burning where he touched it the day we went to Riis Park. I want to walk back into the bathroom and lock the door and wait until he leaves the kitchen to come back out.

But he's seen me. I know now he won't leave the kitchen until I go through.

I take a deep breath and step carefully into the kitchen and walk right past him.

"Don't tell your mom," he says, holding up the ice cream so I can see.

I have no idea how he even got ice cream into this house. But I don't care because Jeremy doesn't reach out toward me. He doesn't even offer me ice cream to not tell my mom about.

I keep walking. "OK," I say. "Good night."

"Good night," he says.

And then I'm safely in my room with the door shut behind me. My heart stops pounding before I even realized it was pounding in the first place.

The spell really is working.

It turns out that even waking up to change the flower isn't a problem. Magically my eyes open and I'm wide awake at two forty-five. I pull my watch out from under my pillow and turn the alarm off so it doesn't wake up Emma. Then I clutch my vial of flowers and Scotch tape and wait for the seconds to tick down. At exactly 2:46:30 I tiptoe into the bathroom and find a perfect five-petaled pink flower. At exactly 2:47:00 I remove the original flower. The new one is taped onto me by 2:47:40. Perfect.

I slip back into my bed and Emma is still sleeping. I reach under my bed and put the vial and the tape in the box with my notebook and other things from the house

I lie on my back on top of my much-less-bumpy pillow and stare at the darkness of the ceiling. Then I realize I'm still smiling. I sigh a happy sigh.

"Lydia?" Emma whispers from the next bed.

I jump, startled. For a second I was feeling so much like my old self I almost forgot she was here. But feeling like my old self makes me like her more too.

I roll onto my side to face her. "Yeah?" I say.

"What was it like?" she asks.

My hand goes to my hip. For a second I worry she's found out somehow about Pan's spell and how I got so happy. But then she says, "I mean, I know you only went to the library. But still. What was it like?"

"Oh," I say. She means riding a motorcycle. "Exciting. Almost like flying except for how much it shook at the red lights."

Emma sighs. "It's not fair," she says.

And I don't say anything back this time. Because this time she may be right. My dad came to me with a motorcycle. Hers is nowhere.

It's quiet for a minute and I think she's fallen back to sleep, but then she says, in the saddest voice I've ever heard come out of her, "My mom had a motorcycle too, you know."

I freeze. Emma hasn't talked about her mom in a long time. When we were little she used to tell me about her all the time. She was a movie star in Hollywood. She was traveling all around the world on a secret mission from the president of the United States. She was a good-for-nothing loser who never had a job.

My mom had a motorcycle seems like the most plausible sentence out of everything she's ever told me about her.

"How do you know?" I ask finally.

"I just do," Emma snaps.

"I'm sorry," I say.

And I finally, finally choose cousins. Maybe the spell makes me. Maybe feeling safe in my skin makes it easier to make the right decisions.

"You must miss her," I say.

Emma doesn't say anything. Her big eyes stare into the darkness between our beds.

"What else do you remember about her?"

Emma doesn't choose cousins back.

"Her motorcycle was even bigger. And faster. And she'd let me ride it every day if she could," she says. Then she turns over and pulls all her blankets with her as if we're sharing a bed and she wants to pull the covers off me.

I touch the flower on my hip and burrow into my bed thinking about Emma's mom.

These spells really work.

Maybe I shouldn't be keeping them to myself.

Maybe there's a different spell that could help Emma.

WHAT MY MOM HAS TOLD ME
ABOUT EMMA'S MOM

SHE WAS TALL, WHICH IS WHY Emma is taller than the rest of the family.

She was black and Emma looked like her, which is why Emma doesn't look like the rest of the family.

She loved Emma. She was a great mom.

Most of what Emma says about her is made up.

CHAPTER 15

THE NEXT DAY DAD IS A few minutes late to pick me up on the motorcycle, which means I'm standing outside waiting for him in just my school uniform—bare legs and arms and neck and wrists and ankles. I feel OK about it. I feel normal. Until Jeremy walks up to the front of the building.

"Lydia, my sweetheart," he says. He holds his arms out like he wants a hug. As soon as he does, I feel the cylinder get hot against the skin on my hip bone. It's almost like it's telling me not to go near him.

I swing my backpack off my shoulder and lean over it as if I need to find a book so that he can't come any closer. "Why aren't you at work?" I ask.

"I got done early with the building on Lincoln Street," Jeremy says with a shrug. "Your mom asked me to do some grocery shopping. She said she left a list on the kitchen counter."

"Oh," I say. I shift from one foot to the other. This is exactly what my mom likes about Jeremy. He participates. He does stuff. He's reliable. I wish I could appreciate it but instead I'm almost panicking. On the one hand, I don't want to be alone anywhere with Jeremy ever, especially not someplace small like an elevator. On the other hand, I have a spell protecting me and Emma is in our apartment all alone. "I'll—I'll go help you find it."

Jeremy smiles so big it makes me itchy. "Well, OK, then!" he says, and his big shoulders shake as he laughs at nothing.

I put my backpack on the front of my body, even though that's weird, and pretend to keep looking in it as we wait for the elevator. My spell must keep working because three other people get on the elevator with us and ride it all the way to the tenth floor. When we get inside our apartment Jeremy hangs up his backpack and stretches out his arms as if he's not just grabbing the grocery list and leaving. Emma comes out of my room.

"Hi," she says, sounding confused.

"Jeremy got done with work early so Mom asked him to go to the grocery store," I say quickly. I walk over to the kitchen counter and find a list written on a pink Post-it.

"Oh," Emma says back just as quickly. "I was just about to go help Ms. Kemp bake some cookies."

"Cool," I say. I force the word not to come out of me like a relieved sigh. Emma won't have to be here alone when Jeremy comes back from the store.

"Found the list!" I say. I hand it to Jeremy and he purpose-fully makes sure the tip of his index finger touches the soft inner part of my wrist when he takes it. My cylinder is practi-cally on fire. I'm safe. "Come on," I say to him. "I'll ride down with you. I'm waiting for my dad."

Emma watches with her eyes wide as we both leave. Emma doesn't usually go to Ms. Kemp's in the school year when she's only home for a few hours before Mom gets home. I don't know if she was really going to bake cookies with her today, but I hope she goes there now, or to another neigh-bor's, or to a friend's. I hope she stays out of the apartment until Mom gets home.

When we get off the elevator I make the mistake of switch-ing my backpack to the correct side again, and when we get outside Jeremy is suddenly hugging me. As usual the hug is too tight and too long. I go limp in it because the only other choices are to squirm away or hug back.

"Thank you for finding the list," Jeremy says as if it were a long-lost family heirloom or something.

I shrug as much as I can with his arms around me. The hug goes on long enough that I start to wonder if my cylinder is working after all. But just as I have the thought, I hear my name. "Lydia?"

It's my dad.

Jeremy lets go and I want to do that thing where I touch all my skin and remind myself it's mine. I want to wipe all his dead skin cells off me.

"Hey, man!" Jeremy says in his usual jolly way. He turns with a big smile and shakes my dad's hand. My dad looks a little confused, but he shakes back. "Molly was asking me to go to the store and I couldn't find the list anywhere. Your little girl saved my butt!" He laughs his jiggly laugh.

My face goes red.

The list wasn't lost. It was right on the kitchen counter like he said my mom told him.

He lied. He lied to my dad. That has to mean there's something wrong. Something real. "That so?" Dad says.

"I'm always losing stuff, man," Jeremy says. "You know how it is. Molly hates that."

He laughs and my dad laughs back. I wonder if Jeremy can tell that my dad's laugh is fake.

"Have fun, you guys," Jeremy says. "I'm off."

He walks down the sidewalk so light he's practically skipping.

My dad is squinting at me.

"What?" I say.

In my head, I beg him to say it. *Tell me if that was weird. Tell me if grown men aren't supposed to hug girls like that, even if the girls did do them a favor (which I didn't). Even if the men are the girls' almost stepfathers. Tell me if something seems off to you. Tell me if it's not all in my head.*

But he just chews his lip and says, "You OK, Lyddie?"

I shrug.

I think I am OK. I think my dad would know if I wasn't.

He would say something if what he saw was weird.

He doesn't.

He says, "How about Prospect Park today? We can go play with the pups at the dog pond?"

I nod. "Sounds good, Dad." He musses my hair in the perfect not-scary touch and hands me my helmet.

My dad loves me.

He knows how to make me feel safe.

If he doesn't think Jeremy is weird, it must really be OK.

Jeremy is leaving right as my dad is dropping me off that night. We both watch him from the motorcycle as he leaves the building and waves at us. Then he disappears around a corner. I have to sit so close to my dad on this motorcycle I almost wonder if he can feel my heart slow down against his back when I realize Jeremy is gone for the evening.

No Jeremy at home makes showering and changing and getting up at 2:47 a.m. all easier to handle.

But as I'm coming out of the bathroom in the middle of the night, a fresh blue flower taped to my hip, I freeze. My mom's voice is loud under her door.

"That's totally unfair, Phil," she says sharply.

She's fighting with my dad at 2:50 a.m. It's almost like my dad still lives here. I don't understand why they had to get a divorce if they're still going to fight all the time. I mean, I hated it when my dad lived here and they fought all the time. I used to hide under the covers and say nursery rhymes under my breath until it stopped. So at least now I don't hear the fights as much.

But if they were still fighting like that, it would mean Dad still lived here. And that would mean Dad still dropped me off at school in the morning. And maybe if the boys saw my dad more, they'd leave me alone. And if Dad still lived here, that would mean Jeremy wasn't here all the time. And then maybe I'd still only be afraid of the fighting and not of the entire world.

"I think I'm aware of exactly what you're implying," Mom says. "Where is this coming from?"

Usually only one of them is loud. If Mom is loud, that usually means Dad is talking calmly and quietly on the other end of the phone.

"This is on another level, Phil. You don't need to get back at me, OK? You won. You get your precious motorcycle."

So my dad is accusing my mom of something. That doesn't happen as much. My mom accuses my dad of not paying child support on time. Or of missing events for me. Or of endangering me on a motorcycle.

"Do *you* really not trust *my* judgment?" my mom says, like it's a joke.

What could my dad be accusing my mom of?

"You can't tell me you're only thinking of our daughter's well-being when you're the one sticking her on a dangerous topsy-turvy machine every second you get. I want to remind you that I've always been the responsible one. I've always made the best decisions for our daughter. She is safe *because* of me."

My face goes red. This sounds like an old old fight. Except that I can't hear my dad's apology.

"I know you know that," Mom says, a little softer. "Thank you, Phil. When it comes to Lydia, you're asking me to trust you." She pauses so he can respond, then says, "Yes, right, you have to trust me, too. Thank you."

I give up and tiptoe back to my room. At least when my dad was here they had other things to fight about. Now every single fight is about me.

I curl up in my bed and wish there were a spell that could stop my parents from fighting. I don't think that spell is in Pan's book, though. I wish I could find Pan and ask her if she could write that spell.

I'm staring at the wall when I feel something thump me in the back.

I roll over. It's a package of gummy worms. My favorite candy. Middle-of-the-night sugar seems like the perfect thing to take my mind off my parents fighting.

I prop my head up on my elbow.

"Thanks!" I say to Emma. "Did you get these for me?"

"No," Emma says. The moonlight catches her face so that her eyes are bright beneath the scarf she wears on her head when she sleeps. "Jeremy brought them back from the store. He gave me some too."

It's like the package turns to real worms.

I toss them back. "You can have them," I say. "Both of them."

Emma shrugs and shoves them under her bed. "Good by me," she says.

After a minute, when we've both turned over to face opposite walls, she says, "Lydia, if the gummy worms were from me, would you eat them?"

"Yeah," I say.

"I thought so," Emma says.

She thought so? What does that mean?

I should ask her. But I'm so tired.

"Good night," I say.

WHY I WON'T EAT JEREMY'S CANDY

IT'S NOT THAT I HATE HIM so much that candy from him grosses me out.

It's that two kids having a secret about a bag of candy is normal . . . but a kid and a grown-up having a secret about a bag of candy is creepy.

I don't want to keep secrets from my mom.

Or maybe sometimes I do.

But I only want to keep kid secrets from my mom.

CHAPTER 16

PAN'S SPELL PROTECTS ME THE REST of the week.

At recess at school, Andrew Quinn and Jason Blackman start to tease us from across the playground while Diamond practices her raps. But it's not like last year.

"Girls think they have such juicy secrets," Andrew says. He wants us to hear but he's talking in a way that he can pretend he doesn't.

"They probably do," Jason says.

They both laugh and Miriam and Diamond turn to roll their eyes at them but they also laugh. I make myself laugh with them. I make myself try to be happy for Miriam and Diamond and Mona who have wanted the attention. I make myself not be scared for them.

Boys paying attention to all of our whispers is one million times better than boys paying attention to my legs.

By the end of the week we're pretending we actually do

have juicy secrets while Andrew and Jason try to throw pine cones into the middle of our little circle.

"I think they're flirting!" Miriam whispers like it's the most exciting thing in the world.

But that's it. Nothing bad happens. Nothing almost bad happens.

Jeremy sleeps at our apartment two more times over the course of the week but I manage to avoid seeing him without my mom there so no more weird touching happens.

Before I know it, it's Saturday. Emma is gone for the day with friends from the school she went to before she moved in. Mom and I are back at the house with paint squares and measuring tape. Mom says it's almost time for us to hire some professional help to clean and fix up what we couldn't.

I start to scope out hiding spots for when that happens. How will I keep the book safe in the special room? How will I make sure I have access to my supplies but none of the professionals see them?

But for now, everything is working fine. Mom has stopped rolling her eyes at my clothes. I've stopped dressing like a weirdo. And the boys at school have stopped making me feel like one.

Except for bringing magic to school, I haven't broken a rule in a long time. I'm a good girl again.

I knew from the second I walked into this house that it would protect me.

And it has.

When Mom goes to the bodega down the street for more garbage bags, I find the key and open the red door. I'm alone in the basement apartment again, a perfect time to renew the spell.

I cut the black and peach strips and glue them onto a new cylinder. I season it with frankincense and cedar and then apply the three perfect alyssum flowers. Then I change the cylinder out with the one on my hip. I change my new flower now too. Four thirty p.m. A much more manageable time to switch my flower every day. I secure the new flower and the new cylinder easily.

Then I page through Pan's book.

Emma was so excited to see her friends today. How excited would she be if I found a spell that could somehow bring her closer to her mom? Can spells do that? Put you in touch with the dead?

I shiver.

That seems more like the magic the nuns are always warning us about. It seems somehow closer to evil. But I don't know why.

I don't know anything about Emma's mom but there's no way she was evil

I look at the table of contents again:

A Spell for Charm
A Spell for Love
A Spell for Fortune

A Spell for Revenge
A Spell for Protection

None of these spells would help Emma. I page through the book and look at the spells written in black and red and blue pen. Most of them are written in the same tiny printed handwriting, but some are suddenly in loopy cursive.

When I turn past the spell for protection I find more writing. I thought the last spell listed in the table of contents would be the last spell in the book, but there are pages and pages after it. Most of these are in the loopy handwriting.

How to Find a Lost Person
How to Banish Bad Spirits
How to Find Better Energy
How to Communicate with a Loved One Who Has Passed On

I freeze. This is it. I could do this for Emma.
I read the first line:

It is essential that this spell be performed by an individual who both loves and is loved by the person who has passed.

I didn't love Emma's mom and she didn't love me. She never even met me.

In order to help Emma I'd have to show her the book and—

"Lydia!" Mom calls from the top of the stairs. She startles me so much I drop the book. It bounces hard off my foot and onto the floor. I bend to pick it up as quickly as I can. The teachers at school always say that Bibles should not be on the floor. *Pan's Personal Book of Spells* feels just as important. Maybe more. I hear my mom's footsteps on the stairs. I stand up so quickly I bang my head on the open desk drawer.

"Are you OK, sweetie?" Mom says. Her voice is much closer now. I throw the book onto the desk and charge out of the little office.

"Sorry," I say. "I was just checking if that little room needed vacuuming but it turns out it's just tile floor so it's OK."

Mom tilts her head at me like she's trying to figure something out. I'm talking way too quickly. I sound suspicious. Mom cannot go in that room right now. I didn't even get a chance to clean it up. *Pan's Personal Book of Spells* is sitting right on the desk.

"Time to go home?" I say, still probably too quickly. "What's for dinner?"

Mom's head goes back to its normal position and she smiles. "I was thinking maybe we can go out to dinner somewhere. Just you and me? Emma's not supposed to be back until eight."

I smile back at her. "Sounds good," I say.

In fact, it sounds great.

It's been forever since I had a whole day with my mom without having to share her with anyone else. No Jeremy. No Emma. Just me and Mom.

"I've missed you," Mom says when our food arrives.

"You have?" I ask. I'm honestly a little shocked. I thought I was the only one noticing the difference in the way things have been.

"Of course!" Mom says. She squeezes a lemon into her water and then takes a long sip. I wait for her to say something else. Something about how things have changed. Something about how it's all not fair to me.

Instead she says, "Did you know when I was nine, Uncle Jack and I had to spend a whole summer with my aunt? I really missed my mom."

"Your aunt?" I ask.

Mom nods. "My aunt Maggie. She lived in Ohio."

"What was it like there?" I asked.

Mom licks her lips. "Part of it was fun. Aunt Maggie raised chickens and I loved to collect their eggs. Plus she had a lot of dogs. And at least your uncle Jack was there with me. I really leaned on him that summer."

"But it wasn't all fun?" I ask.

Mom sighs. "Well, we were used to Brooklyn. The country noises used to keep me up at night! Crickets and branches rustling in the wind. I remember telling Aunt Maggie it was too noisy to sleep. But she laughed and said that it was so much quieter in Ohio than in Brooklyn. And I guess it was.

But still, I'd lived in Brooklyn my whole life. I could sleep through sirens but not crickets. So to me it was louder." Mom almost sounds like she's still arguing with her aunt about this.

"Aunt Maggie didn't get that?" I ask.

Mom shrugs. "Well, she'd never been to Brooklyn. I didn't know her very well."

I lower my eyebrows. "Why were you there if you barely knew her?"

"To be honest," Mom says, keeping her eyes on her plate, "I probably should have told you all about this a long time ago. But it was a really hard part of my childhood and I don't like to think about it."

"Oh," I say. I figure that's it but she keeps talking. And I'm glad. She's talking to me like I'm a grown-up. I love these sorts of conversations. I love having my mom to myself.

"My mom was having a very hard time," Mom says. "She didn't have her priorities straight."

"Priorities?" I ask.

Mom shrugs. "She sort of forgot how to take care of us. She remembered, eventually. But . . . she wasn't the best mom."

I nod. I never met my grandmother, but both my mom and dad have told me that she had some big problems.

"So sometimes, starting when I was nine, she used to send us to Aunt Maggie. I think she was trying to protect us. Or someone was sending us there to protect us . . . I never really understood all the details. And I was so young. And maybe we did need to go there, but . . ."

Mom trails off.

"But?" I prompt.

"But I missed her. Badly. And I missed my normal life. Even though it wasn't perfect. It was my normal. And even though life with Aunt Maggie would have seemed better to everyone else, I missed my normal. Do you think you can understand that?"

I nod. "I can."

Mom pats my hand. "I love you, my good girl," she says.

Dinner is over too quickly.

Later that night when I'm enjoying a minute alone in my room with my Stephen King novel, Emma bursts in the door.

I put the book on my bed and prop myself up on an elbow, forcing myself to be nice. I think about my mom's aunt who suddenly had two kids for a whole summer and didn't know what to do. I think about my mom who was nine that summer and how scared and angry she must have been to be suddenly away from home. It's easier to think about my mom than about Emma for some reason. But still. I know why Mom told me that story. Emma probably misses her normal too.

"How was it?" I ask.

Emma reaches under her bed and pulls out one of the packages of gummy worms. She stares at me, her eyes hard and fierce. "I'm going to eat this right now," she says. "Your mom is in the shower but also, I don't care if she finds out. I don't care if you tell her."

I raise my eyebrows. She sounds mad at me but I know it's not really at me. "I won't," I say. I've never even told on Jeremy having candy and ice cream and I hate those secrets. I don't mind keeping secrets for Emma.

I watch Emma shove two gummy worms into her mouth and she kicks off her sneakers.

"Did you have a bad day?" I ask.

"It would have been a great day," Emma says. "But I live here now."

"Huh?" I say. I would think missing her friends from her old school would make seeing them even more special.

"I didn't get any of their jokes anymore. They have all these stories without me. My friend Kiara had her first kiss and she didn't even tell me about it. I didn't know what they were talking about half the time. I just had to smile. And they all kept asking where my dad is, and you know I couldn't tell them."

"Oh," I say. My face feels hot for some reason. I don't know why she couldn't tell them about her dad because no one has told me anything about him, but I can also tell she doesn't want me to ask. "I'm sorry."

"No, Lydia. You think you're sorry but you can't be. You don't get it. Kiara can't text me to say that Jaquan kissed her because she'd have to text your mom's phone. It's so unfair. It's so unfair that Aunt Molly won't let me have a phone."

"Yeah," I say.

I watch Emma collapse onto her back and suck a green-and-yellow gummy worm into her mouth, tail to head.

"And you know what? You'll probably get a phone first. Just because you're older. When you don't even need a phone."

I don't know what to say to that. She's probably right. She's definitely right that she needs one more than I do. But I don't want to admit that.

"Everything is unfair now," Emma says. Her voice squeaks this time, like her anger is cracking to make a little room for sadness.

I shift in my bed, uncomfortable. I don't think I want to hear Emma's sadness. I don't think I'm ready for it. I don't know what to do with it because her sadness almost suffocates me in guilt.

"I know I love my dad. But he messed everything up."

I freeze, hoping she'll say more. She loves her dad even though he's unsafe? What does it mean that he's unsafe? I have to know this. I'm going to live with him. Why won't anyone tell me?

"I love him and I also hate him," Emma concludes.

"You hate him?" I say slowly. Maybe that will make her tell me something.

She doesn't say anything for a long time. When she does, it's "I wish I could talk to my mom."

I freeze and stare at her. *It is essential that this spell be performed by an individual who both loves and is loved by the person who has passed.*

"Why are you looking at me like that?" Emma snaps.

"I'm sorry you had a bad day." I say.

I should go to her bed and hug her. I should ask her to tell me about her dad. I should open my desk drawer and give her the pack of Mentos I've been stashing in there since last Easter when Miriam gave them to me.

"Everything is unfair," Emma says again.

There's nothing for me to say back because it's true. Everything is unfair. I've been complaining about having to share my mom when she totally lost hers. I've been complaining about having to share my mom when she also lost her dad, her friends, her whole normal. I don't know what to do. How do I make it up to her? How do I give her her normal back?

Emma rolls over to stare at the wall. I look at her back. Finally I go over to my desk drawer and toss the pack of Mentos onto her bed. "In case the gummy worms aren't enough," I say.

She turns and smiles at me, but it's a sad smile. "Thanks," she says.

I shrug. I wish there were more I could do.

It is essential that this spell be performed by an individual who both loves and is loved by the person who has passed.

Do I have to share the spells with Emma?

CHAPTER 17

MONDAY IS THE FIRST TIME I hear "Swing" in seventh grade.

I'm one of the first seventh graders on the playground in the morning. None of my friends are there yet. Emma is on the other side of the playground with the sixth graders. I sit with my back against the big oak tree and take out my homework to check it over. Suddenly I see a pair of sneakers next to my feet.

"Didn't know you were such a nerd, Swing." I look up. It's Andrew.

My hands start to shake before I can help it.

Malik and Tim are standing behind him. They laugh when I look up. "Who checks their homework before school?" Malik says.

"Yeah," Andrew says, "come play football with us so we can watch that skirt swing."

I move so that I'm sitting on my knees and tuck as much of my legs under my skirt as I can. The wood chips I was sitting on dig into my shins but it's better than keeping my legs visible.

"*What do you say?*" Tim says. He holds the football out toward me.

What do I say? Miriam would giggle. Emma would say something rude. How do I get out of this without them seeing my legs any more than they already have?

"No, thank you," I say. I look around for Ms. Banneker or Sister Janice or one of my friends. Someone, anyone, to rescue me. Even though my friends would probably just start giggling. At least they'd pull some of the attention off me.

My face is on fire. Andrew notices.

"Are we embarrassing you, Swing? You don't need to be embarrassed."

"Yeah, we're just enjoying your God-given gifts," Malik says, nodding toward my legs.

I want to dig myself under these wood chips. I want to burrow backward until I am a part of the tree I'm leaning on. I want to be anything but a girl.

Why is this happening? The spell is supposed to protect me.

"Think fast!" Tim says, and throws the ball right at my face. I have to move to catch it, and that exposes half my left and my entire right leg. The boys break down in a fit of laughter.

But when I move, the spell also moves on my hip. I feel it heat up like the movement reminded it to get to work.

"Gentlemen!" we all hear Sister Janice admonish. "Surely

you could be doing something more valuable with your time than bothering this young lady."

The boys run off, laughing. Sister Janice comes over to me and reaches out her hand like she wants to help me up even though I was happy to be sitting down. I let her pull me up.

"Don't let them bother you, Lydia," Sister says. "And if they are, just say a prayer and God will help you to know how to handle them." She winks at me.

The spell on my hip slowly retreats to regular temperature. I'm safe. And no matter what Sister Janice thinks, God had nothing to do with it.

That afternoon it's unusually hot for mid-September. Dad and I ride his motorcycle all the way to Brooklyn Bridge Park. It's only about three miles away but still the farthest we've gone. Mom has stopped complaining about the motorcycle even though I know she doesn't like it.

We play volleyball in the sand courts because my dad loves volleyball and I love him coaching me. I take off my skirt before it can get too sandy and play in just the shorts I wear under it, and my uniform blouse. The hot air scorches my legs and arms and it feels fantastic. I've missed this feeling all summer.

When we're nice and sweaty, we stop at the ice cream stand and get root beer floats. We sit at a picnic table and I tilt my head to the sun before taking the first sweet, creamy sip.

"Your overhand serve is getting fierce!" Dad says.

"You think so?" I ask.

Dad nods. "You should try out for the high school team. I'll have to get you ready for that."

I smile at him and know instantly that I'm going to do it. The thought of my dad in the stands at whatever high school gym I end up playing in is enough to convince me to love volleyball like he does.

Suddenly his face goes dark. We look up and gray clouds are quickly moving to block the sun.

"We better get going," Dad says, even though we have a lot of time left. "I don't want to drive you in the rain."

He runs toward the motorcycle and I shove my skirt into my backpack and run behind him. He puts on his helmet while I put on mine. Then he checks that mine is tight enough and takes off. We've only gone about three blocks when the sky opens up and rain drenches us in seconds. Dad drives through a puddle and mud splashes up, soaking my ankle socks. Then Dad takes an unusual turn and suddenly swerves into a parking spot.

"What are you doing?" I ask.

He cuts the engine so the sound of rain suddenly pounds against my helmet.

"What are you doing?" I say again.

"I can't drive you home in this," he says. "Your mother would have a cow."

He takes off his helmet and steps off the bike but I leave mine on.

"And she'd be right. With rain like this a car is safer."

He puts his arm around me and we huddle together as if we have an umbrella and wait for a cab to show up. It takes seven minutes, and by that time it looks like I dove into a pool with all my clothes on.

"How's this for an adventure?" Dad says when we get in the cab. He smiles at me and runs a hand through his hair so that water runs down the back of his T-shirt. I do the same thing even though it feels like I'm just rearranging the water. "Listen, I'm sorry but I'm going to have to drop you off and leave a little earlier today. I have to get back to the bike before the meter runs out."

"OK," I say. I'm shivering and all I want is a hot shower. I miss the scorching sun as my muscles worked to jump for the volleyball. I miss the sweat. This is what everything with my dad is like. Fantastic for one brief moment, then over.

"And . . . listen," Dad says again, quieter. He speaks so softly I almost can't hear him over my teeth chattering. "Lydia . . ."

My heart sinks before I even hear what he has to say.

"My schedule is getting shifted. It turns out I have to work tomorrow."

I look out the window. I hate this part.

"But hopefully it'll be sunny again next week, right? And we can play more volleyball?"

He promised me he wasn't going to miss days anymore.

"The motorcycle was supposed to fix this," I say.

"I know," he says. "And it has. I'll still be here every time I have a day off."

"What's your new day off?" I ask.

"What?" Dad says.

"You said your schedule shifted. So now you work Tuesdays. What's your new day off?"

Dad sighs. "I have to work six days now. Shorter shifts, but six days."

I chew the inside of my cheek. I watch the brownstones fly by the car window, foggy in the rain. I probably shouldn't be mad at him. It feels like this time it isn't his fault. But it's hard not to be mad at him when so much missed time *was* his fault.

"Does Mom know already?" I ask. Part of the advantage of changing my flower at four thirty every day is that I no longer hear it if they're having three a.m. fights. But that also means I don't know what's going on.

As soon as I ask about her, Dad's phone rings, and when he answers, her voice is angry on the other end.

"Molly, I know," Dad says. "Give me some credit. We're in a cab."

Mom's voice is immediately softer. I can't hear what she's saying. I'm close to tears already and if they started fighting I would definitely cry. I think I hate for them to see me cry even more than they hate for me to see them fight.

"Listen," Dad says. "Do you mind if I just send her up in the elevator? My bike is parked in a meter spot and I want to just take this cab right back. . . . OK? . . . Great, thanks."

Dad hangs up and looks at me. "She says she'll look out the window for you."

I nod.

No one says anything else the rest of the ride home. When we get to my building he reaches for a hug but I just let him pat my shoulder. For the first time I don't want to hug him. No spell could protect me from this.

My time with my dad is getting chopped in half.

I get out of the cab, dragging my soaked backpack behind me. I pull it onto my wet shoulders and pause a minute, letting the rain soak me again. I know Dad will wait until I go inside before telling the driver to go. It's early anyway.

I look at my watch. Five fifteen. I'm supposed to have two more hours with my dad.

Wait . . . five fifteen! My hand goes to my left hip. I forgot to change my flower. I'm already an hour and fifteen minutes late! I have to get upstairs right now!

I run three steps into my building and plow through the lobby—then, *boom*, my wet body runs right into something big and warm.

"Well, isn't this a nice greeting," says a voice. The worst possible voice I could hear when I'm wearing nothing but soaked shorts and short sleeves. Jeremy.

He puts his arms around me like I meant to hug him.

I am so cold I'm shivering against him, which makes it even worse. I try to pull back but he keeps one arm tight around me. "Let's get you to the shower," he says.

It's exactly where I want to go, but in his voice it sounds creepy. This time no one else comes to join us in the elevator.

I pull hard against Jeremy's arm to get some space between us but he keeps it anchored around my shoulder, not budging. His arm is stronger than all of my body. He doesn't move it until he takes out a key to unlock the door to our apartment.

When did he get a key?

Before he opens the door he turns back to look at me again. "You have some rain on your forehead," he says. And then before I can dodge it, he reaches out a finger and traces lightly from my temple to behind my ear.

I'm no longer shivering from the cold.

My inside organs all turn to bugs, split apart, and try desperately to crawl out of my skin. My stomach climbs my rib cage like a ladder, trying to escape through my throat. It only lasts a second but it feels like we stand there an hour with his finger on my face.

Finally Mom calls out, "Lydia, is that you?"

I push past Jeremy and run inside and straight to my room.

I hear Mom greeting Jeremy with a big kiss. "Thank God you're here," she says. "The stove isn't working again and I have to start dinner and they said the super would be here to fix it but of course no one's come yet—"

"Say no more, my lady!" Jeremy booms. "I am here!"

I quickly grab sweatpants and a sweatshirt and a long-sleeved shirt and a sports bra and huge socks and my fluffy robe and stick the vial of flowers in my robe pocket. I hold all the clothes in front of me, blocking my bare skin and wet shirt as I dash for the shower. Once the bathroom door is safely locked, I change my flower. Then I look again at my watch.

5:22.

I'm fifty-eight minutes late.

I think back to Dad telling me that he's not coming tomorrow. I think that was at almost exactly four thirty. The spell broke right on time.

I stare at the new white flower on my hip. "Please work," I whisper to it. "Please make the spell work again."

It doesn't.

At school the next day, things get worse.

Before lunch, Ms. Banneker decides she wants Megan and Andrew to switch seats.

She decides Melina should switch with Treyvon Weston.

So now I'm sitting in front of Andrew, between the window and Treyvon. This is way worse than sitting between Megan and Melina.

At lunch Andrew walks past our table and purposefully bops me on the head with his lunch tray. "Hey, seat buddy!" he says.

Miriam squirms beside me and I try to make myself smile at him because I know that's what a girl is supposed to do. But I don't want to smile at my head being bopped with a lunch tray.

"You're smart, right, Swing?" Andrew asks. "So I can copy off your papers?"

"No!" I scream before I can remember I'm supposed to react like a normal girl would.

But he laughs. Tim and Jason have been standing behind him. They laugh too. I feel my face get red and I'm sure they can see it before they walk to their table.

Around me girls squirm and whisper.

"You're so lucky!" Miriam says. "He was flirting just with you!"

"Andrew is so cute!" Diamond says.

"I wish he'd copy off *my* paper!" Miriam says.

I force myself to smile at her. But I don't like flirting if it's full of lunch trays on my head and boys cheating off of me. I liked it better when the only thing I could be touched with was a pine cone.

After lunch we're back in the classroom copying the week's vocabulary words from the Smart Board when something tickles my neck. I reach up to feel what it is, but nothing's there.

I'm halfway through writing the definition for *flagrant* when I feel it again.

This time my fingers catch the end of it.

Breath.

Andrew Quinn is blowing on my neck.

He has to be sitting so close to me. I know he's not copying from me because what would be the point? I'm just copying from the board.

He blows on the other side of my neck.

I don't know what to do. I just keep writing.

I think I'm supposed to like this.

I think I'm supposed to giggle and find a way to almost touch him back. But to me almost touching is the same as touching and I don't want Andrew Quinn to touch me or to almost touch me.

I wish I could trade seats with Miriam. This would make her so happy because she's normal.

It makes me feel like my own breath is made of fire. Like I'm burning up on the inside and if I don't find a way to fix myself I'm going to explode.

Except I can't explode. No one understands me so I have to pretend to be normal. I have to pretend this is OK. I can't pretend to like it.

I pretend not to feel it. Maybe it'll work this year. Maybe if I ignore him, he will stop.

He doesn't.

That night when it's time to get in the shower, I don't carefully check my watch to make sure the cylinder only leaves my skin for exactly sixty minutes or less. Instead I take it off and rip it to shreds over the sink.

It's stupid, because this is all my fault.

I'm the one who forgot to change my flower.

I'm the one who messed up the spell.

But it seems like a spell meant to protect me should care more about doing its job, right? It shouldn't give up as soon as I make one tiny mistake. What kind of protection is that?

So I'm mad at it. I only have one choice: destroy this spell and sneak back to the house to start all over again.

As I'm coming out of the shower a few minutes later, Mom is in the kitchen. She hands me her cell phone. "You have a text," she says.

I take it into my room and glance at the screen.

Miriam: L, you there?

I text her back. It looks like my mom is texting her because it's on my mom's phone, of course. Miriam has her own phone already.

Molly: hey, it's me.

Molly: Lydia

Molly: what's up

She doesn't answer right away so I dry off and brush my hair and put on my pajamas. Emma is in the living room watching TV so I have the whole room to myself, but it still feels weird to be naked in here. I think the only place I've been naked in my entire apartment is the bathroom ever since Jeremy started sleeping over all the time last spring.

But it's normal to be naked in your room alone and to not even think much about it.

I'm thinking about it but at least I'm not feeling panicked and like I have to rush into my clothes.

Maybe this spell did do something for me.

Maybe I'm a little closer to normal?

Mom's phone buzzes. It buzzes three more times before I can get to my desk to check what she's saying.

Miriam: So? Are you going to let him copy off you??

Miriam: You're so lucky, Andrew is so cute. He has those dimples!

Miriam: Isn't this exciting? I think he likes you!

Miriam: What if it's a real and true and honest CRUSH???

Each text is followed with a string of emojis. I sit on my bed and hold my head in my hands.

If Miriam is normal—and I think she must be because she's just like every other girl in our class—I'm not even close.

She's my best friend and she's forgiven me after a whole summer of ignoring her. I need to find a way to answer.

Molly: I don't want him to copy off of me.

Miriam: Yeah, I get that. But you have to find a flirty way to say it. Let me think . . .

I think while she's thinking. I don't want to find a flirty way to tell a boy not to cheat off me. I don't want to tell him anything. I just want to watch from the sidelines and cheer on Miriam as he flirts with her.

I want to go back to my old body that no one ever blew on or squashed or touched or stroked. I want to own my school-work and my neck and my forehead and behind my ear again.

If this is growing up, I don't want to do it.

Molly: I sorta don't want to flirt with him.

Miriam: Really?? Do you not think he's cute??

Molly: I mean, I guess he is. But like maybe I just don't think about boys like you do.

Miriam: Do you have a crush on anyone?

Molly: No, that's what I'm telling you.

Molly: Why. Do you?

Miriam: YES ♥♥♥♥♥♥♥♥♥♥

I know I'm supposed to ask who. I'm supposed to squeal and beg her to tell me. But I'm scared. What if she has a crush on someone who tortures me? How can my best friend have a crush on a boy like that?

Miriam texts me anyway.

Miriam: I think Andrew Quinn is really hot. But I also like Greg and Treyvon.

Molly: Oh

I'm too tired to make myself act normal when I know I'm not.

Miriam: So . . . are you like . . . sure you don't have a crush? Like on ANYONE?

Maybe this is how she finds out I'm a weirdo.

But I have to answer her. She's my best friend for a second time and I know I can never ignore her again. So I hold my breath and tell the truth.

Molly: I'm sorry. I just don't.

Molly: I don't want that to mean we can't be friends though.

Miriam: Of course we can still be friends.

I can't tell her how relieved I am. I can't tell her this is the closest I will come to letting her know why I disappeared over the summer.

Miriam: I thought maybe you were trying to tell me you

**had a crush on a girl. You can tell me if you do. It's not a
big deal.**

I chew my cheek. To be honest, that didn't occur to me,
but I think about it. I think about Miriam and Diamond and
Mona and my other friends. I like them a lot more than the
boys, but that's mostly because they listen to me and don't
do stupid things like hit me with lunch trays and blow on
my neck and call me Swing. I don't have crushes on any girls,
either.

Molly: No. No crushes. No girls or boys.

Miriam. Oh.

**Miriam: Ok! Well that's ok! Maybe it just hasn't happened
yet.**

**Miriam: I still think you should find a flirty way to tell
Andrew not to copy your papers. It'll be good practice for
when you do like somebody, a boy or a girl.**

Molly: I have to go. My mom needs her phone back.

I type the last thing even though my mom hasn't said anything. I type it because there's nothing to say back. I said *no
crushes* when what I mean is *I'm not normal.*

And I'm pretty sure if boys at my school and men in the
subway and men at baseball games and men who are my
almost stepfather keep touching me when I don't want them
to, I'll never be normal. I'll never be ready. Miriam is my best
friend again, but I don't know how to be the best friend she
wants me to be.

CHAPTER 18

THE NEXT MORNING, I'M FEELING BETTER. Sleepy, but better. I somehow got away with sneaking to the new house in the middle of the night again to perform a brand-new protection spell. This time I won't mess up. I'll never forget to change my flower. Just having the new cylinder hot against my hip makes me more confident as I head into school.

First thing in the morning we have computers. Then it's reading groups and then music, which means it's not until after lunch that we're sitting in our normal rows again. Ms. Banneker gives us a pop quiz in math. Even though I'm protected now, I lean as far over my desk as I can so that Andrew can't copy from my paper or reach my neck with his breath. I'm pretty sure I feel a few whips of air from his mouth anyway but I try to ignore them.

After the quiz, Ms. Banneker starts writing equations on the board for our lesson. I take out a new, sharper pencil and my graph-paper notebook to copy her notes. Just as I'm writing the second equation, I feel something stronger than breath on the back of my neck. It's so ticklish I almost giggle even though giggling is the last thing I ever want to do.

For one horrified second, I think it's Andrew's finger. But when I look back, I find the eraser of his pencil tracing up and down the side of my neck.

I don't turn around. I don't want to encourage him. Instead I shift to the right and angle my neck closer to the wall so maybe he can't reach.

Stop this, I tell my spell. *Make him stop.*

I copy a few more equations before I feel it again.

Now I'm angry.

Is this the kind of thing that would make a normal girl happy? Like Miriam? An eraser on her neck? But I only have to glance at her across the room to know that it would. I have to fix this her way. "Flirty."

When I feel the eraser again, I reach up, fast, and grab his pencil.

I start writing with it.

"Hey!" Andrew cries, interrupting Ms. Banneker. "That was my only pencil."

Ms. Banneker turns so she's facing the class instead of the board. "Is there an issue, Mr. Quinn?"

"Swing—Lydia stole my pencil!" he yells.

The whole class laughs.

"I sincerely doubt Lydia stole your pencil," Ms. Banneker

says. The class laughs again. She walks over to his desk. If she looked at my desk she'd see that I'm using his mechanical pencil now and that the yellow #2 I've been using is sitting beside my notebook.

"It doesn't look like you've been using a pencil for much of anything," Ms. Banneker says. "You haven't written anything down."

"That's because she stole my pencil!" Andrew cries again.

Everyone is still laughing.

My face is burning. My hands are shaking.

He's allowed to blow on me and throw pine cones at me and tickle me in class and if I complain about any of it I'm a weirdo, but he can tell on me for stealing a pencil and everyone is laughing.

I turn around. "Here," I say. "You can use mine."

I want to say, *Just don't touch me with it.*

But more than that, I want this to be over.

"Thank you, Lydia," Ms. Banneker says. She goes back to the board and starts writing a new equation.

I relax. Done. The spell worked.

I hope.

A few minutes go by before I feel anything again. This time it's on my shoulder and it's worse than a breath. It's worse than a pencil.

It's his fingers.

I try to squirm away but then *ping!* It's like a rubber band hits me in the back.

Except it isn't a rubber band.

It's my bra strap.

His fingers were on my bra.

He does it again *ping!*

He puts his fingers inside my shirt, pulls back on my bra strap, and snaps it against my skin.

Before I even know it I'm out of my seat, screaming.

This is not an almost touch. This is not a too-long-for-me hug. This is a *boy* who *touched* my *underwear* at *school*.

I can't stop screaming.

The class chuckles for a minute, then freezes, staring at me.

I force myself to hold in the rest of the scream. I look at Andrew. He cups his right hand with his left as if he's protecting it from me. As if I'm the one hurting him.

My hip is on fire. I can tell the spell tried to work. Andrew was too much for it. It sends half the fire to my shoulder, underneath my bra strap.

"Lydia?" Ms. Banneker says.

"I have . . . I need . . . I need to go to the nurse!" I blurt, and run out of the classroom, the rest of the scream still caught in my stomach.

This cannot be OK.

I cannot live in the world where this is OK.

I run down the third-floor hallway, down two flights of stairs on the side of the building, and into the first floor. I run past the pre-K, kindergarten, and first grade, where all the little girls are still safe. Or at least think they are safe. Or at least don't know how soon they will no longer be safe.

I run into the office at the end of the hall. It's the main office. The nurse uses a small room behind the main desk.

The school secretary, Ms. Gallagher, the gym teacher, Ms. Freemon, and the principal, Sister Janice, are all standing there. They freeze midsentence and stare at me.

"Lydia?" Sister Janice says finally. "I think you should sit down."

"I need to see the nurse!" I blurt.

I have a headache. A stomachache. My period. Something. I have to go home. And then, as soon as Jeremy's off work, I have to leave my home.

I'll go to the new house. I'll sit in Pan's office and read her *Personal Book of Spells.* I'll do anything to be alone. Alone is the only way I'm safe.

I try to dash around the desk toward the nurse's little office without saying anything else.

Except Ms. Freemon catches me by the shoulder. Ms. Freemon is almost six feet tall and has muscles bigger than my dad's and Jeremy's combined. I can't go anywhere.

"No," Sister Janice says. "I need to see you in my office."

She speaks so firmly the rest of the scream dies where it has been festering in my stomach. It almost feels good to have an adult speak so firmly. To remember I'm still a kid and I don't have to be in charge yet.

Ms. Freemon turns me around and I follow Sister Janice across the hall and into the principal's office. I've been going to this school for eight years already and I've never been inside this office. There are posters of cartoon cats all over the walls with sayings like *Hang in there!* and *Keep it up!* It's supposed to be cute, I'm sure. But Sister Janice has been wearing a full brown habit for too long to know what cute is anymore.

She sits behind her big brown desk. In front of it are two small blue chairs like the ones out of the second-grade classroom. She points to them.

"Sit, Lydia," she says.

I squash myself into the chair on the left. The chair is so small my knees practically hit my chin. My hip bones are jammed into the hard plastic. This feels strangely like one of Jeremy's hugs. Not as bad but sort of in the same category. It's another thing I shouldn't be asked to do with my body now that my body is halfway through growing up.

My eyes are wide. My heart is still racing. I can feel sweat beading under my armpits and along my hairline.

I guess that's why Sister Janice says, "You aren't in trouble. At least I don't think you are."

My protection cylinder lights up against my hip again. It's ready to protect me. If it couldn't take on Andrew, will it be any use against Sister Janice?

I nod. I can't say anything.

My wide eyes and sweat and racing heart aren't because I think I'm in trouble. They're because I know I'm in trouble. Maybe not with the school or with Sister Janice. I'm in trouble with the world.

"Do you want to tell me what you're doing here?" Sister Janice asks.

I take a deep breath. I move my arms a little so that I can feel my bra straps, both in the right place, snug against my shoulders.

"I was trying to get to the nurse," I say. "My stomach hurts."

"Ah." Sister Janice nods. "But you see, I have received a hasty call from Ms. Banneker. It appears that Andrew Quinn accused you of stealing a pencil. And then you lent him one of yours. And then a few minutes later, you started screaming uncontrollably and ran out of the classroom. Is this true?"

I nod. I bite my lip. "I was screaming because my stomach hurt?"

"I'm going to be candid with you, Lydia. More so than I usually am with my students. Because I have known you for a long, long time. I have known you since you were just a little girl. And in that time you have never been sent to my office before. I think by now you have earned a little more trust than average. Do you know what *candid* means?"

I nod. Of course I know what *candid* means. Truthful and open.

She should know that that's a fifth-grade vocabulary word.

She should also know how to deal with bigger kids better. We should get chairs our size. And we should be sent to the nurse when we say our stomachs hurt.

"Ms. Banneker and I—all the adults in the school really— are having a little trouble with Andrew," Sister Janice says.

"We're working with him and his parents to mold him into a man of the Lord. But he has some . . . rebellious tendencies."

My face burns. She shouldn't be telling me this. It's none of my business.

"He has been bothering the younger kids at recess. And he has been speaking back to the teachers. And, well, you were there to witness the lunchroom incident last year."

I know she means when he threw his milk carton into the ceiling fan and milk sprayed all over the second graders.

This is even worse than that.

"It is imperative that you tell me what he did to cause your screaming. It is imperative not just for your own well-being but for his." She pauses. "Do you know what *imperative* means?"

I nod. Of course. Sixth-grade word. *Imperative: Of utmost importance.*

I think about what she wants me to do. She wants me to say he touched my bra.

She is trying to mold him into a man of the Lord. Whatever that means, I'm sure a man of the Lord doesn't go around touching girls' underwear.

But I haven't said any of this stuff out loud to anyone. Can I really start by telling my principal?

"I was screaming because my stomach hurt so badly," I say.

Sister Janice clucks her tongue. "I'm not sure I believe you," she says.

I bite my lip.

"Would you like to know why?"

I don't answer but she keeps talking anyway.

"You see, it took you a very long time to answer the question as to why you started screaming. And you are no longer screaming. If you were truly in stomach distress, I don't believe you could be sitting so calmly with me now."

I stare past her, out the window. Now I'm mad at her, too. I add her to the list of people who make it hard to pretend to be a normal person.

But then she says something else. Something different.

"You know, Lydia," she says, "he doesn't need you to protect him."

I shift my gaze so that I'm looking at her out of the side of my eyes. I can't help it. How does she know I was sort of protecting him? Even if it was only to protect myself.

"He is a boy. A privileged boy, at that. Of course, he's still a child. He needs guidance and strength like all children. . . . But you, young lady, are a girl. Life will already be infinitely harder for you than it will for him. Life will always be harder for you than it will for the boys and men around you."

There are tears in the corners of my eyes. Is this finally someone who gets it? Is this the person who is going to understand me? Not my mom or my cousin or my best friend, but my principal? My principal who is a nun?

I open my mouth. Then I close it again.

"That!" Sister Janice says. "Whatever you were about to say. I need to hear it."

So I look at my beat-up loafers and I whisper, "He touched my bra."

Sister Janice's eyes go wide and she launches back from the table. She only loses her composure for a second, but it's enough to remind me that I should never have said anything. I shouldn't have said a word.

"Explain, dear," she says, as quietly as she can. Like she's trying not to scare me. "This happened in the hallway? On the playground?"

There's a lump of dread so big in my throat I can barely get the words around it. What Andrew did made Sister Janice almost jump out of her chair. She will kick him out of the school.

Everyone will hate me.

"Class," I manage.

I have to tell the truth now. My protection cylinder snuggles into my hip, encouraging me. It's time to tell the truth.

"He touched you in class?" she repeats.

I nod.

"How did he manage to get his hand on your breast in the classroom?" Sister Janice asks.

"No!" I say too quickly. My ears are on fire with embarrassment. "I didn't say he touched me . . . there."

Sister Janice nods. "Explain."

"I said he touched my bra . . . not my . . ." I can't say the rest of the sentence. There's no way the word *breast* can make it from my brain to my mouth.

"Ah," Sister Janice says. "So, which part of the bra?"

"The strap," I say, voice shaking. "He snapped the strap against my shoulder. Twice. In the middle of class. With his bare fingers."

"Aha," Sister Janice says. "You know, it is always best to be precise with our language. Snapping bra straps is not quite the same as touching bras."

"But my bra strap is a part of my bra," I say. He *did* touch my bra. And what does it matter precisely what happened if I don't want him touching me at all?

She takes a deep breath like she's trying to erase her smile. When she talks again, the smile is smaller but it's still there. "I can see how that would bother you, Lydia," she says. "And I'm sorry that it did."

I nod. I don't understand what's going on. It seems like she suddenly doesn't care that the boy she wants to mold into a "man of the Lord" is touching my underwear. It seems like she suddenly has a problem with me instead.

I already told her more than I've told anyone. So I gather up all the courage in me. All the bravery in my heart and lungs and stomach. I push it out of my throat and into these words: "Why are you smiling?"

"Ah," she says. "I'm sorry about that. I don't mean to be. If I'm going to continue to be candid with you, I must admit I was worried you were going to say something quite a bit worse. So I am smiling with relief."

"Worse?" I say. What could be worse?

"Lydia, I'm afraid seventh-grade boys have been snapping seventh-grade girls' bra straps since the beginning of time."

My jaw drops open. I don't understand what's happening.

"Little boys snapped my bra straps in junior high school."

A little boy didn't snap my bra. Andrew snapped my bra. Andrew who has been tormenting me for months now.

"And my mother's. And if you ask her, I'm sure you'll find that boys snapped your own mother's bras too."

My mom? No.

Or maybe my mom was just normal about it.

"Do you remember what I said a little bit ago? About how life will be infinitely easier for Andrew and for people like him than it will ever be for you?"

I nod.

That was the only reason I told her anything. And now look what happened.

"Well, unfortunately, that means we have to prepare you both for that life," Sister Janice says. "You will have to deal with men like Andrew as your bosses and as the authorities on all sorts of things. You are going to have to show some . . . flexibility . . . when they treat you in a way you don't want to be treated. You will need to pick your battles. You have to learn that sometimes it's better to live with a little mistreatment in order to keep living the life you want to live."

But this is not the life I want to live.

"That's not the way God wants the world," Sister Janice says. "But it's the way the world is. Find God in it and he will make these things easier."

She says *he* for God.

And if God is real, he ignored me all last spring when I begged him to make the boys stop with that nickname. If God is real, he's seen and heard everything they've been doing to me. And Jeremy's been doing to me. And the men on the subway. And the man at the baseball game. And Jeremy again and again. Now Andrew, again. If God is real, he must be a *he*. He sure doesn't care about us. About girls.

Sister Janice stands. "Let's get you back to class," she says.

I don't move. "That's it?" I say.

"I'm afraid we have bigger fish to fry with Mr. Quinn. He's been doing so much better controlling his anger at recess and responding to redirection in the classroom. I can't let this get in the way of the progress we're making in other areas."

I want to scream. But what about me? What about my fish?

I follow Sister Janice out of the office and all the way to my classroom. My protection cylinder is no longer hot. It's like it ran out of batteries. I have no protection.

When we stand outside the seventh-grade room, she whispers to me what she always said last year. "Just try to ignore him. He's doing it for your attention."

Then she sends me back to my seat like it's nothing. I'm almost in tears but I don't think Ms. Banneker and Sister Janice take their eyes off Andrew long enough to notice. Sister

Janice stays in the back of the classroom and watches for about fifteen minutes. Andrew is perfect behind me.

As soon as she leaves he snaps my bra again.

I scoot forward in my chair until the desk attached to it is digging inches into my stomach. He can only reach when Ms. Banneker makes us pass our papers forward or back. It still happens four more times before the end of the school day. That's seven bra-snaps total.

I do what Sister Janice says. I ignore him.

Not because I think that'll work to make him stop.

It won't.

He'll go from snapping bras to sitting too close to girls on subways and rubbing his knees against them at baseball games. He'll grow from Andrew into Jeremy.

No one even tries to stop it.

HOW TO TURN INTO A BAD GIRL

FIRST, STOP FEELING SAFE IN YOUR own skin.

Second, stop trusting any adult to fix it.

Third, start breaking rules so obvious your mother has never even bothered to talk to you about them.

Fourth, get caught.

CHAPTER 19

AFTER DINNER THAT NIGHT, MOM COMES into my room with her cell phone in her hand. I still feel like my shoulder blade is burning where Andrew's fingers were underneath my shirt.

I'm lying on my bed sort of half doing my math homework. I look up at my mom. Can I tell her about the bra-strap snapping? What if Sister Janice is right? What if the same thing happened to my mom and she really does think it's no big deal?

"Miriam is on the phone," Mom says. "She asked if you're all right?"

I smile like I'm happy.

"Why wouldn't I be all right?" I ask. I didn't realize until this moment that a question could be a lie.

Mom lowers her eyebrows at me. "Did something happen in school today?" she asks.

"No," I say. I reach up for the phone. I don't want to talk

to Miriam. Miriam heard me screaming. But I want to talk to my mom even less.

She stares at me for a minute.

"Can I have it?" I ask.

Mom nods and hands the phone over. I wait until she's out of the room to unmute it.

"What's up?" I ask.

It's super weird for Miriam to call me. Usually she texts me or chats me or something. Still, I make my voice light and chipper.

"I wanted to see if you're OK," she says.

"I'm fine," I say. "I just don't like Andrew."

I expect Miriam to argue with me, to tell me he's one of the cutest boys in the class or something. Instead she says, "What happened today?"

"He was bugging me," I say. "It wasn't a big deal."

At least you wouldn't think it was a big deal.

"You were screaming, though," she says.

I sigh. Should I try to tell her how it felt? Just thinking about it makes me feel dirty all over. He's the one who did something wrong but I feel like there's something wrong with *me.*

"You know he was probably just flirting, right?" Miriam says.

It'd be so easy to say *I know.* It'd be easy to keep pretending to be normal. But Miriam is my best friend. And I'm so tired.

"Yeah maybe . . . but . . ."

"But what?" Miriam asks, softly.

"But I didn't like it."

"Oh!" she says, like this is just occurring to her. And also like this is totally acceptable. Like I could have said *I don't like it* about flirting ages ago and we would still be totally normal best friends.

I'm so surprised I almost miss the next thing she says. "Well, the good news is he knows that now." She laughs.

"Knows what?" I ask.

"I mean, anyone who heard you scream would know you didn't like whatever he was doing."

"Yeah," I say.

"So I bet he'll stop now that he knows."

I bite my lip. She sounds so happy. Breezy. She really believes that.

This is why I never wanted to talk to her. I don't want to ruin that breezy voice. But now there's no turning back.

"He already knew, Miri," I say.

"Huh?" she says.

"I've never smiled when he does this stuff. I've never laughed. I've always moved away. He keeps going."

She doesn't say anything for a minute. Then she says, "No . . ." super slowly.

"Plus . . . he didn't stop. Even after I was screaming. He did it like three more times."

"But what? What did he do?" Miriam says.

I take a deep breath. I'm going to tell her. I tried to tell Sister Janice and it did no good. Maybe telling Miriam will go better. "He snapped my bra strap."

"What!?" Miriam says. But it's not an angry *what*. It's an excited *what* with maybe a hint of jealousy.

Somewhere there's a universe where I could squeal about this with her. Somewhere in her she's wishing I could be that best friend the same way I'm wishing I could be that girl. But I can't.

"You think that's OK?" I ask.

Miriam makes a sucking sound like she's swallowing her excitement. "No, I don't. I actually don't. Not if you didn't like it. Did you tell him to stop?"

"Do you think that would work?" I ask. "I mean, I screamed."

Miriam clucks her tongue. "True. Maybe you could ask Ms. Banneker for a new seat."

"I'm just going to keep doing what I've been doing," I say. "If I didn't have that spell maybe something worse would have happened."

"Spell?" Miriam says.

I sigh. "Remember that day when we did the spells? I didn't want to do the one for fortune because I wanted to do the one for protection. Because the boys—mostly Andrew, but also all of them—are always bothering me."

"Spells?" Miriam says. "You've been bringing spells to school?" *Now* she sounds scared. *Now* she sounds like this is a huge deal. I don't understand how a boy touching my bra at school could be "just flirting" but me bringing a spell could make her sound that way.

"Well, yeah," I say.

"You can't do that, Lydia. What if Ms. Banneker found it?"

"I have to," I say.

"What if Sister Janice found it? You can't bring spells to school. You'd be in huge trouble!"

"I have to," I say again.

"No," she says. "Talk to Ms. Banneker. Talk to a grown-up. They'll get Andrew to stop."

I want to tell her that I tried that but she's still talking.

"What if someone found the spell and then you get kicked out of school for letting the devil in or something? I don't want you to get kicked out."

"It's OK!" I say. "I'm not going to get kicked out of school. It's just a toilet-paper roll."

At least that's how it would look to an outsider. To me it's a lifesaver.

"Lydia," she says. "Promise me you won't bring that book to school. We'll find another way to get Andrew to leave you alone."

"OK," I say. "I promise." But there is no other way. Miriam doesn't know that. But I've tried everything else.

Technically I'll keep my promise that I won't bring the book. I can't even get it out of the room.

But I will bring the spells.

* * *

213

I manage to fall asleep that night until my watch alarm wakes me up at two thirty a.m. I tiptoe out of my room and throw on the heavy black coat. I slip into my sneakers, grab the keys, and slide out the door. It's getting too easy. I shouldn't be this good at sneaking out.

The spell didn't work today but maybe if I didn't have it something worse would have happened. I have to keep believing in it because I don't have anything else left to believe in. I have to do it again so it can be stronger. I need it to be stronger.

I let myself in through my new front door and take a minute to breathe in the spookiness. It feels like misty wisps of ghosts go through my nostrils and into my lungs. I feel my shoulders relax away from my ears. I feel my jaw unhinge. I'm safe here.

I feel even safer in the little room in the basement among all of Pan's extracts and dried herbs. I open the book and reread the instructions to be sure I am doing everything correctly. The last line renews my hope.

If results are mixed, try doubling or tripling the spell to make it more potent.

Maybe Andrew was too much for my little protection cylinder. But maybe he wouldn't be too much for two of them.

Or three of them.

Or four of them.

I'm about to open the desk drawer to start pulling out the black and peach tissue paper when I hear something so terrifying I cannot move.

The doorbell rings.

At first I hide under the desk. My lonely little exhausted protection cylinder tries to vibrate against my hip, but I can tell it's out of power. I have to deal with whatever is on the other side of the door alone.

A few minutes go by. Maybe more. It's hard to tell how much time goes by under this little desk when my breath is coming like ocean waves and my heart is beating a thousand times a minute.

Maybe the person went away.

Maybe it was just the wind or something.

Maybe I dreamed it.

I start to crawl out from under the desk when the doorbell rings again. Then again. Then again.

My cylinder tries to vibrate.

It's like it's telling me something. The house is telling me something. I hear it loud and clear: someone knows I'm here.

Whoever is on the other side of the door knows I'm here.

I'm in one of the scary movies or Stephen King novels that always help me escape the fears in my own life. Except this actually is my own life.

I know I should stay where I am.

The doorbell keeps ringing.

But if I'm in one of those scary movies, I'm going to do the thing I shouldn't do anyway. I get up from under the desk and tiptoe up the stairs. The doorbell will not stop ringing.

Maybe no one is there. Maybe it's just broken.

I tiptoe through the kitchen and glance out the front windows next to the door. Night is beyond them. It's Brooklyn, though, so all the streetlights are on and the lights from Manhattan bleed into the sky. It's not completely dark. Tree branches reach out to each other across the quiet street. A sole car drives past. When it does, the doorbell goes crazy. The first bell doesn't stop before the next one starts.

DingdongDingdongDingdongDingdongDingdong

I tiptoe across the living room and take a deep breath. Then I stretch my hand up and move aside the little peephole cover as slowly and quietly as I can. I hope that whatever murderer is on the other side can't hear it slide across the metal door. I stand on my tiptoes and squint through the little circle.

I don't see a murderer.

I see a multicolored satin scarf wrapped around a girl's hair. Her hands are shaking as they reach for the doorbell again.

I swing open the door and pull Emma inside, then lock it, bolt it, and chain it behind us.

"What are you doing here?" I whisper fiercely.

At the same time Emma says, "Are you trying to get us killed?"

We're having the kind of conversation that should be shouted, but instead we're whispering. I think we're both that scared.

"Does your mom know you're here?" Emma says. "Is this your plot so you can finally get away from me or something?"

She's still shaking. I've never seen her face look so broken. I have no choice, really, this time, when I choose cousins.

"No!" I say. "Mom doesn't know I'm here. And it's not . . . it has nothing to do with you."

She takes a deep breath and tries shaking her shoulders on purpose as if that can rid her body of some of the fear. Then she sits on the bottom stair. "You've been sneaking out in the middle of the night. We share a room. Did you think I wouldn't notice?"

I shrug.

Emma takes off the hot-pink sweatshirt she's been wearing. Hot pink is not a great color for sneaking out into the night. I can tell she didn't really want to do this.

I realize then how hot it is in this house without the air-conditioning. I take off my jacket and sit next to her on the stair.

She speaks. "I'm sorry, Lydia, but I'm just not that cool."

"Huh?" I say. I have no idea what coolness has to do with anything. And anyone can see that she's infinitely cooler than I am.

"I couldn't let you keep sneaking out in the middle of the night in the middle of Brooklyn without getting super worried about where you were going or what you were doing. It almost reminded me of when things went bad with my dad. He would sneak out and then . . ."

I lean forward, desperate for whatever comes next. Her dad snuck out? Why would a grown-up ever need to sneak?

She doesn't say any more about him though.

"I don't know. I only had two choices. Follow you or tell your mom."

I give her a half smile. "I guess I'm glad you followed me, then," I say.

She gives me back a half laugh.

"You have to tell me what's going on," Emma says. "I need to know. Now."

"What do you mean?" I ask.

Emma shrugs. "At first I thought you were looking for attention. And I thought you have both your parents and all your friends and get to go to the same school and live in the same city. There's no way you could have problems that are really big like mine. The extra clothes didn't seem like such a big deal and I thought it was about . . . I don't know. Acting strange so people would notice, or something. But then you being sneaky doesn't make sense. Sneaking is about people not noticing."

"I didn't want anyone to notice," I confirm.

"You're acting really weird, Lyddie."

I don't know what to say, so I nod. I am acting weird. But I don't think I can really talk to Emma about it. I don't think I can tell her I'm afraid of the boys at school. That sounds so weak and pathetic and I don't want her to know how much weaker I am than her. I can't tell her I'm afraid of Jeremy when she's still taking his candy and giving him bear hugs. And I definitely can't tell her I'm afraid of her dad.

"And it's not fair," she says. "You know everything about

me. You know all my problems. It's time for you to tell me your problems. If we're ever going to be close again, we need to make it even."

I lower my eyebrows at her. "I don't know your problems. I don't know anything. No one tells me anything."

"You do," Emma says. "You know all about my messed-up parents . . . parent. My mom . . . well, you know about her, too."

I shake my head. "I don't, Em. My mom hasn't told me anything. She just says that your dad couldn't keep you safe."

Emma's eyes go wide. "Really?" she says.

I nod. "That's it. And now your unsafe dad is going to live with us."

Emma shakes her head. "I thought she told you everything," she says. "You're her daughter."

"No," I say, quiet.

"And my dad isn't unsafe."

I almost laugh. "Well, then I really don't know anything," I say.

Emma looks at her feet. She's wearing flip-flops. Another not-so-great fashion choice for sneaking out in the middle of the night. They're named after the sound they make. Sneakers are an obviously better option.

"If I tell you . . . ," she says. "If I tell you about my dad . . . I've never told anyone before. I don't know."

I nod. "You don't have to tell me," I say. I want to know, but I understand secrets better than anyone.

"But I miss you!" Emma says.

She looks from her flip-flops into my face and there are tears in her eyes.

Suddenly all the Emma-feelings I've been ignoring for the past year come rushing through my bloodstream. They race through all of my veins and into my mouth until it feels like it's on fire. I can't even stop myself. "I miss you, too!" I say. "I don't understand how I can miss you when you're right here, but—"

Emma cuts me off. "I miss everyone! I miss my dad. I miss my mom. I miss all my old friends. I don't get why I have to miss you, too."

We stare at each other, frozen. A mix of shock and embarrassment fills the air and I can't tell which feeling is hers and which is mine or if we're sharing them both. I wonder if she can also feel the ghosts celebrating around us. I wonder if she knows we're surrounded by spirits who have been trying to make us choose cousins for a long time now.

She says, "I'll tell you about my dad, OK? I'll tell you what's going on with me. But then you have to tell me, too. Why you're here. Why all the clothes in the summer. What's going on."

I squint at her. "But . . . but I'm embarrassed."

Emma nods. "Me too."

"It all makes me seem not . . . not . . . normal."

Emma nods. "Me too," she says. "But we already aren't

normal. We already snuck out of a perfectly posh apartment to hang out in a creepy house in the middle of the night. Let's be not normal together."

I can hear the ghosts cheering her on. I take a deep breath and say, "OK."

Then she takes her hand away from my knee and looks back at her flip-flops. I don't move. She said she'd go first, so I wait. A lot of time goes by, though, and I really do want to know what happened to her dad. Actually, I *need* to know. I'm going to live with this man. I need to know.

"You said your dad isn't unsafe?" I remind her.

"No," Emma says. "I mean, not really. I mean, he never put me in danger or anything."

"Oh," I say.

"But like . . . he's sometimes not safe with himself." She pauses. Finally she says, "He's been . . . he's been in rehab, OK? For drugs."

"Oh!" I say, because that makes a lot of the puzzle pieces come together.

"But, like, he never hurt me or left me in danger. He had this girlfriend who took care of me until . . . She wasn't great but she was safe. He tried. He says he tried."

"Tried what?" I ask.

"To get clean," Emma says. "For me . . . I don't know. I'm never going to do drugs."

"Me neither," I say.

221

"He didn't want to be addicted. It's not like he loves drugs more than he loves me. It's not like that. Or at least that's what he says now."

"But he never . . . he never did anything to hurt you? Or anyone?" I can see the sadness in her eyes. I focus on that. I focus on feeling sad for my cousin who has had to live away from her dad.

I ignore my own relief.

"No!" Emma says. "No way. The only thing he did was . . . well, one time after his girlfriend left him . . . just one time . . ."

"What?" I ask. Because I can think of plenty of things that are terrible to do just one time.

"I don't want to say it. It makes him sound so awful. But . . ." She pauses. "He left me alone at night."

I let out all of my breath. I nod.

"That's it. And I was OK, really. I knew how to microwave dinner and put myself to bed. But then the social worker came that night and . . . I don't know. I don't think she believed me that it was only one time. Maybe someone at my old school called the authorities on us? Maybe Dad's ex-girlfriend called? Anyway, you aren't allowed to leave your kid alone all night long. So they took me away. And then my dad went away. And then I had to come live with you guys for so long. But he went to rehab for three months and he's clean now. Then he went to a sober-living place. So he's been clean for almost a year. They said that once he's clean for a year, I can live with him again."

"Wow," I say.

Emma nods. "But I guess . . . I guess we're not going back home. Ever. I guess he's going to live here with you guys and with me? I know that's not what you want."

"No, I—" I try to tell her that it wasn't that I didn't want her around. I mean, sometimes I didn't but I always understood that she had to be. That we're family. I try to tell her it wasn't her at all. I was just afraid of her dad. Not even him specifically. I was afraid of the idea of another man.

She cuts me off too fast. "But listen, you don't have to watch yourself around my dad or anything. He isn't . . . I mean, even when he wasn't clean he wasn't . . . you know, he's not like . . . like Jeremy."

I'm so surprised I actually gasp.

"Like Jeremy how?" I say.

Emma looks like she's struggling for words. "Like . . . creepy. Like . . . all touchy and stuff. My dad is like your dad. Nice. A little clueless. Not creepy."

I should be relieved. In a little corner of my brain I am relieved. But I'm too shocked to process it.

"You *know* about Jeremy?" I ask.

Emma shifts. "What do you mean, know about him? I see him just as much as you do."

I nod vigorously. "Yeah, but you . . . you let him hug you."

"So do you," Emma says. "It's not like I like it or anything."

"Right," I say. "But I mean, you hug him back."

Emma shrugs. She rubs her hands on her face the way she

did when she was a little kid and someone said something mean about her. "I don't know. Sometimes it's easier to pretend I want to hug him than to think about what's happening. If I hug him first it all feels less gross." She looks at me. "Or less scary," she admits.

"Wow," I whisper.

"And, you know, your mom thinks he's—"

"But you eat his candy!" I interrupt.

"It's candy!" Emma says. "And your mom never lets us have candy. My dad's girlfriend I just told you about? She always said that you have to take what you can from men because they're going to take what they can from you."

I stare at her with my jaw dropped. How is it that she's noticed the same thing about Jeremy but responded so differently? How is it that we've both been tiptoeing around him without even talking to each other about it?

"Wait!" Emma says. "Is that what all this is about? Is *that* what's going on with you? Jeremy?"

I shrug. "Sort of," I say.

"The clothes were so he wouldn't touch you?"

"Yeah. Well, him and . . . other boys. And men," I say. "It didn't work, though."

Emma turns so her whole body is facing me. "Did he do something?" she demands. "Like something worse than a creepy hug or whatever?"

"No!" I say. "No . . . he didn't. I guess the creepy hugs are enough to mess me up. Like a lot."

"Oh," Emma says. She leans back and puts her elbow on the stair above us.

"I told you. I'm weird."

I should be able to eat the candy he gives us. I should be able to come up with a way to make being around him feel OK in my head.

"No. He is pretty gross," Emma says. "I wish your mom would dump him."

"He's only part of it, though," I say.

"There's someone else?" Emma asks.

"There's everyone else," I say. "I notice all the things and . . . I can't react to them normally."

I tell her about the guy at the baseball game who kept invading my space while he acted like I wasn't even there.

"I hate when men are all up in my space like that too," Emma says.

"You do?" I ask, shocked.

"Yeah," she says. "But I guess I thought I was supposed to deal with it."

"That's what Sister Janice said," I say.

"Sister Janice?" Emma squeals. "You wouldn't talk to me about any of this stuff but you told Sister Janice?"

I laugh.

Then I stop because it all really isn't funny. I tell her about Andrew snapping my bra.

"That's different, though!" Emma says. "Andrew isn't an adult. He's your equal! You don't have to take that! You should tell on him."

"I did," I say. "Sister Janice says I need to get used to it because men will always have easier lives than us or something stupid like that."

"What!" Emma says. "We have to let boys treat us however they want because their life is easier?"

"I guess," I say. "That's what she said."

"That's stupid. We need to do something. We can't do anything about Jeremy or all the creepy men out there. But we should be able to take on Andrew."

I squint at her. This is the final bit. The last piece I haven't told her.

I'm nervous to let her in. But also I'm excited. I've been feeling so lonely. I've been carrying around way too many secrets. It feels so good to be close to someone again.

"I was about to do something," I say. "Before you rang the doorbell."

Emma's eyebrows jump. "Right. Why are you here?"

"Listen. I'll show you. But you can't . . ." I stop. I was about to say you can't make fun of me. But I think about the past few months Emma has lived with us. It's been hard and I've been weird, but when I think back I realize she hasn't made fun of me once. Not one time. I need to trust her. "But . . . do you believe in magic?" I say.

Emma smiles. "Sometimes I think I do," she says. "Sometimes I think I have to. Because no matter what happens, I always believe things will get better with my dad."

I smile back at her. I feel the hope pouring out of her like too much perfume. I take a sniff and let it pour out of me, too. I hope hope hope for her that everything will get better with her dad.

"And . . . this is a little embarrassing. But also? I always believe my mom can hear me. Like, she's around me all the time. Like, she's looking out for me. Is that stupid?"

"No," I say. I pause. I think about the ghosts who have been orchestrating this long-overdue conversation. "I maybe even sometimes feel her too. Oh!" I say, remembering the other spell in the back of the book. The one for communicating with a passed loved one. "I may have something to help." I grab her hand. "Come on!" I say. I pull her to the red door and we go giggling down the stairs.

The stairs that will soon be the passageway between my cousin and me.

The stairs that will let my cousin get her dad back.

I see it all so differently now.

We spend the next hour giggling together and perfecting cylinders in the little office. Emma makes a spell for communicating with passed loved ones, and I hope it helps her feel even closer to her mom. I make seven protection spells—that has to be enough. I will wear them all the way around my hips and one on each shoulder under my bra straps.

I hope it's enough. Just enough to help me take on Andrew tomorrow.

Just enough to protect me—us—from Jeremy.

CHAPTER 20

THE CRACKING OF THUNDER OUTSIDE OUR big glass windows wakes me up the next morning before my alarm goes off. I roll over in my bed to find Emma already smiling at me.

"We got this," she says. "We have magic. Andrew has nothing."

On the subway on the way to school, she sits close to me and whispers, "I think mine worked."

I turn to her, my eyes wide. "Really?" I ask.

She nods.

"Did you dream about her? Did you hear her voice?"

Emma shakes her head. "No," she says. "It's something else."

Goose bumps crawl across my arms and legs. "What?" I whisper.

She shakes her head. "It'll sound too crazy. I'll tell you later."

When the school day starts, no one is sitting behind me.

It's possible that my seven protection cylinders are so power-ful they made Andrew sick so he's absent from school. Or maybe they made him mess up Sister Janice's man-of-the-Lord plan in a big enough way that he's never coming back. I keep readjusting my sweater to make sure that the two cylin-ders on my shoulders aren't showing for the rest of the class behind me to see. I keep wiggling in my seat to keep the five at my hip from poking me in the thigh. But otherwise I can learn in peace.

Worth it.

An hour into the school day, though, while we're supposed to be silently reading our science text books, the back door to the classroom opens and Andrew walks in, flanked by his mom and Sister Janice. The whole class turns to look at the three of them like we always do when someone walks in in the middle of the day.

"Back to work!" Sister Janice commands.

My classmates turn back around but I shift in my seat try-ing to catch her eye. Were they talking about me after all? Did Sister Janice tell Andrew's mom about him touching my bra? Did he at least get a strong warning not to do it again?

Did my cylinders do something?

They feel normal against my skin though. Not vibrating. Not even a little bit of heat.

Andrew hangs up his coat and bag on the hooks at the back of the classroom and walks toward his desk. Toward me.

I finally manage to catch Sister Janice's eye, but she looks away from me so fast. She doesn't tell me to get back to work. She doesn't even give me a *get back to work* look. She looks away.

Almost like she's ashamed.

Of me. Or for me.

Andrew's mom and Sister Janice stay in the back of the classroom and keep their eyes on him. I take that time to try to get comfortable on the front edge of my chair, farthest from Andrew, so that maybe he can't reach me when they do leave. But when I sit all squashed up like that, the cylinders against my hip climb higher into my shirt. I wiggle around to try to get them into place.

Andrew slumps behind me and ignores me.

I push my science book to the far edge of my desk and cross my legs to try to make the cylinders rest across my thigh.

I don't even realize one has slipped until it hits the floor.

It rolls one, two, three, four times. Backward. In Andrew's direction. Almost like it's trying to get to him. Almost like he needs protection more than me. Almost like it's turned on me, same as the rest of the world.

Andrew leans out of his desk and in one horrified instant I realize he's reaching for it. The words in Pan's handwriting run through my brain:

> *DO NOT let the cylinder touch another mortal or the spell will be reversed and danger will be imminent. You will both be doomed.*

"No!" I scream, and lunge out of my chair toward my protection spell.

The whole class watches as I scoop it safely into my palm. *He didn't touch it. He didn't touch it.* Then I stare at it. It's in my hand. It can't be in my hand. It's supposed to be on my hip. How do I get it back on my hip in the middle of class?

"I was just trying to help," Andrew says under his breath. He adds "Weirdo" so quietly no one but me can hear it.

I look at Miriam. Maybe she will know what to do. But she's staring at me with her jaw dropped. Her head is going back and forth, slow slow slow.

I can't figure out what she's trying to tell me until suddenly there's a freezing-cold hand under mine.

I look up into the hard, angry eyes of Sister Janice. She puts her other hand on top of the cylinder—*doomed*—and takes it from me.

"Lydia," she says slowly. "What is this?"

She picks up my spell and holds it carefully in both hands. She turns as if she wants to hold it toward the light. "Lydia . . . ," she says.

"It's just . . ." I try to come up with something quickly. Something that isn't magic. Something she won't think is evil.

She peers inside. "Is this . . ."

I glance back at Miriam. Her eyes are wide and she's frozen. She doesn't know how to help me either.

Sister Janice breathes in suddenly through her nose, like

she's trying to smell something. "Oh no!" she says.

She's figured it out.

She shoves the cylinder away from her face. "You need to come with me."

Something about the way she says it makes my bones shake like her voice.

"Oooohl" the class says.

I stare at her. She touched my spell. She touched my spell. We're both doomed.

What did Pan even mean by *doomed*? What happens now?

She takes a step toward the back door. I half expect to suddenly be on fire. To suddenly be at the bottom of the ocean. To not be here anymore.

"Lydia," Sister Janice says.

I don't move. I can't. I have four more cylinders precariously pinched in my waistband. I don't know what will happen if I move.

"Now!" she says.

Finally all six of the cylinders I have left heat up a little bit. Are they trying to protect me from Andrew? From Sister Janice? From the doomed part of the spell she's holding?

"Lydia!" Sister Janice says. She's yelling at me now. The only other grown-up to ever yell at me has been my mom. "Get up now!"

I don't move, though. I can't.

"Lydia?" Ms. Banneker says.

I can feel everyone's eyes on me, digging into me. Miriam's.

Ms. Banneker's. Andrew's. Andrew's mom's. The rest of the class.

I know I'm in the most trouble I've ever been in, beyond being doomed. But I also know I shouldn't be. I know deep down that I should not be the one who is getting in trouble.

I'm going to be in trouble for trying to protect myself.

"Lydia," Sister Janice says. "Now!"

I slide my bottom across my seat and try to stand as slowly as I can. But two more cylinders fall and bounce across the floor. Andrew reaches again to pick one up.

"Stop!" Sister Janice yells at him. "Don't touch that."

Andrew looks at her, his eyebrows knitted together. "It's a toilet-paper roll," he says, as if she's stupid.

Sister Janice squats and picks up the other two.

"No, Andrew," she says. "I know exactly what it is."

All I hear on the way back to the office are Miriam's words. *You'll get in such big trouble. You'll get in such big trouble.*

My face is hot like my body is ashamed even though my brain is telling it not to be. I didn't do anything wrong.

When we get back to her office, Sister Janice stands me in front of her.

"I don't know what happened to you, Lydia," she says. "You used to be such a godly young lady."

That's not true, really. I was just a good girl. God had nothing to do with it.

"You've been going to this school since kindergarten. You

have received a robust Catholic education. You know what comes from God and what comes from the devil," she says.

I look at my shoes. I don't believe that. I don't even think I believe in a devil. But I do know magic isn't allowed at school. I'm enough of a good girl still to feel a little ashamed.

She pulls out the two cylinders that are left in my waistband. Then she softly pats around my sides and shoulders. When she finds the ones fastened to my bra straps she stops and stares at me, her eyes a little less cold, her face a little open.

"This is dangerous," she says. "More dangerous than you could understand."

"I was just—" I say.

As soon as I start talking her face closes up again. "There are no excuses for this, Lydia."

"I didn't want—"

"None," she says.

She pulls the cylinder out from under my right bra strap. My strap *pings* against my skin and my face burns even though I know Sister Janice is not snapping my bra strap. But the *ping* feels the same.

Sister Janice won't help me.

God won't help me.

Spells won't help me.

I'm doomed to constant bra-strap pinging forever.

It's exactly like what Sister Janice said: I'm doomed just by being a girl.

"Go sit in the hallway," Sister says once she has all my cylinders. I wonder what she's going to do with them. "We'll call your parents to pick you up," Sister Janice finishes.

"Pick me up?" I say, surprised.

I figured now that she had all the cylinders I'd get a lecture and be sent back to class.

Sister nods. "You're suspended, Lydia. At least suspended. I need a day or two to think about how to address this so that I can trust you to come into my school again without bringing the devil in with you."

"At *least* suspended?" I say. What's worse than suspended?

She doesn't say anything.

Something in my body is getting hot. But it's not the cylinders. It's not some spell. It's not coming from Pan. It's coming from me.

My stomach is getting hot.

My stomach is angry.

It's like my stomach wants *me* to do the job that adults wouldn't do and God wouldn't do and protection items wouldn't do and now spells won't do.

I try to listen to my stomach. I try try try to say something. Anything.

"Go sit in the hallway," Sister Janice says.

I'm weak and alone.

I sit on the old church pew that has been outside Sister Janice's office ever since I started school here. I've walked by this bench on my way to lunch every single school day of my life and never had to sit on it. I'd always look at the kids who got sent here and wonder what they could have done that was so terrible to have to sit at the principal's office.

Now I am that terrible kid.

Those are my choices.

Either let boys touch my bra. Or be a terrible kid.

A lot of time goes by. I watch the first grade walk past in a line on their way to lunch. I watch the fifth grade walk past. I pull my sweater tight and cross my legs, trying to hide them, when the eighth grade walks past.

Sister Janice comes out of her office. "You will be picked up in a few minutes," she says. "You will not eat here today."

I don't answer her even though my stomach is growling.

When the seventh grade walks past, Miriam pauses in front of me, trying to talk to me with her eyes.

Her eyes say, *Are you OK?*

I can't make my eyes say anything. I should have talked to her earlier, I realize. I should have talked to Emma about this stuff sooner. I should have told Miriam that I don't have a crush because the way boys "flirt" makes me feel dirty and worthless. I should have talked to Diamond and Mona. I should have talked to everyone. Because Emma is dealing with it too. And if Emma is dealing with it, Miriam probably is too. Everyone is. We just don't talk about it because we all deal with it differently.

My mom. She's the person I'm going to talk to first. As soon as she gets here. Now.

The rest of the class walks by and Andrew doesn't look at me.

Down the hallway I can see the sixth grade, Emma's class, approaching.

I fold my hands in my lap and practice it in my head. *Mom, I'm in trouble because Andrew snapped my bra. And I act weird sometimes because I don't like the way people touch me. Boys. Men . . . Jeremy.*

I hear the front door to the school open and the words in my brain start to shake. I'm nervous. But I know I'm finally going to say it.

Except I forgot that Sister Janice touched my spell and now I'm doomed.

"Well, sweetheart," Jeremy says. "You're in trouble now, huh?"

I look up at him. He's huge standing over me, almost leaning over me, already too close even here in this school.

Sister Janice comes out of her office and he backs up and of course she doesn't notice.

"Molly asked me to come get her," Jeremy says.

"Grand," Sister Janice says. "Sign her out and take her home. She's suspended the rest of the week. I will call Molly to discuss the details this afternoon."

Jeremy shifts on his feet. "She screwed up that badly, huh? That's not like my kid."

"I'm not your kid," I say. But it's quiet. So quiet I maybe didn't even say it out loud.

CHAPTER 21

WHEN WE WALK OUT THE FRONT door of the school, I start to head toward the subway.

"No," Jeremy says. "This way."

He walks in the opposite direction and I can see his beat-up old car parked on the street in front of the church next to the school. He opens the passenger door and waits for me to get in.

I hesitate. "I'll just sit in the back," I say.

"Why?" he asks.

I shrug like it's no big deal. My brain is sounding alarms. Last time I sat in the front with him he kept his hand on my knee. My knee is freezing cold just thinking about it. "Mom says that's safe."

"Really?" he says. "You can gallivant all over the city on a motorcycle but driving in my car with airbags galore makes you nervous?"

I look up at him, my eyes wide.

Yes, of course. The world thinks cars are safer than motorcycles. But not this car. Not that motorcycle.

He stares at me. He's never challenged me this directly before. I start to shake in my loafers.

He opens the front passenger door. "Get in," he says.

I bite my lip. Emma is at school. Miriam is at school. Dad is all the way in Manhattan. Mom is at work. There is no one who can save me this time. I have to do everything he says. I slowly walk to the car and sit in the passenger seat.

Jeremy turns on the car and I press my head and shoulder blades back into the fabric behind me as far as I can. I squeeze my legs together from ankles to knees to inner thighs. I try to make myself as small as possible.

Jeremy leans across my lap and opens the glove compartment. I try to shove myself back even farther as his big arm hovers in front of me but I can feel the heat coming off him. It's impossible to get far enough away.

He takes out a package of gummy worms and throws them into my lap.

"Eat them," he says.

I stare at them.

"No, thank you," I say.

They used to be my favorite. Now I know I will never be able to look at them again.

"I know they're your favorite," he says. "Just like I know

you always want to sit in the front seat of the car. I know you, Lydia. I know you very well by now. I know what a good girl you are. I know you didn't mean to get in trouble at school."

I swallow.

"So sit and eat," he says.

I still don't move. "Eat," he says again.

"No, thank you," I say. "I'm not hungry."

"Lydia, I'm in charge. Your mom put me in charge. And I'm asking you to eat the gummy worms."

I still don't move.

"You're a good girl," Jeremy repeats, softening his voice in a way that somehow makes it worse. "I know you don't want to be suspended. I know you don't want to hurt my feelings. I know you don't want your mom to hear about how after you got suspended you also wouldn't listen to me."

I stare at him, wide-eyed.

He looks right in my eyes. His are so far above me. It's like with that look he's trying to remind me how much bigger he is than me. "Eat."

My hands shake as I pick up the bag and rip it open. I slowly put one orange-and-green gummy worm into my mouth.

Jeremy smiles, suddenly different. "There," he says. "Enjoy. Because you probably won't be getting too many treats now that you're suspended from school."

Where is my mom? Her office is close to the school. Any-time I've ever had to go home sick she's always been there.

Where is she now?

I blink hard to keep the tears in my eyes. The sugar is burning my tongue.

Jeremy finally starts driving. The gummy worm manages to slip down my throat.

"Delicious, right?" Jeremy asks. "Right?" he repeats, louder, when I don't say anything.

"Yes," I squeak.

"I knew you'd think so," he says. "I know you so well by now." I don't say anything. "Have another," he says. He reaches across the console and opens the bag on my lap. He takes out another worm and holds it up. Then we're at a stoplight.

At first I think he's going to eat it, but instead he says, "Open up" and holds it in front of my face.

I blink hard to make sure no tears fall; then I open my mouth and let him put the gummy worm inside. He puts his thumb under my chin to close my mouth and then lets it rest on my lips for just a second. I'm afraid I'm going to puke on his hand.

I don't know what he'll do to me but I know I can't hurt his feelings. He has complete power over me in this car. If he's angry it'll be worse.

He puts his hand on my knee. For the rest of the ride he keeps it there except to feed me gummy worms. I keep my eyes closed as tight as I can, trying not to see or hear or feel or taste what's happening. But he doesn't notice.

Finally we park and I open my eyes.

My brain is going crazy. How can I keep from being alone with him until my mom comes home? When will my mom come home? What will he do to me in the apartment? How much creepier will it get than what happened in the car?

I reach for the door handle but his arm reaches all the way across me to stop me from opening it.

"We shouldn't have done that, Lydia," he says. "We both should have known better, huh?"

My eyes are wide. I have to do what he wants. I nod.

"You know better than to eat candy when you're suspended from school, don't you?"

He's trying to manipulate me. I'm too scared to do anything but pretend to be manipulated. I nod again.

"So we won't tell your mom, will we?" he asks.

I shake my head as fast as I can.

I'm going to tell her. I have to tell her. And lying makes me a bad girl just like sneaking out and bringing spells to school. But for now I have to lie.

"That's right, Lydia. You're a good girl."

He smiles at me and it looks so genuine it makes my stomach flip.

"All right," Jeremy says. Then he opens my door. "You go on upstairs. I have to go back to work. Act grounded or something."

I get out of the car faster than I've ever done anything.

He's not coming up with me.

I can go lock my door and pretend to be asleep before he gets home.

I walk as fast as I can to the door to our building. Then I hear him call out behind me, "Hey! You forgot my hug."

I glance back, stupidly, and see that he's gotten out of his car and is standing next to it with his arms outstretched.

But I don't go to him. I turn and run.

HOW TO PROTECT YOURSELF
WHEN EVERYTHING ELSE FAILS

CHECK UNDER EVERY BED. CHECK INSIDE every cabinet. Make sure you are absolutely alone.

Lock and padlock and triple-lock the door.

Turn the water on in the shower as hot as it will go. Use a whole bottle of body wash. Use a whole bottle of shampoo. Rub your knee and lips with the loofah until they bleed.

Gather as many snacks as possible and pile them under your bed.

Lock your bedroom door. Barricade it with your dresser.

Promise yourself that you are never coming out. That you are never opening the door for anyone except your cousin. That you will stay in this room forever.

CHAPTER 22

"HEY," EMMA WHISPERS AROUND TWO A.M. I don't know how she knows I'm awake. But I am. Wide awake feeling like bugs are crawling all over my body.

Mom got home late and said I needed to eat in my room, which was fine. She said she didn't feel like dealing with me until tomorrow. I didn't know where she'd been and she didn't bother to tell me. It's really weird for my mom to come home so late and I think it's even weirder for her to do that on a day I got in trouble at school. But I didn't ask about it. Through my locked door I heard Jeremy come in with his big jolly voice. He made my mom laugh all through dinner. Then I let Emma in the room. She asked if I wanted to talk about it, but I put on headphones and looked out the window.

Now I roll over, the sheets that were so soft yesterday scratching against my skin. "Hey," I say. Part of me wants to get up and get back in the shower. Maybe with more soap. Maybe with more lotion. Maybe never.

"Did Jeremy do something?" she asks. "Or Andrew?"

"Both," I say.

Emma breathes in through her teeth like me saying that hurts her physically.

"Do you want to talk about it?" she asks.

I blink at her. I can see her eyes and not much else. The moon is just a sliver out our window.

I sort of want to talk about it. But I can't. I don't feel worthy of talking.

She sits. "Do you want to go talk about it somewhere else?"

My breath speeds up a little bit. Just enough for the bugs to pause their constant roaming around my body hair.

I know exactly what she means. It didn't occur to me that she would want to go back there.

I sit up too. "Yes," I say.

I go to Emma's drawer and toss her a black hoodie. "This is better than hot pink," I say.

She giggles and a few of the bugs die.

Together we slip on sneakers and pull hoods tight around our heads. I don't have a protection spell pressed against me as we walk out the automatic doors of our building and the cool air hits my face. But I think it turns out the spell was never protecting me anyway.

We walk down our block silently, then cross the street.

"I'm sorry," I say.

Her eyes are big when she looks at me. "You're sorry?" she says. "I should be."

"No." I shake my head. "You couldn't do anything," I say. "We're powerless."

Emma shakes her head but doesn't answer me for a while. Finally she says, "Why are you sorry?"

We're crossing the next street. Still five more to go before we reach the house. There are more cars driving by than I remember in the past. And we cross paths with a group of college-age boys who don't move over on the sidewalk to make room for us so we have to scoot by them, our hips pressed into the parallel-parked cars.

I glare at their backs when they are past. I bet they would scoot into our seats in the subway. I bet they'd think nothing of snapping the bra strap of some college girl. I bet they didn't even see us.

"What are you sorry for?" Emma asks again.

"I don't know. Maybe you didn't really believe in the spells. But I did. But now I think they were all stupid. I shouldn't have pulled you into something so stupid."

Emma stops on the sidewalk and grabs my shoulder so I stop too, facing her. The trees and streetlights above her make leaf-shaped patterns on her face.

"She came to me, Lydia. Last night. You were sleeping but I wasn't. It wasn't a dream, I know it. I was sitting up in bed and you were right there sleeping and the whole world felt different and I knew my mom had always been there and I knew that everything was going to be OK with my dad." Emma smiles. "The spells. They work. That's why I thought we were going back. I thought you needed another spell."

I lower my eyebrows. "What did she look like? Just like herself or like . . . ghostlike?"

Emma shakes her head. "I didn't see her," she says.

"Well, what did she say?" I ask.

She shakes her head again. "It was more like . . . a feeling. I just knew. She was there and always has been."

"Oh," I say. Then I stop. I don't want to tell Emma that the spells don't work. That her having a feeling in the middle of the night when she may have been asleep is not enough evidence to counterbalance Sister Janice confiscating all my protection spells and ruining them without saying a word to Andrew. Emma will figure it out on her own. Maybe her mom does watch over her, but not because of a spell.

We start walking but then Emma whispers something. "You're going to think I'm crazy but . . . I smelled her."

"Huh?" I say.

"That's how I know. I smelled her. It was the strongest smell in the world. Stronger than when you walk into Ample Hills Creamery, you know? Stronger than when you sit next to someone who needs a shower on the subway."

"Oh," I say. "What did she smell like?"

Emma stops walking and looks toward the sliver of moon with a sigh. "Lilac and green apple. Lilac hair conditioner.

Green apple body lotion. No one else has ever used those two smells together."

I nod at her. I still think it could have been a dream. Or a coincidence. Or the mixture of Emma's own body lotion and all the candy she hides in our room or something. But at least I can agree with her. "I've never met anyone who smelled like both of those at once," I say.

Emma whispers, almost to herself, "It was her."

We walk a few blocks in silence, then turn the corner onto what will be our new block.

It's like walking into a wall. The smell hits me so hard I flinch. It's physical.

Lilac. And green apple.

Emma looks at me, her eyes wide. "I smell it again," she says

I nod. "So do I," I say.

Does this mean Emma's mom will look out for me, too?

"See, the spells do work," Emma says.

I look at her.

They do. They must.

Miriam and I found the hundred-dollar bills.

Emma found her dead mother.

"Maybe they sort of work, but they aren't powerful enough to stop . . . everything."

Emma nods. "Maybe." She pauses. "But maybe we can try to just stop one thing?"

"Huh?" I say.

"Maybe there's a spell we can use to keep Jeremy away from us?"

I take a deep breath and nod. It's worth a try.

But then Emma stops in her tracks and a sob escapes from her mouth. I follow her eyes to the front of the house and freeze. Tears spring to the corners of my eyes.

The front stoop of the house is gone. The door looks like it's just floating there, four feet in the air. There are work permits stapled all over the front door. The windows are boarded over. We can't even get inside.

And now I know why Mom was out late. The work started on the house. She was there to get it started.

It will be months until we can get inside again, and when we do it will be completely different.

"What if they find Pan's book and spells?" I cry.

Emma puts her arm around me. We stay like that for a few minutes, looking at the house that will transform before we can set foot into it again.

We walk home in silence.

Just as we are reaching the automatic glass doors of our building, Emma grabs my arm.

"Let's make a pact, OK? Let's be each other's protection spell. Let's not leave each other alone, whenever we can help it. Let's promise to always believe each other."

My heart quiets down just a little and something inside me

feels warm where it's been cold all summer, even through all the sweat and ninety-degree days in turtlenecks.

I hold out my hand to her. "Deal," I say.

She shakes it. "Deal."

We put our arms around each other and don't let go as we ride up in the elevator and slip our shoes off outside our apartment door. But then Emma points under the door.

"Is the light on?" she whispers.

Just then the door swings open. Mom stands there with eyes so wide and mouth hanging open so low it's impossible to read the expression on her face.

Emma looks at me. I start to shake.

Mom puts her hand to her ear and that's when I see that she's holding her cell phone. "Never mind, they're back," she says, and hangs up.

She drops her hands over our shoulders and pulls us into a hug. She doesn't even move as the heavy metal door bumps her from behind. "I've never been so mad at you in my life," she hisses into my ear.

I don't know how to feel. I'm frozen. Numb.

I'm suspended from school.

I snuck out in the middle of the night.

I don't even feel like myself anymore.

"I'm sorry," I say.

Mom straightens up and opens the door all the way. She points to the couch. "Sit. Now," she says. "Both of you."

We sit side by side on the couch, and the weight of Emma's body next to mine feels like something physical I can hold on to. We have a pact.

"I don't even know what to say," Mom says.

Then she stays quiet for so long the bugs start to crawl back up my skin.

"Were you talking to Dad?" I ask.

"No," Mom says. "I was talking to the police. I thought you'd been kidnapped."

Red-hot guilt crawls out of the collar of my big black jacket, lighting up my neck and face.

"I'm so sorry, Aunt Molly," Emma says. "We didn't mean to scare you. We were just—"

"Did you girls think this was funny? To trick me or something? To prove you can sneak out in the middle of the night? Don't you know what would have happened, Emma, if they thought I couldn't take care of you? Don't you know the consequences?"

"Don't yell at Emma," I say. The pact makes me say it. "I started it."

Mom looks at me. "Oh, believe me, I'm plenty mad at you, too. But I expect Emma to know better."

It's a sentence that would have stung a long time ago. Emma is younger than me. Why should she know something I don't?

But I get it more now. That age and knowledge don't always go together. That knowing things isn't always fun.

"Was this worth it?" Mom says. "For a fun little prank?"

"It wasn't for fun," Emma says.

I shift in my seat.

"It wasn't fun," Emma says again. "It was . . . necessary."

Mom raises her eyebrows. "Necessary for you to put yourselves in danger?"

Neither of us says anything.

"Where were you?" Mom says again.

I answer. "We were at the house. Our new house."

Mom's eyebrows drop. "The house?" she says. "Why? What did you do to it?"

"Nothing," I say. "I just . . . I wanted to be there. Emma followed me."

"Lydia!" Mom says. "This is maddening. And why, why, why are you suspended from school?"

I pause. I swallow and look at her. "Sister Janice didn't tell you?"

Mom shakes her head. "She says I need to come in for a meeting tomorrow. Without you. So that we can discuss your future at that school, if you have one. What could you possibly have done?"

I say it quietly. I almost can't say it. It seems so tiny compared to sneaking out in the middle of the night. It seems so stupid.

"Magic," I say.

"What?" Mom cries. "What does that even mean?"

"I . . . I tried to do magic at school."

"She suspended you for that?" Mom asks, like she doesn't believe me.

"She said it was from the devil," I say.

"She always says stuff like that," Emma says.

"So she caught me doing a spell and . . . and now I'm suspended."

Mom shakes her head like she's trying to clear it out or something. "This makes no sense."

I don't say anything.

"A spell?" she says. "What kind of spell?"

I freeze.

What if I tell my mom what Andrew did and she tells me it doesn't matter? That boys always snap girls' bras? That I have to get used to it because my life will always be harder? My heart beats loudly against my ribs. I'm surprised my mom can't hear it. I don't know what I'll do if my mom joins my friends and my principal and God and magic in the long list of things that don't help. I don't know how I'll be in the world.

Finally, Emma says, "There's a boy at school who has been . . . bothering Lydia. It's really not good."

Mom's face softens. "What do you mean?" she says.

Emma scoots closer to me so our elbows are touching. She is totally, completely choosing cousins in this moment. She looks at me. "You can tell her," she says. It's a promise.

I start at the beginning. "Last spring the boys gave me a nickname I didn't like," I say. "They started calling me Swing."

"Swing?" Mom says.

"Because of the way my skirt swings when I walk."

Mom's face breaks open and with it my nerves break away. "No," she whispers. "Lydia, that's not OK."

Emma bumps my elbow as if to say, *I told you you could tell her.*

So I do. I tell my mom the whole story. How the boys did all sorts of things that I hated but that my friends called flirting and how I didn't know how to stop them. How I found a book of spells in the house but I wanted to keep them to myself. How I screamed when Andrew snapped my bra but Sister Janice took his side. How I tried to perform a spell to keep him away from me and how Sister Janice found out and suspended me. I even admit to going to the house multiple times. I let it all out. Almost all of it.

"Lydia," Mom says, hushed. "Why didn't you tell me? I can help you."

I look at my feet.

I can't answer.

There's no way I can answer.

There's no way I can tell her that I believed Sister Janice when she said my mom would think it was no big deal.

Because I can't tell her why.

Because I still don't know if she'd believe me about the biggest deal of all.

Emma puts her hand on my back. "It's hard to talk about this stuff."

The pact.

The pact means there is a real problem with Jeremy.

The pact means it hasn't all been in my head the whole time.

But the pact also means I have some help. Finally.

CHAPTER 23

THE NEXT MORNING MOM IS KNOCKING loudly on our door before the usual time my alarm goes off. Does she not realize we've only been in bed a few hours?

"Get up," she calls through the door. "We're going to school."

Emma and I both half sit up in bed, rubbing our eyes. Mom opens the door and sticks her head in. "But don't wear your uniforms, OK? Wear whatever you want."

"*Whatever* I want?" I ask.

Mom nods. "Whatever."

An hour later all three of us are sitting in Sister Janice's office waiting for her to be finished with the morning announcements and come in and talk to us. Mom still hasn't said anything about everything I told her last night. The last real thing she said to me was to ask why I didn't go to her for help. So I don't know what she's going to say to my principal. Mom is wearing a skirt suit because she's going to work later today. Emma is wearing capri pants and a black T-shirt with white print that says *I ❤ TACOS* because even in late September it's still over seventy degrees outside. I'm wearing jeans, long socks, a turtleneck, and a sweatshirt on top of it. Underneath is a not-very-pingable sports bra.

Whatever I want.

Sister Janice comes into her office in her usual calm way.

"Mrs. Wexler," she says. "I didn't mean for you—"

"It's Ms. Wexler," Mom says. "Or Molly."

Sister Janice looks ruffled for only half a second. "Regardless. I didn't mean for you to bring these two with you. Lydia is suspended, and Emma, you should be in class. Let me find a uniform pass—"

"Sister, they need to be here," Mom says. "Both of them."

Sister Janice's green eyes bore into Mom's face like she's debating how to respond. Finally she says, "I'm afraid I have to insist Lydia show me she has not brought evil into the building again. Stand up, dear."

I do. But then Mom says, "Sit, Lydia," so I do that instead.

She looks at Sister Janice. "You'll keep your hands off my daughter," she says. "She has been violated enough in this school."

Sister Janice's eyes go wide and for once she has nothing to say.

I don't blame her. I've never seen my mom like this, I realize. This isn't mom mode. This is lawyer mode. My mom is my lawyer.

Sister Janice puts her hands in the air for half a second like she's going to argue. Then she lets them drop to her side and closes her mouth. She walks behind her desk but looks at me before sitting. "Lydia, do you have any . . . offending items on you today?"

Mom answers before I can. She stands. "Do you mean like this?" she says.

She reaches into her briefcase and pulls out something and slams it onto Sister Janice's desk.

Sister Janice almost screams in horror.

I almost scream in surprise.

The black leather binding and the shiny gold letters look so out of place in the principal's office of my Catholic school. *Pan's Personal Book of Spells.*

It's here! It's safe!

Emma reaches past my mom's chair to grab my arm. She looks at me with wide eyes, as if to say, *How did she know about it? How did she get it out of that little room? How did she get it here?*

Sister Janice folds her hands together as if she's praying. Then she slowly opens the book, right to the middle. A smell fills the room, thick and true. Lilac and green apple.

Emma clutches my arm tighter. We both have our mothers here fighting for us.

"This," Mom says, closing the book and sliding it back across the desk so that it's closer to us than it is to Sister Janice, "is a child's imagination. A desperate child's imagination."

That description doesn't sound like Pan. It sounds like me. Or Emma. Or Miriam.

It sounds like every girl in the world.

"You knew her?" Emma asks.

"No," Mom says. "But I can—"

"I did," Sister Janice says.

Mom, Emma, and I all look at her in stunned silence.

"How?" I whisper.

Sister Janice is shaking her head back and forth as if that would stop us from seeing the tears in her eyes. "Penelope. She was my niece," she says. "It seems that you have bought my sister's old house."

Emma and I are too stunned to say anything.

"It's no wonder that house corrupted your daughter."

"Sister," my mom says in her warning voice. I've never heard her use her warning voice on an adult before.

"My sister and my niece lived there a long time before my niece turned . . . well, started, this evil. And then you probably know what happened. To the house. To them."

"You're saying your niece is evil?" Mom asks.

"No." Sister bites her lip. "I'm saying she got seduced by magic . . . before she died. And magic is evil."

Emma and I look at each other. So that's what happened in that house. That's why one room was perfect and the rest destroyed. A family was broken there.

"When?" Emma whispers.

"A long time ago," Sister Janice answers. "My niece was a child but she'd be closer to your mom's age than yours by now. I was shocked when my sister told me that that house had finally sold. She'd been unable to even look at it ever since. I thought all this magic had . . . well . . ."

"Sister," Mom says, "we're very sorry for your loss, of course, but this book did not kill your niece."

"No," Sister Janice says. "She was sick. But if she'd turned to God instead of the devil—"

"Actually," Mom interrupts, "I've read this entire book and there's not a single mention of the devil."

"Well, I . . . ," Sister Janice says slowly. I realize that in all the years I've known her I've never seen her not be in charge of the room she's in.

"In fact, if you look at it out of context, it reads simply like a children's crafts book. Are you going to suspend my daughter for bringing a craft to school?"

"It's not—"

"And," Mom adds, "that's before we even discuss why she brought it."

"It's unacceptable to—"

"This is a yes-or-no question," Mom says. "When my daughter told you she was being violated by a boy in her class, did you protect him instead of her? And when she looked for another, desperate way to protect herself, did you *suspend* her for it while still refusing to address it with the boy?"

My mom sees this the way I do. Exactly the way I do. Sister Janice takes a deep breath and sits.

"It's a yes-or-no question," Mom says again.

Sister Janice doesn't say anything for a minute. When she speaks again, she's back to her calm, collected, in-charge self. She says, "I'll kindly ask you to remove that book from my desk, Ms. Wexler."

Mom looks uncertain and my heart starts to race again. Mom takes the book, puts it back in her briefcase, and sits.

"Ms. Wexler, I'd like to remind you that in a Catholic institution it should be self-evident that any sort of magic—even if it's simply created by a child with a wild imagination—is strictly forbidden—"

Mom leans forward to interrupt. "But bodily violation is not expressly forbidden?"

Sister Janice leans back in her chair. "I'd hardly call it violation," she says. "It was mild flirting. There's hardly a way to outlaw all flirting among seventh- and eighth-grade students."

"You called it mild," Mom says through clenched teeth, "when my daughter was screaming."

"I simply told her that we have bigger fish to fry with Andrew than typical seventh-grade boy behavior."

"Typical?" Mom says.

"Well—" Sister Janice starts.

"So boys pulling girls' bra straps is typical in this school?" Mom says.

"When—"

"What else is typical?" Mom asks.

Sister doesn't answer right away, ready for Mom to interrupt again. Then she says, "I'm not sure what you mean, Ms. Wexler."

"Is commenting on girls' bodies typical?"

Sister Janice clears her throat.

"Is touching their legs?"

"No!" she says.

"How about touching other parts of their bras? Their underwear? Their—"

"Ms. Wexler! Stop!" Sister Janice exclaims.

Mom takes a breath and slows her voice. "My point is, if you let pulling bra straps be typical," Mom says, "what's next? Touching girls when they don't want to be touched becomes typical? Then holding them down against their will? Then what else?"

Emma and I squirm in our chairs. Why can Mom see this all so clearly at school? Why hasn't she noticed that she's also letting things be typical when they shouldn't be? Things like extra-long hugs and forced hand-holding during grace. Why can't she see we are balancing on this same slippery slope at home?

Sister Janice pauses.

"I think it is common sense what behavior is typical and what is deviant," Sister Janice says finally.

"Then please explain it to me," Mom says. "Because I don't

seem to have common sense."

Sister Janice takes a deep breath. "Ms. Wexler, was your bra snapped when you were a little girl?"

"Of course," Mom says.

My jaw drops.

"So was mine," Sister Janice says. "I was simply pointing out that we went through the same thing and we are fine and—"

"Are we fine?" Mom says.

Sister Janice looks surprised. "Huh?" she says.

I can't believe my mom made her say *huh*.

"Maybe it didn't matter to you when boys pulled your bra straps in school. Or called you names. Maybe you were one of the girls who didn't mind."

It mattered to me.

"I'm not saying—"

Mom interrupts her. "But I'm sure something did matter, right?"

"I don't understand," Sister Janice says.

"For a second, just think about what did matter," Mom says. "Think about when you weren't fine. Every time you weren't fine. Think about every time a man commented on your body. Or your face. Or your skin. Think about every time a man looked at you in a way that terrified you. Every time one invaded your space or touched you in a way you didn't like but you were too afraid to say anything." Mom pauses. "Don't tell me being a nun protects you from all of it."

Sister Janice's face is red inside her brown habit. Her eyes are on her lap. She looks almost like a little girl. "No," she says. "Of course it doesn't."

"So are you really fine?" Mom asks.

Sister Janice doesn't answer but she doesn't need to.

Everyone is silent for a minute.

I breathe in the silence and something deep inside me stops shaking. Something that has been shaking since the first time Andrew called me Swing. Something that has been shaking since the first time Jeremy handed me a piece of candy. Something that has been shaking every time my space has been invaded for the past year or more. Something in me quiets.

Everyone in this room understands what it feels like to be touched when you don't want to be. My cousin. My mom. My principal, who is a nun.

It's not that I don't *fit* into the world.

It's that the world is *broken*.

"Sister," my mom says, her tone almost pleading, "what if you had gotten the message that your body is your own from the very first time someone snapped your bra? What if the boy who snapped your bra had learned that *no* violation is OK? What if we didn't let our boys get away with this stuff?"

Sister swallows. She looks at my mom. "This was supposed to be a conversation about magic."

Mom shakes her head. "Maybe. But I'm going to force you to talk about the real issue. Look at how my daughter and niece are dressed," Mom says.

Sister Janice squints. "Not in uniform," she says.

Mom almost laughs. "And yet in these outfits they picked out themselves they are less likely to be victims of ogling and bra-strap snapping."

Sister Janice shakes her head. "They must be in uniform."

Mom nods. "And they will be. As soon as you create and facilitate a zero-tolerance sexual-harassment program that involves both education and consequences for all forms of bodily violations. Until you do that, both my girls will show up in the clothes that make them feel protected and comfortable. That's hardly magic," Mom says. "But it does make my girls feel safer."

My eyes go wide. No uniforms? How will she pull that off?

"I need to show Lydia how to stop looking for answers in magic and God and other things that haven't worked for women for centuries. She needs to look inside herself. She needs to use her intuition and her voice. Right now her voice is her clothes."

I look at up at my mom. This is a different thought completely.

Me. I'm the answer.

I need to protect myself.

I can protect myself.

I can use my voice.

Sister Janice lowers her eyebrows. "We can . . . we can look into some of your concerns, Ms. Wexler," she says. "But uniforms are required for all students. And Lydia is suspended."

"No," Mom says. "We've agreed that there was no magic.

That Lydia was trying desperately to protect herself from having her bra pulled at in class."

"I understand that was her intention but—"

"Sister," Mom says. "You have suspended a girl who was trying to keep her bra from being pulled. Do you know how quickly we could sue the school over not having an effective sexual-harassment policy?"

Sister Janice's eyes are so wide they look like they might roll out of her face.

She takes a long time to answer but when she does she says, "OK, girls. Go to the hallway and wait a minute. I will get you a uniform pass."

Emma and I both gasp audibly, then scurry into the hallway. We throw our arms around each other and jump up and down, squealing.

"Your mom was incredible in there!" Emma says.

"I think yours helped," I say.

Emma smiles. "You could smell her too?"

"I could," I say.

Sister Janice comes out of her office and gives Emma and me each a late slip and a uniform pass. I walk up to class with no books or pens or pencils or anything but that's OK.

I walk into the classroom, give my note to Ms. Banneker, and don't even care as I feel the eyes of all my classmates on all my clothes.

I sit in my seat. The class is working on math equations

that are projected on the board. Everyone will be able to hear but I don't care. Or maybe it's even better that way.

I turn to Andrew, look him in the eyes, and say, "Don't touch me today. Don't even try it."

He doesn't.

CHAPTER 24

EMMA AND I PRACTICALLY BOUNCE HOME from school. We're still riding the high of seeing my mom so powerful. We're still basking in the glow of controlling our school principal by wearing whatever we want until she does what she needs to do.

But as soon as we open the door, the look on my mom's face drops us back to earth.

"You're still in trouble, girls," Mom says. "Big trouble."

Then she steps aside to let us into the apartment. I'm so surprised by what I see behind her I almost fall over.

My dad is sitting on the couch.

"It's Friday!" I say.

"I'm not here for a celebration," Dad says. "I'm here for an intervention."

"That's right," Mom says. "And Emma, I've arranged a call with your father soon too."

Emma swallows. I've never seen her look so negative at the mention of her dad.

"Sneaking out in the middle of the night is terrifying and will not be tolerated. We need to have some serious discussions later tonight," Mom says.

Then the buzzer buzzes. Mom walks over toward it. "But first, dinner," she says as Jeremy's voice booms "hello" through the speaker.

"Later tonight we will discuss your choices. For now we will all pause our anger and enjoy each other's company. Understand?"

My dad jumps up and smiles at me. "Understood," he says.

He crosses the room to hug me as Mom lets Jeremy in the door.

Emma raises her eyebrows at me. I nod back. We'll have to tell my mom another time.

The mood at dinner is lighter like Mom asked. She has pulled up two extra tray tables to make an extra-big fake table. She's set five places.

She's made pan-seared scallops with white wine sauce. I can smell chocolate, also. So it's like tonight is a special occasion.

Mom is humming under her breath as she sets the final dishes on the table. Jeremy is chuckling as he recounts his day. He doesn't say anything about grace tonight. I decide that if Mom is pausing her anger, I'm going to pause mine, too. And my nervousness about whatever my parents are going to do to me. And my shame for breaking so many rules.

I'm sitting between Mom and Dad. It feels good to have them sitting on either side of me at dinner, even though I know they're not getting back together. It feels good to have them talking cordially. It feels good because I need them both.

"So you should be aware," Mom says to Dad as she starts dishing scallops and pasta and vegetables onto everyone's plates, "that I've arranged it so that Lydia doesn't have to wear her school uniform to school next week."

"What?" Dad says with a chuckle. "How did you manage that?"

"Uncle Phil, you should have seen Aunt Molly!" Emma says gleefully. "She was a beast!"

"Really?" Mom says, sitting back down. "A beast?"

"A total beast!" Emma exclaims.

"She was incredible," I say seriously, looking at her.

Will she be just as incredible when I try to tell her about Jeremy?

"Thank you," Mom says, looking right back at me. "But you know I'd do anything for you, right?"

I smile at her.

I hope so.

"So what are the terms?" Dad asks. "How long is Lydia out of uniform?"

"Emma too!" I say.

Dad smiles. "Even more impressive."

"Only until the school initiates a proper sexual-harassment policy," Mom says. "One that encompasses education for both boys and girls, and consequences when students are violated by other students or anyone else."

"Sexual-harassment policy?" Jeremy asks. "I thought every place had one of those these days."

"Well, apparently not everyone realizes they're important for seventh graders," Mom says. "Even when seventh-grade boys are snapping bra straps."

Jeremy chuckles. "Seventh-grade boys will always snap bra straps," he says.

My fork freezes halfway to my mouth.

"That's not sexual harassment," he concludes.

Dad lowers his eyebrows at Jeremy. But then he looks at my mom.

Mom slowly sets down her water cup. She looks at Jeremy.

What will she say?

What will he say?

Say something worse, I beg him in my head. *Say something awful. Show her if you are what Emma and I think you are.*

"It *is* sexual harassment if the girl doesn't want her bra strap snapped," Mom says slowly.

"Boys shouldn't be touching girls' underwear in school," Dad adds. "Girls need to be safe at school."

Jeremy laughs again. "You make it sound like he's reaching up her skirt or something."

Mom clears her throat. "I happen to think that bra-strap snapping is on the same continuum."

"Come on," Jeremy says. "Really?"

Dad is staring at his scallops, frozen. I can see Mom's face getting a little pink. Jeremy is embarrassing her.

"Yes, really," Mom says.

"You honestly think that's necessary?" Jeremy says. "A sexual-harassment policy for kids?" He says that like he's talking about the most ridiculous thing of all time.

"I do," Mom says.

"Don't you think that's a bit of a slippery slope?" Jeremy asks. "We start punishing boys for snapping bra straps? What's next?"

"I do think it's a slippery slope," Mom says. "If we do nothing, what happens to the girl?"

"Come on," Jeremy says. "A little bra-strap snapping never hurt anyone."

I look up from my plate very slowly. I look him in the eyes for the first time since before he started giving me candy. Maybe even before that. Maybe the first time ever.

This is the bravest thing I'll ever do. Braver than telling Andrew not to touch me. Braver than what I have to say to Mom before Jeremy has a chance to get to me again.

I look Jeremy in the eyes and say, "It hurt me."

Jeremy closes his mouth.

"There you go," Mom says.

Jeremy nods and changes the subject.

Emma raises her eyebrows like she can't believe how brave I am.

Suddenly my dinner smells like lilac and green apples.

After dinner, Jeremy gets in the shower, which is good because he smells like floor polish again. I sit between Mom and Dad on the couch. Emma sits across from us.

"Emma," Mom says. She looks up. Mom hands her her phone. "Your dad is expecting your call."

She goes into our bedroom with Mom's phone.

Mom barely waits until the door is shut before she starts yelling at me. "Do you understand how idiotic it is to sneak out into the middle of the night as a young girl *alone*? You were doing the opposite of protecting yourself! A million terrible things could have happened to you."

I don't say anything. These aren't real questions. I don't think I'm supposed to answer.

"What if you were kidnapped?" Mom says. "Or worse?"

Dad nods while Mom is talking.

"I haven't been able to breathe since I found you missing last night, Lyddie. I thought I might have an actual heart attack."

That makes me feel guilty but her point doesn't stand. Not really. When someone dangerous is in my own house, it doesn't feel as dangerous to sneak out.

"Your mom told me what you were doing," Dad says quietly. "I'm heartbroken that you were going through that at school. I just don't understand why you didn't tell us."

Here it comes. The question I haven't been able to answer. The same one Mom left me with last night.

Why didn't you just tell me what was going on? Why didn't you let me help you?

"You know," Dad says, "if you ever have something you need help with, you can talk to me, too. Me *and* your mom, we're on your side. If you feel for any reason that you can't talk to your mom, you can always call me."

My mom shocks me with her answer. "That's true," she says.

Dad keeps talking but I can't hear anything he's saying through the ringing in my ears.

Neither of them can tell, but suddenly I'm angry. My heart is shaking. My veins are shaking. My blood is fire.

I think about how my mom used words with Sister Janice earlier today. I think about how my words worked with Andrew. How they made Jeremy change the subject at dinner tonight. I open my mouth and I let my words come out.

"No, I can't," I say.

Dad stops talking midsentence. "You can't what?" he asks.

"You said I can call you anytime I need help. But I can't."

Dad takes my hand in both of his as if that will help somehow. "Yes," he says. "Yes, you can, Lydia. You are the most important thing to me. You can call anytime."

I pull my hand away. "No," I say. "I tried that. I tried to call once when I needed help. And it didn't work."

"Huh?" Dad says. "You tried to call me before sneaking out?"

"Another time," I say. "I called and you were working. And then you didn't listen to me and then you hung up."

Mom's eyes are big. "When was this, honey?" she asks.

"When—" I stop myself.

When Jeremy drove me home from the beach with his hand on my knee and you were going to let him take care of me for two nights and I knew that was going to be bad bad bad.

She believed me so quickly about Andrew but she doesn't love Andrew. Andrew doesn't make her laugh. She doesn't talk all the time about how Andrew makes her life easier. She doesn't slow-dance with Andrew in the kitchen.

Could she possibly believe me about Jeremy just as quickly?

"When Dad hung up I called Miriam and she helped me," I say.

Mom nods once but her face tells me she isn't really following. "Miriam knows about the spells?"

"Yes," I say.

"So Miriam suggested you sneak out in the middle of the night?"

"No!" I say. I don't want Miriam in trouble also.

"How exactly did Miriam help you, then?" Dad asks.

I look at my shoes. Maybe I can help them figure it out without saying anything. Maybe if they figure it out on their own they will believe me. "She invited me to sleep over."

Everything is quiet for a second. Mom closes her eyes and I can see the wheels in her brain moving. She's going to figure it out. She's going to.

This is all going to be over.

"Aunt Molly!" Emma calls from the bedroom. "Dad wants you to come get on the phone so that you can properly gang up on me."

Mom opens her eyes. "I'll be right back," she says. She looks at Dad. "Try to get to the bottom of this."

I watch them look at each other. I realize that this is the first time in a long time that we've felt something like family. It should feel good to have my parents working together, on the same side. Except I can't enjoy it because it somehow feels like I'm on the other side. It's always two against one. I want it to be three against zero.

Mom goes into the bedroom and Dad says, "Lydia, I never want you to feel like you can't come to me when you need help. When did you call me and then sleep over at Miriam's? I don't remember this at all."

"This summer," I say. "Toward the end of summer."

Dad nods. "And why couldn't you talk to Mom that time?"

I chew the inside of my cheek. "Because she was visiting Uncle Jack with Emma. And it was supposed to be your day anyway but you canceled at the last minute and I was left all alone."

"Oh!" Dad swallows. He remembers now. "But you were with Jeremy, right?" Dad says, like it's nothing.

I nod. I make my eyes big. I beg him to ask the next question so I don't have to say it.

Just then the bathroom door opens. "Did I hear my name?"

Jeremy calls across the kitchen.

It's like his voice sets off a million fireworks in Dad's brain. His head shoots up. His eyes go wider than I've ever seen.

"She said you'd be fine and then . . . oh no . . . oh Lord, no . . . Lydia?" he says. It's not a question. It's a plea.

He knows. He finally knows. But he doesn't want to know. He wants me to tell him everything is OK. But I won't. It's not.

"Oh, Lydia!" he pleads again.

He can't say any more because Jeremy is standing behind us, hair still dripping wet onto his T-shirt.

"You folks OK?" he asks.

We ignore him.

Dad puts an arm around me and pulls me close. "I'm so sorry," he whispers low into my ear. So low I can barely hear it and there's no way Jeremy can. "I'm so, so sorry. Whatever's going on . . . I'm so sorry. And whatever it is, it's over. You have me now. One hundred percent. I promise."

I nod. "It wasn't . . . it hasn't . . . I'm not, like, physically hurt. Yet," I say.

"Did it . . . did Miriam help?"

I know what he means. I nod against his chest. "Do you want me to tell your mother?" he asks.

I shake my head against his shoulder. I'm so glad he would talk to her for me. But I don't want them to fight. Besides: "I should do it," I say.

"OK," Dad says. "As long as he's anywhere near you, I'll be by your side."

He's whispering, but this is more than a secret. It's a promise.

Late that night, Emma whispers across the space between our beds to wake me up.

"Hey! Hey, Lydia!"

I prop myself up on my elbow.

"What's up?" I ask.

She smiles at me, her eyes shining with relief. "Thanks," she whispers.

"Thanks?" I say.

"Your dad's asleep on the couch."

I nod.

"I know he said it was too dark to ride his motorcycle back to Manhattan tonight but . . . you told him, didn't you?"

"Yeah," I say. "Sort of. He sort of figured it out."

"Finally!" Emma whispers. She collapses back down into her pillow. "Is he going to tell your mom?"

"Nope," I say. "I have to do that tomorrow."

"We," Emma says.

"Huh?" I say.

"The pact, remember? *We* have to tell her tomorrow. Together."

CHAPTER 25

JEREMY IS GONE BY THE TIME we wake up the next morning. I find Dad asleep on the couch. He smiles at me. Then he says Mom said she wants to spend the day with us but that I should just call if I need him and he'll be here in a jiffy.

Once he's gone Mom gives Emma and me each a plate of roast chicken and rice pilaf for breakfast. She doesn't turn on her cooking shows like on a regular weekend morning. Instead she sits across from us and squeezes a lemon onto her own breakfast.

"You're both grounded," she says. "And I'm installing an alarm on the front door so there will be no more sneaking out. This front door and the new front door."

I nod. That makes sense. It's embarrassing, though. I've never been grounded before.

"But I don't believe in grounding for grounding's sake," Mom says.

Emma slurps a bite of rice. I don't know how she's able to eat. Seeing my mom's disappointment in me makes my stomach turn.

I think of all of Jeremy's candy. Emma has always been able to eat things that make my stomach turn. It doesn't mean she's OK with everything. I've learned that now.

"What does that mean?" Emma says.

"It means you're grounded so that we can spend time together. It means you're grounded from all fun except family fun. I've missed too much going on in your heads," Mom says. "We need to spend some time as a family. So that's the terms of the grounding. Family time. No friends. No phone calls. Nothing but school and family time. Emma, I've canceled your sleepover for tonight. Lydia, I've let Miriam's dad know so that she doesn't think you're mad at her or anything when you don't call her all weekend."

"How long are we grounded?" I ask.

Mom shrugs. "Until it works," she says.

Emma shifts beside me. She's stopped eating. "No phone calls?" she says.

"Ah," Mom says, "I forgot the exception. Emma, you may of course call your father."

Now it's my turn to shift. Mom remembers a beat too late.

"And Lydia. You may call your father too. Parent phone calls are allowed. It's family grounding, after all."

"Family grounding," I say. "Does that mean you're grounded too?"

Mom smiles around a bit of chicken. "I suppose it does," she says.

I look at her. I sort of think she deserves to be grounded with us. I want her to be grounded from Jeremy.

I have to do it myself. I have to do it today.

"I want you two dressed and ready by ten a.m. Lydia, you may wear whatever you want. And Emma, I don't want to hear it."

Emma looks up quickly from her plate.

"I don't care what Lydia wears," she says.

Mom stumbles for a second. So do I.

We were both expecting Emma to say, *Family day? I'm not even really in this family.*

But she doesn't.

It's like the thought doesn't even occur to her.

The day doesn't feel much like a grounding. We go get mani-pedis at the salon that does them for half price if you show up before noon. We go to a deli and get huge sandwiches for lunch, which we eat on the bench outside. It's a sunny day and I'm wearing capri pants and regular long sleeves. My ankles are showing.

I feel sort of OK about that now that my mom understands the part of me that feels sort of not OK about it.

After lunch we go to a free art class at the public library, where we paint bowls of fruit. Emma turns hers into cartoon fruit and the teacher says that wasn't the point but Mom just laughs and puts her arm around Emma. And I don't feel even the tiniest bit jealous.

Then we have dinner in the booth at the Chinese restaurant.

The day is almost over. I have to tell Mom now or else Dad will have to tell her. I want to be the one to do it and I want to do it with Emma. I'm terrified of Mom not believing me, but even if she doesn't, I have Dad. And if she does believe me, I want to see it happen.

I'm looking at Emma and she's looking at me. We're serious. We aren't blowing straws or giggling like usual.

"What?" Mom says. "What's going on?"

I think about what she told Sister Janice. It's not God or spells or protection items or magic that can save me. It's something smaller and bigger all at once.

It's me.

Emma nods.

I take a deep breath and then I say it. "Mom, there's someone who scares me even more than Andrew."

"Me too," Emma says.

Mom lowers her eyebrows. "Someone has done something worse than pulling your bra strap?"

I chew my cheek. I guess feeding me candy isn't technically worse, but it feels worse because Andrew is just a boy and Jeremy is a—

his arms around my body

his fingertip stroking my wrist

his fingers brushing my hair behind my ear

his hand on my knee
his thumb on my lips

Mom interrupts my thoughts. "I was afraid of this, Lydia. Tell me. Tell me what else is happening. I will help you."

I blink and blink and blink. I won't let the tears fall. I know it's going to hurt her, what I have to say.

And if it doesn't hurt her, it will hurt me. Which is worse. Because that would mean she didn't believe me.

"What else did those boys do?"

"Not the boys," Emma says. She nudges me with her elbow. Pact. Cousins.

Mom's eyes go even wider. "Not the boys at school?"

"Not boys at all," I say.

"What do you mean?" Mom asks. "A man?"

I nod. Emma nods.

"A man has hurt you?"

Emma and I nod.

Mom's eyebrows knit together. "Who?" she says so fiercely we both jump a little in our seats. "A teacher?" she asks. "One of our doormen? That old librarian?"

We shake our heads.

"It's bad, Mom," I finally say. "I'm afraid to tell you."

"Who?" she says. "Who?"

I whisper it. It's the best I can do. I'm so quiet I'm not even sure if all the syllables make it out of my mouth.

"Jer . . . e . . . my."

But they must because Mom's face breaks open. It goes through a thousand expressions in half a second. It lands on loving. "Lydia," she whispers. "Emma. Did he touch you?"

We look at each other. Mom has seen Jeremy hug me and put his arm around me. So I know she doesn't mean did he touch us at all. She means did he . . . I can't even think about it.

Emma and I both shrug.

"His hugs are really long," Emma says finally. "But only when you aren't in the room."

"And he grabs my knee under the table sometimes when we're eating," I say.

Mom is still calming herself with her breath but her face is broken in half. I can't tell if she believes us. I can't tell if we sound crazy.

"And he, like, strokes my wrist sometimes when we say grace," Emma says. She shudders.

I shudder back. "Yeah," I say. "That too. And he gives us candy."

"Candy?" Mom says.

Emma and I nod. "I can show you the wrappers when we get home. Lydia never eats it. It's sort of creepy. He knows it's not allowed."

"Candy," Mom says again, like that's the most shocking part. She shakes her head.

Mom looks right at me with her broken face. The face that I broke. "What's the worst thing?" she asks. "What's the worst thing he did?"

It's the question I've been dreading. Because the worst thing feels so bad—it feels like a million bees in my stomach and climbing all over my tongue; it feels like blood pooling out from behind my fingernails; it feels like my knee disappears off my body when I think about it. It feels so bad. But it doesn't sound bad enough.

"The worst thing," Mom says again. "I need to know."

Then she takes one of those breaths again. She takes my hand and for a second I let that feel good. Because it will feel so bad if she doesn't believe me. Or if she acts like what I'm about to say is no big deal. I let it feel good in case this is the last time my mom touching me ever feels good.

"Lydia," she says, "I believe you. I believe you completely. Jeremy will never set foot in my house again."

There are tears in her eyes. Tears climb into mine, too. I'm so relieved.

"When I was a little girl . . . something happened. Something . . . something like this. Something worse than the bra-strap pulling," she says. "My uncle . . . he lived with us. He was . . . he should never have been allowed to be alone with me. He . . . my mom didn't believe me. That's why I had to go live with my aunt for a while." Mom takes a shaky breath. She's blinking a lot. She won't let the tears fall because she doesn't want me to see them. She wants to be strong for me.

I don't have to be strong for her.

"I've promised myself your entire life that no matter how hard it is, I would not be like my mom in this way. I'd be like my aunt Maggie. I will always believe you. I believe you." She looks at Emma. "And I believe you, too. I just need to know the worst thing so that I know what to do. So that I know if it's more than changing the locks on the front door."

Now I take the same shaky breath my mom just did. I can tell her. She went through this as a little girl and it's over now. Now she can be strong for me.

"He made me ride in the front seat all the way home from school the other day. And he forced me to eat gummy worms from his hand. And he kept putting his thumb on my lips and his hand on my knee."

And now that I say it out loud I know it *is* bad. It's worse. It's awful. It's gross.

Emma gasps. I guess she didn't realize how far it had gotten for me.

Mom is really crying now but pretending she doesn't notice she's crying so that maybe I won't notice too. "What did you do?" she asks.

I bite my lip. I'm ashamed. "I froze," I say. "I didn't say anything. I didn't know how to yet."

Mom pulls me into her arms and we cry together. It's the best hug in the world.

"I didn't know," I say. "I didn't know if he was being wrong or if I was just being weird. I didn't know what's allowed and what's not."

Mom pulls back so that her hands frame my face. "Lydia," she says. "That's up to you. That's always up to you."

"What's up to me?" I ask through my tears.

"Who touches you. And how," Mom says. "It doesn't matter what anyone else says is OK. You get to decide for you. There are no other rules. It's your body, so you make the rules."

"I make the rules," I say.

Mom nods. "You have to promise me that if anyone ever touches you in a way you don't like again, you'll tell me right away. It doesn't matter who says it's OK. If you say it's not, it's not OK."

I nod. This feels so good.

It doesn't matter if I'm normal or not.

It doesn't matter what other people feel when people touch their bodies.

The way my body is treated is up to me.

"You make the rules," Mom says. "And while you're under my roof, I'll enforce them. I promise. I'll do better."

Then she buries me in a hug again and I cry on her shoulder as I feel each inch of my skin come back to life. It starts with my forehead and spreads down through my scalp and face. It spreads over my neck and collarbone, my chest and back and stomach and arms. It spreads through my fingers and down my legs into my ankles and feet and toes. I own every bit of this skin.

I make the rules.

HOW TO BE A GIRL IN THE WORLD

IT'S THE SIMPLEST THING, BUT IT can be hard to remember

Especially when the world tells you in a million tiny ways that it's not true.

So, to survive the world, say it every single day.

Tell yourself:

You matter.

Your thoughts matter. Your feelings matter. Your body matters.

You matter just as much as anyone else.

To yourself, you can matter the most.

SIX MONTHS LATER

WE STAND ON THE SIDEWALK HOLDING hands, our eyes squeezed shut. There are more of us this time. Dad, me, Emma, Mom, Uncle Jack. We stand and breathe in unison. Only Mom is allowed to have her eyes open.

"Ready?" Mom says. "One, two, three!"

My eyelids fly apart and a breath catches in my throat. The house in front of us is beautiful. The green aluminum siding has been replaced by beautiful gray wooden shingles. The windows each have two perfectly white shutters. The stoop is solid and inviting.

I stare and I can see the future. Emma and Miriam and me sitting out there in the early summer evenings, giggling. Emma, Mom, Uncle Jack, and me sharing sandwiches on a Saturday afternoon. Dad pulling up on his motorcycle to take me on adventures.

"Wow," I whisper.

"Wait until you see the inside," Mom says.

I smile at her.

"We don't have all day!" Dad says. "Let's get you ladies moved in!"

He turns to walk toward the moving van parked on the street. He's not going to live here, of course, but he's here for the day to help us move. He's rearranged his hours at work so that he has every Sunday and Monday off. Which means I get to see him all day on Sunday and Mondays after school. I even got to spend the night with him last night since most of our furniture was moved into our new house yesterday. Dad said he learned a lesson from me. He said he had to use his voice to stand up to his boss, and since he did he has been able to see me way more often.

He's been around a lot, lot more since Jeremy and Mom broke up. Sometimes I wish Dad would get back together with my mom but I mostly know that's never going to happen. I'm mostly just glad to have him around, to have them both with me on Sundays without anybody fighting.

Uncle Jack and Mom join Dad in opening the back of the U-Haul.

Emma and I glance at each other. "Ready?" she says. "One! Two! Three!"

We race toward the front door. There will be time to help the grown-ups unpack later. For now we have to see the inside. We rush up the front steps and into the new living room. It has a shining hardwood floor and a brand-new blue couch right in the center. I barely take time to notice, though, in my rush to get up the stairs.

It takes a second before I realize Emma isn't behind me. She ran off toward the basement. Of course. That's where she's going to live. That's where her room will be.

I pause halfway up the stairs. I'm going to miss her in my room, I realize. I'm going to miss her even though she's only two flights of stairs away from me. How did I ever think we could go back to the normal kind of cousins who only see each other every once in a while? She's so much more than that now.

I take the rest of the stairs slowly and pause at the first door when I reach the top. The door is different. It's now white and chiseled. It looks good against the gray wall and hardwood floor of the hallway.

Still, I know this is going to be my room. Mom didn't tell me but she didn't have to. It's the room that was Pan's. Penelope's. It's the room that was covered in pink teddy bears. I take a breath and slowly open the door.

It's different. No pink. No canopy. No frills. No teddy bears.

It looks like me. Not like Pan. But I can still feel her in here. The memory of her. The way her memory made me brave.

My bed from the old apartment is shoved against the wall with a new pale blue bedspread on it. My white desk and nightstand and dresser are here. I have a new blue-and-white rug in the center of the room.

If I squint, I can see what it will look like. How my clothes will look in Pan's closet. How my pictures will look hung up on her walls. How this room is mine and not hers anymore.

I slip off my shoes and let my bare feet walk across the new carpet. It's soft and cozy and mine.

It doesn't feel haunted. Not one tiny bit.

I sit on my bed and breathe in. It smells like new carpet and a hint of drying paint. It's new, I think. The ghosts are gone.

But that's OK. I don't think I need them. I have a mom and a dad and an uncle Jack. I have a cousin. I have a best friend.

I don't need magic anymore.

I have me.

ACKNOWLEDGMENTS

With a full heart I want to offer my deepest thanks to so many folks who helped this book come to fruition.

Karen Chaplin, thank you so much for your careful critiques, your patience, and your enthusiasm. This is our fourth book together and there is no doubt that I am a much better writer because of it.

Cindy Hamilton, Patty Rosati, Katie Dutton, Vaishali Nayak, Jessica Berg, Bria Ragin, and everyone at Harper, thank you so much for the thoughtful discussions, the passionate ideas, and the enthusiasm you put behind this book. And Molly Fehr, thank you for the beautiful cover design!

Kate McKean, thank you for being an advocate, a confidant, and a fantastic agent.

Amy Ewing, Corey Haydu, Jess Verdi, and Alyson Gerber, thank you for being my early readers and literary discussers without whom my brain would rot.

Molly Donnelly and Mike Collona, thank you. You know what you did.

My parents, Bill and Beth Carter, and all my family and friends, thank you for the endless support, enthusiasm, and for friend-ing and family-ing so damn well.

Elijah and Maebh, thank you for being you and reminding me daily of why I need to keep doing what I do.

And, Greg, thank you for everything. Every single thing.

Turn the page for a sneak peek at critically acclaimed
author Caela Carter's next middle grade novel!

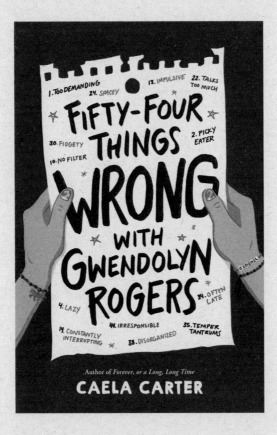

1

HEART SPLINTERS

"**C**upcake."

My mom's soft voice and her hand on the back of my head startle me awake. I jump so high I almost hit the ceiling.

"You fell asleep with your light on again," Mom says, stroking my hair.

I wiggle my hand from where it was resting on my pillow and snake it down under my comforter until I feel the pages. *Still there. Still hidden.* My heartbeat evens out and I'm able to talk to Mom in my regular voice.

"Sorry," I say. "I was reading . . ."

I pat the book next to me on the pillow. It's some corny book about middle school popular crowds and crushes, and I'd never read it, but Mom bought it for me at the school book fair so I keep it there on my pillow to distract from what I really read at night.

"It's OK, honey," Mom says. "But now you should turn

your light off. You get better rest that way."

"OK," I say.

Mom can't turn my light off because my bed is lofted and she's standing on the ladder leading up to it. The reading light is above my head, attached to the other side of my bed. The lofted bed was the perfect solution when I started to get homework and wanted a desk in my tiny room. My desk and my chair and Mr. Jojo's tank fit perfectly beneath my bed, and there's still enough room by the window for Zombie and Marshmallow's aquarium. But it does make it difficult to get in and out of bed in the middle of the night.

"Turn it off, OK, honey?" Mom says. She sounds tired. Her eyes are red. She pushes her bangs off her forehead like she has a headache. Which she does. She always does. Because she cries. She always cries.

I make her cry.

She thinks I don't know because she waits until I'm in this lofted bed to start crying but I hear her while I read my list.

I hand Mom the book, which is how I pretend I'm going to turn the light off when she leaves the room but luckily Mom never comes back to check if I actually turn it off.

"Will you tuck me tighter?" I wait until she's off the ladder to ask her so that I don't have to see the way the etches in her tired face get deeper when she hears the question.

"Oh, Gwendolyn, really? It's almost midnight." I make her so tired.

"It helps me sleep," I say.

I don't know how anyone sleeps the way people in movies and TV (and my mom) always seem to sleep. Like the blankets are resting on top of them and could slide any direction at any minute.

Usually it takes longer to convince her, but Mom must realize she never gets away without tucking me in tighter because she climbs up the ladder again and reaches to the bottom of my mattress, pulling my sheets and blankets snug around my feet. She does the same with the top and folds it so the sheet is exactly under my chin.

I can still wiggle my toes a little, though.

"Tighter?" I say.

Mom sighs but does it. Then she kisses my forehead and I try not to wince at the way her bangs brush the bridge of my nose.

As soon as she leaves the room, I pull my hand out from under the blankets and spread the pages in front of my face. I leave my light on. I hear Mr. Jojo running around in his cage beneath me. I love having a hamster. I love that someone is awake with me when I read this list in the middle of the night.

The pages are delicate because I shuffle through them constantly and I carry them with me everywhere, every day. I have to. Reminding myself is the only way I'll ever get better.

Tonight the papers are warm and guilty from being under my blankets. I have to sneak them because, even though it was about me, I was never supposed to read that old IEP educational assessment report when the school mailed it home.

But I did read it.

Then I wrote a list.

Now I have a list.

And now I need the list.

Even though it's wrong and bad like everything else I do and everything else I need.

I wiggle to my side, careful not to let the blanket loosen too much, and start over from the top, reading until my eyes get heavy.

FIFTY-FOUR THINGS WRONG WITH GWENDOLYN ROGERS

1. Too demanding
2. Picky eater
3. Attention-seeking
4. Lazy
5. Will only do what she wants to do
6. Socially inept

My eyes close. I'll start again at number 7 tomorrow night.

The next day, it's a regular normal day and we are on the way to school and Mom is talking. The mornings are always the best because I haven't had a chance to mess anything up yet. My list is folded up super tiny and tucked inside my shoe as always. I try to focus on the way it's poking into the arch of my foot. Sometimes when I focus on one thing—*bam*—I can magically focus on something else. Today it's not working. I'm trying to pay attention, but Mom's words dance across my brain like brown and gray horses galloping in red and pink saddles.

"Oh, Mom!" I say, launching my head in between the front seats of our car. I like to sit in the middle of the back because that means I'm the farthest from all the windows, but I can see out them all at the same time. "I forgot to tell you something!"

"Gwendolyn, you just interrupted me," Mom says.

14. Constantly interrupting

22. Talks too much

"No, I didn't," I say.

28. Argumentative

Maybe I did interrupt. But there was so much going on in my brain before my mom started talking it felt like she was interrupting me.

"Anyway, do you know what my brother said?"

Mom sighs. "I really need you to pay attention. What I was saying was important."

I don't answer her because what I had to say was important too. I imagine Dandelion. My favorite horse. The one I used to ride all the time. I imagine what her hair felt like when I would run a brush over it.

"What did Tyler say?" Mom asks finally. "And after you tell me, please listen to what I was saying."

"OK," I say. "Well you know Tyler is in PowerKids with me, right? Well he does the summer camps too. Like me. And he said that this year there's going to be a whole week at Crux-man Stables for anyone who wants to learn to ride horses. He's going to do it and I want to do it too! Sign me up, OK?

Mom gets quiet like she always does when I talk about Tyler. Which isn't fair. He's my brother even if Mom doesn't like it.

We turn right and the trees and fields we've been driving past disappear behind the buildings of downtown Madison. We're almost at school.

"Honey," Mom says. "I've told you I'm not ready to discuss this summer yet. We have to concentrate on this afternoon first. I need you to be on your best behavior in PowerKids after school today, OK?"

"And you get to brush them!" I say.

"Brush what?" Mom says.

"The horses."

"We aren't talking about horses, G. We need to talk about this afternoon."

"You know I used to brush Dandelion," I say.

"I *really* don't want to discuss Dandelion," Mom says.

Bad memories flood my body making me shivering cold and chasing the good warm ones away. I don't know why she had to do that. Mom never lets me have the good memories without bringing up the bad ones. She knows I'll remember even if she doesn't bring it up.

50. Demonstrates a strong working memory but is unable to use it to her advantage

54. Above average intelligence but not so much as to be
    exceptional

Neither of us says anything for too long and it gets colder and colder in the car.

"Well I liked to brush her," I say finally.

"Gwendolyn!" Mom says, like I just said something terrible. "We have to talk about this afternoon, OK? I need you to focus and—"

7. Inattentive

"I know, best behavior. I know. You say it every day."

Mom does say it every day. PowerKids is our after-school program, and in the summer, it turns into camp, or a lot of different camps, and if you're a PowerKid you get to choose which one you want to go to week to week to week. I've been a PowerKid for a long time because PowerKids ran the after-school program at my elementary school too. And I love it. I do love it. Even if I'm terrible at it. I'm also sometimes not a good student or daughter or person in general. But Mom mostly talks about PowerKids. I don't know why and I also don't ask her because I don't like to talk about the things inside me that jump and poke and make me not good.

Mom turns left and pulls around the outside of my school.

"I say the same thing every day but then I get calls—"

"I know! I'll be good today, OK?"

"How do I know that?" Mom asks as she parks the car in the parking lot.

I don't know how she knows that. I don't even know how

I know that. I just know that right now I'm not going to get in trouble today.

"Because . . . I heard you," I say.

"You heard me?" Mom says.

"Yes," I say.

"So you'll behave today because you heard me?"

"Yes!" I say.

"Does that mean you don't hear me other days?"

"Mom!"

"Gwennie!" Mom mimics my tone.

"Can I go to horse camp?" I blurt.

10. *No filter.* (That one means I don't watch what I say.)

Mom sighs. "Cupcake," she says. Then stops.

"What?" I say. "I want to go to horse camp. It's just one week of summer. Please."

Mom shakes her head and gives me a little smile. "I love you," she says. "No matter what."

I tilt my head at her. *I love you* is nice. But I don't know what the *what* is in the *no matter what.*

"Now listen to me. You know how to behave, right?'

"Right," I say.

Mom is always asking me if I know how to behave and I do. Like if anyone gave me a test on it, like a math test, I'd get a 100 percent. But I sometimes don't behave anyway, and what I don't know is why I don't behave when I could totally get a 100 percent on any sort of behaving test. So when adults ask if I know how to behave, I just say yes.

I'd rather think about horses.

I spot a purple backpack in the group of students crowding around the school entrance.

"Tyler!" I call. Mom flinches. She'll say she's flinching because I'm being loud but I know it's also partly because she doesn't want me to love my brother the way I love my brother.

"He can't hear you, Gwen. The car windows are closed," Mom says.

"I know," I say. Even though it's April, it's freezing and there's still snow on the ground. That's life in Wisconsin. I'm always asking Mom if we can move to Florida or Arizona and she thinks it's because I hate the cold but that's only a little bit of it. It's mostly because I hate losing my gloves at school every day and then having Mom yell at me because my gloves are lost again.

I watch a tiny, faraway Tyler run up the school steps and then back down. I open the car door and start to run.

"Gwen!" I hear behind me. "Gwen!" I turn. Mom is standing outside the car. "You forgot something," she says.

"Oh yeah," I say. I run back and throw my arms around her. A hug. "Bye, Mom."

"That's nice," she says. "But I also meant this."

She holds up my blue backpack. The one full of all the homework I did yesterday. All the homework we fought about last night. "Oh," I say.

Mom sighs and shakes her head and a little piece of my heart breaks off and falls, sharp, down my torso and legs all the way into my heels.

I disappointed her. Again.

"Have a good day," she says. "And behave!"

Then she gets in the car and she's gone.

The disappointment splinter is small this time. It was just one disappointed look. It's small enough that I can ignore it sticking in my foot as I run across the parking lot toward my brother. But I worry that my heart breaking apart so much is the reason I have trouble being a whole person sometimes. A good person. A person who acts like she would get a 100 percent on a behavior quiz.

I wish I could stop disappointing my mom. I wish I could stop getting in trouble. I wish I could be the kind of kid whose mom says yes right away when she asks about horse camp with Tyler or a hangout with Hettie.

But I'm not that kind of kid.

I'm a splinter-heart kid.

2

ANGER AND HIS SHELL

At outdoor break a few hours later Tyler and I sit huddled under the big oak tree in the schoolyard. *Outdoor break* is just the middle school word for *recess*. It means the school forces us to go outside for half an hour after we eat lunch. They used to even call it recess, Tyler says, but then a lot of kids complained about being treated like babies and being forced to play outside even in the freezing winter. Well, they still make us go outside and all they changed was the name so I think I'm supposed to hate outdoor break like some of my classmates do, but I actually don't mind it.

We go to a charter school, which means they do things a little differently. Most of the kids in my elementary school go here, too, but Tyler went to private elementary school.

This has been my outdoor break routine—Tyler and the big oak tree—since I first found out he was my long-lost brother in the beginning of fifth grade. In fourth grade, I spent recess with Hettie and her friends. It's OK though because I still spend most of PowerKids with Hettie because her other friends go home after school. Hettie is my only friend.

6. Socially inept

Kids are running in every direction around us and Tyler is sitting on his heels bouncing up and down and the bare branches above us are shaking in the wind making patterns on his face and I can't hear what he's saying.

I close my eyes and build a glass wall. It's pretend. But that doesn't mean it's not important. I make it go from the ground behind Tyler's feet to the tree branches. I make it a circle so it grows around me and Tyler and the tree and, sure no one else knows about it except me, but it fixed everything anyway because my brother and I are alone inside this glass tube with our tree and all of the commotion is outside and I can finally hear him.

"The best one is Midnight," he's saying.

I can hear him, but I still have no clue what he's talking about.

7. Inattentive

"Will you redo my braids?" I ask him. Back in the fall he started doing that for me every day at outdoor break. At first, I didn't think he'd be able to get them as tight as mom does, but Tyler loves to do hair and he's really good at it, and he can almost always get them tighter. "They're too loose already," I say.

25. Picky about her appearance

Every morning my mom folds my blond hair into twin French braids because that's the only way my head feels right. Otherwise it feels all loose and I can't concentrate without the pulling on my skull. I always have to tell Mom to redo them tighter and tighter, and she tells me we're going to be late to school or wherever we're going, and I tell her I can't go to school or wherever we're going with loose braids, and eventually she does them tight enough, and then we're late or almost late to school, and then, by the middle of the day, my braids are too loose again anyway.

5. Will only do what she wants to do

31. Poor sense of time

"Sure," Tyler says. He kneels behind me and I start to feel the tug of my hair pulling my ear closer to the top of my head. I sigh with relief. Tyler's own jitters calm down with the pulling and twisting so it's easier to understand him.

We haven't talked about it, but I've noticed: Tyler is like me. There's something(s) wrong with him too. He has the same things inside him poking and jumping and turning him into a bad kid all the time. He's a splinter-heart kid too.

Those bad pokey things—they must come from our dad. Neither of us have ever met our dad, at least not that we can remember. But he's still what makes us brother and sister.

"Did you talk to your mom about horse camp?" Tyler asks, excited.

"Yeah," I say. "It didn't go too well."

"It didn't?" Tyler sounds alarmed. He does this thing with

his tongue where it sticks out the side of his mouth and sort of clicks. He always does that when he's nervous, and sometimes Hettie says some mean things about it behind his back, but I don't mind the clicking because he's my brother.

"What did your mom say?" I ask.

"I didn't get to see her yesterday," Tyler says. His mom works at the university like mine, although I didn't realize that until this fall. It isn't surprising though because it feels like almost every adult in this town works at the university. But I guess my mom didn't even know Tyler's mom also lived in Madison, Wisconsin, until this fall, when we ran into each other at Back-to-School Night and my mom's jaw dropped so far you could see all the way down her throat. She told me later that she never thought she'd see Ms. Christakos again. She told me that she didn't think I needed to know Tyler since she had never considered that there was a chance he could actually be in my life. She told me that she had no idea his mom was sort of her coworker for years.

My mom used a strange voice when she said all of this. And she spoke in shorter sentences than she usually does. It was weird.

The things that are wrong with my mom are different from the things that are wrong with me. Which means my mom has a filter. Which means I don't know how much of that story is the absolute exact truth.

And even though our moms work in the same place it's different because Tyler's mom works as a professor in the psychology department and sometimes ends up working all night long. They live in a big house with people Tyler calls *au pairs* and *housekeepers*, so I think she makes a lot of money. My mom is a receptionist for the admissions department, and Mom and I live in a two-bedroom apartment that could fit inside Tyler's living room. I think that part makes Mom mad, but I like our apartment better than their big stone house.

"It doesn't matter, though," Tyler is saying. "We know my mom will say yes. She loves whenever I want to do anything outside."

"Really?" I ask. "She'll say yes no matter what?"

I can feel my hair go up and down as Tyler shrugs.

"Why wouldn't she?" Tyler asks.

"But . . ." I trail off. I don't want to say it. I don't think Tyler wants me to say it.

Before I can help it the words are out of my mouth.

10. No filter

"But what about what happened yesterday?"

Tyler and I talk about animals and braids and I listen while he talks about outer space and dinosaurs and ninjas and video games. We don't talk about the biggest sign that he's my brother. We don't talk about things inside us that jump and poke and make us into bad kids.

And we aren't usual brother/sister. Not like my best friend Hettie and her younger brother, Nolan, who live in the same house and get on each other's nerves all the time, who are also sort of like partners because they've been together for as long as anyone can remember. Tyler and I are siblings because of a stranger.

Tyler is in sixth grade and I'm in fifth, so he's a year older than me. But it seems like I matter to him as much as he matters to me. We both only had a mom, no one else in our family, until we found each other. Our moms know we love each other but they don't understand why it matters so much to have a sibling.

"What do you mean?" he asks. "What happened yesterday?"

I move my head against the pressure of the braid he's currently pulling on. "You know . . . at PowerKids?"

I'm talking about what I saw from the fifth-grade table. I'm talking about when Tyler purposefully slammed his foot down on Ms. Hayley's toes and then ran away when he was supposed to be playing chess.

His brain cracked.

When my brain cracks my mom says no to everything. Horse camp. Vacations. Hanging out with Hettie or Tyler. Dessert. My iPad. Everything.

Tyler's brain cracked but he still thinks his mom will say yes to horse camp.

Tyler shrugs. "She doesn't know about that," he says.

My face burns. "Ms. Hayley didn't call your mom?" I ask.